A devil in disguise . . .

"Look at me, Rebecca," he demanded, trying to ease the naked shame that burned upon her face. "I do care for you, or else that emerald gown would have been lying on the floor since Fleet Street. If I had no real regard for you I would be taking everything that you have to offer . . . and more." His eyes swept her body and he took a ragged breath. "It is not because I do not want you, Rebecca Creighton. At this moment, I find that I desire you more than anyone that I have ever wanted in my life."

"You must think me no better than I should be—a tease," Rebecca whispered, feeling the bitterness of shame rising up in her throat. "A desperate spinster, a fraud."

"I see a woman, Rebecca," he said, trying to make her believe that he spoke the truth. "A woman of valor, who has not yet realized that her worth is beyond pearls." He smiled at her look of surprise. "My apologies to 'Ecclesiastes.' You see, the devil does quote scripture to make his points. You esteem yourself too little, but I cannot." His fingers brushed her kiss-stung lips with regret. "I cannot count you so cheap, Miss Creighton."

SIGNET REGENCY ROMANCE
Coming in February 1999

Karen Harbaugh
Cupid's Kiss

Patricia Oliver
The Lady in Gray

Emily Hendrickson
Miss Timothy Perseveres

The Poet and the Paragon

Rita Boucher

A SIGNET BOOK

SIGNET
Published by the Penguin Group
Penguin Putnam Inc., 375 Hudson Street,
New York, New York 10014, U.S.A.
Penguin Books Ltd, 27 Wrights Lane,
London W8 5TZ, England
Penguin Books Australia Ltd, Ringwood,
Victoria, Australia
Penguin Books Canada Ltd, 10 Alcorn Avenue,
Toronto, Ontario, Canada M4V 3B2
Penguin Books (N.Z.) Ltd, 182-190 Wairau Road,
Auckland 10, New Zealand

Penguin Books Ltd, Registered Offices:
Harmondsworth, Middlesex, England

First published by Signet, an imprint of Dutton NAL,
a member of Penguin Putnam Inc.

First Printing, January, 1999
10 9 8 7 6 5 4 3 2 1

To Binnie, dear friend and book midwife, and my husband
and kids who suffered through the labor.

Prologue

Yorkshire, 1806

It was time to abandon hope.

He would not come.

Rebecca Creighton schooled her expression, knowing that every person in the church was watching her, storing away each detail, a tidbit of gossip to savor for their afternoon tea. She met the stares of her father's congregants squarely and forced a resigned smile, hoping that there was no evidence in her eyes of shame, no trace of the wreckage of her crumbling dreams. Beneath the rising hum of the wedding guests, she could already hear fragmented whispers magnified by the acoustics of the church nave.

". . . aimed too high . . ."

"Pity . . . never thought her the sort of gel for a fellow like Rowley."

". . . shame . . . almost pretty . . . does well for the dressing . . ."

". . . poor dear thing . . . Ollie should be horsewhipped . . ."

". . . jilted at the altar."

Rebecca closed her eyes, knowing that soon every home in the county and beyond would know the tale.

". . . think Miss Creighton will cry?"

Her lids flew open. By heaven, she would not give them that satisfaction. Though her throat was constricted with misery, Rebecca determined that she would not shed a public tear for Oliver Rowley. Besides, Rebecca's stepmother had already begun to make up for any deficiency on her stepdaughter's part.

Lydia Creighton was weeping copiously into her husband's new surplice, and Sarah, Rebecca's sister, had already joined in the lamentations, bawling into their stepmother's skirts. Even the Reverend Creighton seemed to be having some difficulty in keeping his upper lip steady as he patted his pregnant wife's arm in an awkward, comforting gesture.

Strangely enough, not a one of them seemed to think that the bride might be in need of some consolation. Perhaps that was fortunate, since a kind word or a condoling hand would have sufficed to breach the bulwark of Rebecca's precariously built defenses. Unconsciously, she pleated the skirt of her dusky pink gown, crumpling the delicately embroidered trim between her nerveless fingers.

Her first London gown . . . Lydia had insisted that her stepdaughter not appear the gapeseed. Rebecca moaned inwardly as she reckoned the other costs that Lydia had mandated so that Rebecca might be fired off in a style befitting her new estate.

Waiting at the rector's manse was an enormous wedding breakfast, a reckless extravagance of champagne and lobster patties. As for the lavish trousseau that Lydia had assembled, Rebecca knew full well that she would wear none of it. All of those glorious garments were suitable for a viscount's bride, not a vicar's daughter who spent her time visiting the sick and needy.

A fitting end to vanity, Rebecca thought, forcing her betraying hands to be still and wishing for the concealing refuge of pockets; but there were none in the frivolous confection that she wore. When she had seen herself in the mirror this morning, she had scarcely dared to presume that the woman in the glass was the vicar's eldest daughter.

It would have been self-deception to describe the reflection as beautiful. Still, with her chestnut curls tumbling free from her usual austere knot, her oval face glowing with excitement and anticipation, and her slim figure enhanced by the cunning cut of a modish gown, she had actually begun to believe that Oliver might actually find her pleasing, even pretty. "Vanity of vanities," quoth Ecclesiastes.

An awkward quiet fell as Oliver's father advanced slowly toward the front of church, his usual attitude of confident command shattered. "Arthur . . ." he began hesitantly, making his closest friend's name into a plea for understanding, for forgiveness. "I shall make this right, Arthur, I swear it."

"Can you?" the Reverend Creighton asked softly, looking past his daughter's calm demeanor and reading the turmoil in her tawny eyes. "Can you, indeed, milord?"

Chapter 1

The tall cove pulled a piece of paper from the pocket of his greatcoat. His deep brown eyes narrowed as he squinted in the morning sun, as if he could scarcely read what was written there. Like a golden nugget in the middle of a muddy stream, the gentleman's clothing and aristocratic bearing marked him, causing the palms of the flash gents to itch. Mayfair and Bond Street, no doubt of it, though they could only wonder why one of the Quality was out of his bed at so early an hour, much less roaming lost in Whitechapel. Too good to be true, it was.

Still, the more wary would-be thieves evaluated him with care before making their strike. As the wind whipped his coat against his body, there was a bulge that had the suspicious look of a barking iron. But it was not just the possibility of the pistol that caused them to shrink back into the shadows. As the gentleman looked up, his craggy features tightened into a hard line, dark brows arching speculatively below a sweep of coal black hair. His discerning look seemed almost amused; but held within that gaze was a barely veiled threat.

Though his tan was faded, the Mayfair cove's face was not the pasty white that typified the gentry. India or the Peninsula they speculated, the weather-beaten countenance of an ex-soldier? Instinctively, they knew that those hands were driven by corded muscle, just as they were nearly certain that no tailor's foolery enhanced the athletic figure glimpsed as those long legs rapidly ate the distance. This was a man who would give chase and fight rather than call for Charley and the catch club. Trouble on two feet. In the dark, they might have chanced a go at him, but in the broad light of day, cutpurse wisdom prevailed, and they let the mark pass.

"Got a penny for a man what fought for king and country?" A beggar stretched out his good hand; the ragged remnants of a uniform hung empty from the other shoulder.

"Regiment?" Michael Fairgrove asked quietly, his hand plunging into his pocket to seek a coin. Unfortunately, these days there were red-coated mendicants aplenty who were using the uniform to solicit alms, yet they had never set foot on the battlefield.

"Sixth, sir," the beggar responded, straightening unconsciously at the air of command in the other man's voice. "Name's Eager. I did for Lieutenant James Robertson, sir, if you knowed him, rest his soul."

"Aye, I knew James. Charleroi, was it not?" Michael questioned, watching the man's eyes closely to see if he would react to the deliberate lie. If Eager was telling the truth, he would know the details. If not, bad luck that he had chosen an officer that Michael had happened to know.

"Nay." Eager shook his head, vehemently. " 'Twas Hougemont, where the major went down. Buried my arm with him, they tole me. Don't know if it's true."

Satisfied, Michael's fingers slid from the smaller silver tanner to a golden guinea. "Would you work, if you could?"

Eager laughed bitterly. "A one-armed man, sir? Naught left but the street or the almshouse for the likes o' me."

"If you want to work, there is a place in Marylebone called 'Soldier's Sanctuary,' " Michael said, sliding the coin discreetly into the man's hand. " 'Tis not far from the church across from where the old gardens used to be. Tell them Fairgrove sent you by."

"Fairgrove?" Eager asked, a catch in his voice as he saw the gold glinting in his palm. "Wouldn't be Major Fairgrove would it? The hero of Vittoria?"

"We were all heroes, Eager," Michael said with a sad smile. "You and Robertson much more than I, in the end.

Now, you could do me a favor if you would? Is there an apothecary hereabouts?"

Eager dipped his head. "Aye, Old Deems's shop, just down the street a bit. Wouldn't trust him to grind a powder for a cat, though. As like to give a man hemlock as horehound, he is."

"I am not seeking a cure, but an old friend," Michael assured him. "Is there a new lodger above his shop?"

"Aye," Eager said, "a big 'un. Light hair? A bruiser, by the look of him?"

Michael nodded. "That would be him." He pulled out another coin, this time silver. "Remember, Soldier's Sanctuary in Marylebone."

The beggar gave a rusty smile. "Aye, might be I will."

Michael made his way to Deems's shop, conscious of watching eyes and glad of the pistol in his pocket. Eager's words began to echo in his head. *Buried my arm with 'im, they tole me.* Eager and Robertson—now there was a tale that deserved telling; a perfect end to his Hougemont canto. Relentlessly, Michael put aside the lines that were suddenly spinning themselves into being. Somehow, he knew that they would still be there when the time came to put them to paper tonight.

Instead, he forced himself to concentrate on the here and now. The rank stench of poverty permeated the dim hallway; sweat, boiled cabbage, and stale urine mingled with the odor of frying fish from the cookshop next door. A far cry from Piccadilly, Michael thought grimly.

He mounted the stairs slowly, his frown deepening with each rickety step. If ever a man had relished skating on the edge of disaster, it was Oliver Rowley, Viscount Elmont. However, it appeared that this time he might not have managed to halt himself at the brink. Oliver had disappeared in the dead of night, leaving the proprietors of the Albany to join the growing legions of his debtors. It had taken Michael and his ex-soldier friends better than a week to trace his tracks.

Though Michael pounded the dilapidated door for several minutes, screams and curses from the flat below and the din from the street masked any reply that might have come from within. Once again, Michael folded his fingers into a fist, battering at the entry with all the force of his frustration and a sudden niggling sense of fear.

Abruptly, the door gave way, swinging open with a squealing protest of rusty hinges before slamming up against the wall. A glance at the doorpost revealed no sign of a damaged lock; the latch had been open all along. "Idiot," Michael muttered in a mix of annoyance and affection.

Oliver had always been better with his fists than with his wits, but now it would seem that his attic had gone entirely vacant. The neighbors here would gut a man for a ha'penny; not that they would find much worth the trouble of taking these days. In the past few weeks, most of Oliver's possessions had either found a new home beneath the golden balls of the pawnshop or been sold outright.

Still, as Michael entered warily, there was no mistaking that this was Oliver's den. Whitechapel or Mayfair, the shabby chamber had already assumed the ambience of a nursery that had been left too long without a nanny. Weston's work was strewn everywhere, jackets, vests, and trousers. Oliver's valet had obviously tired of working for promises. The table was littered with an assortment of crockery bearing the congealed remnants of meals.

Even with the windows shut against the morning chill, the cacophony from the busy street outside merged with the hullabaloo from the hall. Little wonder that his knocking had gone unnoticed. Michael exhaled a sigh of relief as he heard a familiar sound rasping above the din.

In the corner of the room, his fair head pillowed upon the papers that covered his battered escritoire, Oliver slept, a half-drained bottle perched precariously by his elbow and another empty one nestled near his boots. Michael crossed the room and took a whiff of the contents. Gin? Matters were grave indeed if cheap blue ruin had become Oliver's drink of choice.

"Ollie!" Michael called, grasping his friend by the shoulder, trying to bring his sizable bulk to an upright position "Get up, you oaf."

"Tell old Nosey I shall be there shortly," Oliver mumbled. He blinked bleary-eyed as he tried to focus on the wavering shadow that swam before him. "Inform my man that my horse must be readied at once."

"Your horse went on the block at Tattersall's last month," Michael said, cupping Oliver's chin in his palm. "As to Nosey, he has no more need of either of us, if you recall. Hougemont? Waterloo? Boney is living out the remainder of his miserable life on St. Helena. He is utterly exploded."

"My head, too." Oliver moaned softly as he rose unsteadily to his feet, his meaty hands suddenly clutching at his stomach.

"Not on my Hessians, Ollie," Michael warned, taking a cautious step back. Hastily, he grabbed a large bowl from the table and shoved it in his friend's direction. As Oliver cast up his accounts, Michael set aside his coat and automatically began setting things to rights.

"Ain't at Eton any longer, Michael," Oliver reminded him gruffly, wiping the corners of his mouth with a handkerchief of dubious cleanliness. "Don't have to fag for me anymore."

"Aye, it is somewhat like the old days at Eton, is it not?" Michael remarked with a fond smile. "You shooting the cat, and me mopping up after you," Michael recollected as he began to pile up the crockery.

"Must have been the smallest runt in Eton's history. You came into your own soon enough, though," Oliver allowed. "A wicked set of fives on you, Michael."

"Still, if we are reckoning obligations, then the tally is still weighted in your favor," Michael said, grimacing as he saw a suspicious gray shadow skittering about in the corner of the room.

"More than made up for it, I should say," Oliver mumbled, blinking his blue eyes against the light. "Bailed me out more times than I care to count and now . . . by heaven, if you can track me down, then the duns won't be too far behind."

"A week," Michael said, "perhaps more since they have to rely on inferior information."

"Aye, those pet soldiers of yours are everywhere, ain't they?" Oliver said, shaking his head and moaning at the ache that resulted. "Should have known that you would find me in the end. Well, I might as well tell you that I have been a fool, Michael, an utter fool."

"The mille you lost?" Michael asked.

"Heard the news already, have you?" Oliver sat down heavily, his head in his hands.

"How could you expect it to be otherwise?" Michael asked, setting the dishes aside in exasperation and running a nervous hand through his hair. "A thousand pounds on the turn of a card? The *ton* laps up such lunacy as a cat savors cream! You swore to me the last time . . ."

"Know I did," Oliver said miserably. "But the cards were in my favor, Michael. Hell, I *knew*—"

"You always *know*," Michael said, painfully recalling the past few months and Oliver's ever-mounting losses. Oliver was one of those soldiers who had spent the better part of his life at war and now that peace had come he had not the vaguest idea how to go on. "Unfortunately, you have been wrong more often than not these days."

"Already admitted to being a fool," Oliver said, blinking owl-like. "What more do you want? Swear I won't ask again, if you could just . . ."

Michael knew the question that was surely to come by the look of abject shame in his friend's eyes. Steeling himself, he decided to spare Oliver the humiliation of the asking. "This time, I fear that I cannot tow you out of Tick, my friend."

"Why not?" Oliver asked petulantly, rising from his chair, only to fall back once again, cradling his aching head. "Become so much the blooming Cit these days, with your connections in the bourse, the Patronesses will barely let you squeeze past Almack's sacred portals."

"Indeed?" Michael remarked with a wry smile. "Perhaps I

ought to dine with Nathan Rothschild and Isaac DeSilva more often. Maybe they will bar me altogether."

"DeSilva wouldn't lend me a sou, for all he's a friend of yours," Oliver grumbled. "Sentiment don't butter bread with a man like that."

"You went to Isaac DeSilva to borrow to pay your gambling debts?" Michael asked, shaking his head in sheer incredulity. "By heaven, man, he and Rothschild helped to finance Wellington's war!"

"Still a moneylender, ain't he?" Oliver argued doggedly. "Besides, you don't know how much I owe." He reached back and grabbed a batch of papers from the desk, letting them sift from his fingers to the floor.

Michael bent and picked up some of the notes, holding his breath as he mentally calculating the sum. He let out a slow whistle.

"My debts. Twenty thousand, Michael, and I ain't even reckoned what I owe you," Oliver said, his expression boyishly woebegone. "Aye, almost out-Prinnied Prinny. Couldn't get past DeSilva's clerk till I mentioned your name. Then it was all 'Yes, milord.' 'Good to see you, milord.' 'Can I help you, milord?' The old Jew holds you high, seems to me; else he would never have sat me down and spoke like he did," Oliver remarked. "Told me that m'father sent a letter to every bourse in town; told them that they were fools if they lent me more than a tuppence. As it stands, the earl would as soon throw anything that ain't entailed into the Thames as leave it in my hands."

"And now I suspect that there is not a cent-percenter who is unaware of those sentiments," Michael observed.

"Might as well have had it sung as a penny-ballad on the street corners," Oliver agreed with a groan.

"I wish I could help you, Ollie," Michael said, seating himself on a Chippendale chair that had likely been too wobbly to pawn. "However, though my pockets are not to let, they are less than full these days, unless, I succeed in interesting a publisher in 'On the Fields of Waterloo,' that is."

"Do as well to try and milk a pigeon, as depend on the sale of your verse," Oliver said, smiling sourly at what had long become a private joke. "Especially when they ain't sold but two copies of your first volume."

"*A Soldier's Journey* did not exactly set the world afire," Michael admitted.

"Ain't the sort of stuff to make the ladies swoon," Oliver said. "Might be if you would put your name on it, instead of just saying 'by a Gentleman.' Mebbe limp about like you were wounded."

"Wear a brooding expression, like George Gordon, as if the world weighed oh so heavily upon my shoulders," Michael said, effecting a melancholy air and lifting a dramatic hand to his brow.

Oliver laughed weakly. "I think not. World couldn't stand another Byron. Your verse is far better than his, in any case."

"Well, now I know who purchased at least one of the copies that were sold," Michael said, his own humor fading as he regarded his friend. "Would that I might help you, Ollie, but you have gone beyond any line that I might throw you."

"Wouldn't have asked unless I thought you were flush with the ready. Between your inheritance and your everlasting Funds and those estates of yours, I was believing you kin to Croesus," Oliver continued, eyeing his friend searchingly. "Dammit, it's that place in Marylebone again, ain't it? Bleeding you dry again, are they?"

Michael smiled, knowing that Oliver was entirely unconscious of the irony in that statement. "There was a fire that totally destroyed the kitchens."

"And you let those soldiers pick your pockets! A soft touch, Michael, that's what you are, and those men at Soldier's Sanctuary know it," Oliver said, admonishing him with a wagging finger.

"No doubt you are sorry that they got to my purse before you did," Michael remarked with a wry twist of his lips.

Oliver flushed. "Aye, true enough," he admitted, running a sheepish hand through his blond curls. "But if you can't frank me, Michael, I suppose there ain't much in the way of choice for me. Can't say as I'd blame you, though, even if you had the blunt. Enough of my vowels in your pockets to fill old Johnson's dictionary."

"Maybe it will not come to debtors' prison," Michael said, walking to the escritoire and sifting through the assortment of bills and demands for payment. "Perhaps if I might talk to some of your creditors? Any agreement would require strict economy on your part, Ollie. No more gambling or visits to Weston."

"Might as well be in Fleet if life out here ain't worth three half pence," Oliver groaned, his chin jutting out with the aspect of a pugnacious child. "If a man can't dress decent or play a friendly game of cards now and then, what is there? Won't be choked to death by the purse strings, Michael. I won't."

Michael came to his feet in annoyance, letting the papers slip back on to the desk as he folded his arms across his chest. "What choices do you have, Ollie? I doubt that there is a man in London who will loan you the time of day. Your alternatives seem limited to two options: Fleet or a run for France, my friend. As for the latter, it seems to me that we spent too many bloody years fighting so that we could get ourselves home again in one piece. Are you that much of an idiot?"

"Never call me an idiot!" Oliver roared, his face darkening, fists curling menacingly as he rose.

"Idiot!" Michael repeated, holding his ground. "You are no more than an imbecile if you would exile yourself from England because of the duns, Ollie. And for all that the fashionable world makes light of Fleet, it is still a prison."

Oliver's anger subsided as Michael's baritone faded to a hoarse whisper. Even though Oliver was half befuddled, the naked pain in his friend's eyes jarred him back into awareness. Slowly, his fists slipped to his sides. "Forgot, Michael, about that time," he said, remorseful.

"I never shall," Michael said, turning away and walking to the window. Clearing his throat, he forced himself to continue, trying to make Oliver understand. "Though I spent only a few days in that Spanish hellhole, it might as well have been an eternity. You cannot know what it is to lose your freedom, Ollie. It is only a matter of time before your creditors locate your new lodgings. So, if you still refuse to let me help you fend them off, I can, at the least, cover your fare across the Channel. Perhaps your father will eventually relent."

Oliver snorted. "When hens make holy water! Had a letter from my dear pater just before I cut and run from the Albany." He shuffled unsteadily to the escritoire, searching desultorily through the pile of papers before culling a piece of embossed vellum from the heap and thrusting it into Michael's hands. "Wrote him that I was under the hatches. Read that, if you would!"

Michael frowned as he held the letter up to the wan sunlight, swiftly scanning the elegant script. "It appears that he has heard of your losses on the baize."

"Aye, don't see how he would go on without me if I cross the Channel. Won't be half so much fun to scold me if I am in France," Oliver complained. "Father was due to take Holy Orders, you know, before my uncle turned his toes up without an heir. Every letter is a virtual sermon."

"I vow, I can almost smell the brimstone," Michael said, turning the page over.

"Don't even bother to finish the text," Oliver told him. "I didn't. But as you can see, there is no chance of him throwing so much as a copper in my collection plate."

"I believe such contributions are supposed to come from the penitent," Michael murmured as he traced the last paragraph. "Ollie, you did not read this, you say?" he asked, a grin gradually dawning as he finished the earl's closing statement.

"Never do; his prosings are always the same," Oliver said, lifting the half-empty bottle and taking a swig. "Have a bit of the hair of the dog?" he offered.

"Indeed, I shall," Michael said, taking the bottle and lifting it high. "I propose a toast, Ollie. To debts paid." He took a short pull, letting the raw fire burn down his throat. DeSilva had recommended a sweet deal, but without the funds, Michael had been forced to let the investment pass him by. Now, if the earl was willing to buy up his son's vowels, Michael would have the capital he needed to buy his way in. Within a few weeks, he might be a very rich man, indeed. "No, better still, to wedded bliss, a prison more permanent than Fleet."

"The devil, you say?" Oliver guffawed as Michael took another drink and handed back the bottle. "You? The man who swore he would never wed? Fancy you, caught in the parson's mousetrap. I'll drink to that, I will." He tipped back the bottle, taking a long swallow.

"No, Ollie," Michael said, his eyes glinting, an effect of the crudely refined alcohol. "Not I. You. Your father has offered you marriage as a way to redeem yourself."

Oliver choked, gin spewing from his mouth. "Who?" he coughed. "What?"

"You really ought to read your mail," Michael said as he hastily began to pound the hulking man's back. "It seems that the earl has found you a true paragon of virtue; an example of feminine rectitude and probity who will surely turn you from your wicked ways. 'Tis neither Fleet nor France for you, Ollie. For, if you will just wed the female, your father will pay all your debts, including, I assume, what you currently owe me. Allow me to be the first to wish you happy."

Oliver grabbed the letter and traced out the last lines with his meaty finger. "Her? No!" His ruddy face paled. "Rather go to Fleet," he croaked, letting the paper drift to the ground.

Rebecca Creighton sat at her desk, one hand absently disarranging her curls into a disheveled tumble as she stared into the hearth. Slowly, she nibbled her afternoon snack, making the remaining scone linger as long as she might. Her tea had long since gone cold; nonetheless she sipped, knowing all the while that the inevitable could not be forever postponed. A rest, that was all that she needed, she told herself as she massaged the bridge of her nose.

With a sigh, Rebecca replaced her spectacles, frowning as the paragraphs that she had just completed jumped into sharp focus. Though she had hoped that the respite would prove her intuitions wrong, the lines were clearly beyond redemption, a pap of regurgitated ideas and stale concepts. Her late father's friend, the Reverend Havermill, would doubtless accept them, embrace them eagerly, in fact, due to the growing success of her Penny Tracts.

However, the tragic figure of the tale, *Cathy of Covent Garden,* was emerging as a mindless twit. The villain who was wiling the heroine into a life of sinful abandon was emerging as the most appealing character in the story. Rebecca was beginning to like him entirely too much for comfort. By comparison, her hero, Jack Valiant, had all the appeal. of a cold pease porridge. No, that would not do at all. There was only one means of forestalling temptation. Rebecca took the sheaf of pages in hand and went to kneel by the hearth. One by one she fed the sheets into the flames.

Unfortunately, there had been far too many afternoons like this of late, hours where words eluded her entirely. But worse were times like today, when sentences poured from her pen like drivel from the mouth of an infant. Perhaps it was just as well, since Mr. Havermill had heartily disapproved the subject matter that she had selected. Still, she could not muster any enthusiasm about his topic of choice, the evils of gossip.

As the last piece of paper withered to ash, she rose to pace the length of the faded Turkey carpet, noting the threadbare spots that could not be entirely obscured by judicious placement of furnishings. Though the deep burgundy draperies had been cunningly mended and patched, their shabby state, too, was beyond concealment. As Rebecca pulled the hangings aside, a cloud of dust rose into the air. Sneezing, she waved her hands futilely at the motes, stirring them to dance mockingly in the sunlight.

Like it or not, Rebecca conceded a point to her stepmother. Lydia had long maintained that Creighton House had become entirely too great a burden for their reduced staff to manage.

Mentally, Rebecca marched out the figures on her household ledgers for review, matching them pound and pence against her expectations of income. Thoughtful, she gnawed upon her fingernail as she considered the costs of board and salary for one more maid and its likely impact upon the fragile balance of her accounts.

There was still Sarah to consider. Due to the Reverend Creighton's untimely death, her younger sister's introduction to the fashionable world had already been postponed once. Yet, even before their father's demise, Rebecca had entertained serious doubts regarding their ability to bear that enormous financial burden.

Now, though the income from her writings had been rising steadily, the loss of her father's living had cast them adrift in perilous financial waters. Without the subsidy of the moneys from his parish as their anchor, even the strictest economies might not suffice to withstand the formidable expenses of Sarah's upcoming Season. Rebecca stared at the pile of blank paper sitting like a silent rebuke upon her father's mahogany desk. She could almost hear her father's voice. *What are you doing, Rebecca, idling your time away?*

Still, Rebecca turned to press her nose against the windowpane, gazing at the street like a child who had been forbidden to go out and play. Had spring arrived so suddenly that the leaves had begun to unfurl without her notice? A passing wind slipped through the trees, whipping the swelling buds. How long had it been since she had allowed herself the simple pleasure of a walk? The idea was tempting . . . tempting beyond measure to sneak out through the mews without even bothering to take a maid for company.

A deliciously scandalous idea: Rebecca Creighton, abroad without so much as a servant to give her countenance! To go out into the world alone, unwatched. What would it be to walk and to keep on walking until she came to a place where no one had ever heard of Miss Rebecca Creighton and her worthy tracts? Did a somewhere exist where no seminary for young ladies had ever performed her edifying play, *Lucy's Valuable Lesson*?

A boyish shout from below brought Harry to mind. Harry . . . It was well past time to begin thinking of her brother's future. Though he was doing well enough now, it was inevitable that the precocious boy would outstrip his half sister's limited knowledge. He would need more than the smattering of Latin, Hebrew, Greek, and mathematics that Rebecca had thus far been able to give him. Father had always intended for Harry to follow in his footsteps at Eton and then on to Oxford. Money would have to be found for that as well. It was no less than her duty.

Duty . . . first and foremost.

Rebecca forced herself to return to the desk and stared up at the Reverend Creighton's portrait. She sat herself down once more and stared at the blank sheet of paper, but though the minutes ticked by, the only thing she had to show for her effort was a crick in her back. Rebecca rose in relief as she heard the sound of footsteps in the hall, glad of the excuse to leave her work.

"Oh, bother, where is the footman?" Lydia's voice floated up the stairs. "There is no time to wait. We shall just have to do it ourselves!"

The curious haste in Lydia's voice roused her stepdaughter's suspicions. With a groan, Rebecca capped the inkwell. As she opened the library door, she saw her sister, Sarah, and Lydia, their stepmother, standing in the entry. Their maid, Ellen, had already begun to ascend the stairs, a veritable mountain of parcels and bandboxes in her arms.

"It might be easier if you made several trips," Rebecca said, her lips pursing as she took some of the packages from the maid's hands.

"Bless you, miss," Ellen said gratefully. "If I might leave a few here, it will make it much easier."

"Indeed," Rebecca said with deceptive mildness. "I am surprised that you are juggling the entire pile in one trip, Ellen. Why could you not wait for the footman for help? One might almost think that there was a particular need to rush." The maid's look of distress was an answer to Rebecca's question. There was not a servant in the house who was unaware of their need to practice strict economy and to follow her inflexible rules that governed every purchase that the Creighton family made, down to the last loaf of sugar.

"Lydia? Sarah?" Raising an inquisitive eyebrow, Rebecca looked beyond the servant and addressed herself to her stepmother and sister.

Lydia flushed; her eyes dropped. "Dearest, I had thought that you were to address Lady Shand's afternoon tea today." Her voice held the faintest hint of a tremor.

The guilty glance that flew between Lydia and Sarah spoke volumes. Anger and weariness warred within Rebecca. Had she become so much the martinet of late that the two of them feared to even speak to her? Rebecca forced herself to smile. "Lady Shand sent a footman by with a note soon after you left. Apparently there have been rumors of unrest in London. The poor woman is forever in fear of a riot since that sorry business with the Corn Laws just last March. Orator Hunt and his friends stir up yet more trouble, and the thought of another uprising terrifies her."

"Pooh," Sarah said, dismissing Lady Shand's worries with a negligent wave of her hand. "If one paid attention to all the radical talk these days, we would lock ourselves in our houses and never come out again."

"That may be so," Rebecca agreed, "but whether her feelings are justified or not is of little import. My lecture must be postponed."

"Reverend Havermill will be most disappointed," Lydia said. "He had expected that quite a few of the ladies there would be interested in purchasing copies of your pamphlets."

"I suppose that means we must all make do on less for the while," Rebecca said, eyeing the parcels significantly. "I *do* hope that all of these things are on the list of absolute necessities that we agreed upon for Sarah's debut."

"We only meant to look. Truly, Becky," Sarah spoke up,

suddenly aware of the tawny glint in her sister's amber eyes, like a tiger about to pounce. "It was such a beautiful sunny day, perfect for viewing the windows on Bond Street."

"And we saw this cunning bonnet in the corner of the milliner's window. I vow, we could hardly help but go in and see," Lydia chimed in. "Show her, Sarah," she urged.

Sarah hastened to loosen the ribbons on one of the band-boxes, pulling out a straw bonnet delicately framed with pink rosebuds.

"Try it on, Becky," Lydia said. "I know that it will suit."

"For me?" Rebecca asked, surprise causing her breath to catch in her throat.

"No, for Prinny!" Lydia laughed. "Of course it is for you, dearest. When the mountain will not travel, one must drag it to Mohamet."

"I believe that goes the mountain cannot go to Mohamet, therefore, Mohamet must go to the mountain," Rebecca corrected, touching the brim in disbelief.

"Indeed, I just said so!" Lydia exclaimed, "but since we know that you would sooner visit Bedlam than spend an hour on Bond Street, Becky, we must bring Bond Street to you."

"There is a gown for you, too!" Sarah said, her rosy face alight with pleasure. "It is of the same shade as the trim on the hat's brim. Madame Robard had it on hand, and it was a splendid bargain! It seems that her customer could not manage to pay."

"No more than we can," Rebecca murmured, toting up the expense. "Indeed, we are still in mourning for Father. Such an excess of color—"

"Will be right and proper in less than two weeks' time," Lydia interjected, her blue eyes meeting Rebecca's stormy amber glare squarely. "It will be a year, you know. He would not have wished us all to wear black forever, dearest. And with Sarah's Season so rapidly approaching, you shall need an appropriate wardrobe."

This time it was Rebecca who lowered her eyes. "I shall do well enough with what I have. It was most kind of you both, but I doubt the dress will fit anyway," Rebecca said, "especially if you used Sarah as your dressing doll."

"We were not that foolish!" Lydia laughed once more. "One of Madame Robard's girls was pressed into service; she was much of the same size as yourself."

"Poor girl," Rebecca said. "The figure of a lumpy washboard, with little bosom and hardly any hips to speak of."

"Far better than being an Amazon, like I am!" Sarah retorted. "There is hardly a man in London who can look me in the eye. I suspect that I shall be looking at the tops of their heads when I go to Almack's."

"And Madame herself promised that she would alter the dress to suit you," Lydia coaxed, pulling the box from the pile and sweeping off the lid. "Please, Becky, just let Ellen help you try it on."

The folds of silk were the shadowy color of blossoms at dusk. Despite herself, Rebecca reached out to touch the shimmering folds. It was a dream of a gown, almost the same color as her wedding dress . . . Firmly, she put those long-ago regrets aside.

"It was kind of you," she said, trying to keep the old pain from creeping into her voice, "both of you, but bargain though your purchase might be, we must all continue to observe strict economy and purchase only what is unequivocally necessary."

"But Rebecca—" Lydia began.

"I shall make do with what I already have," Rebecca interrupted, putting up her hand, demanding a halt to any further argument. "After all, I doubt that anyone will spare me a second glance with Sarah on the scene. But there are other matters to consider." She looked at her stepmother. "I find that you are right, Lydia. We ought to increase the household staff this spring. We must not make a shabby appearance."

"I knew you would see the sense of it," Lydia said, mercurially shifting from peevishness to delight.

"In order to afford an additional maid and bear some of the expenses of the Season, we will cease to keep our own coach;

a hired carriage will have to suffice," Rebecca said, trying to keep her tones even in the face of Lydia's dawning consternation. "It costs us four pounds, sixteen shillings in annual servant taxes for the mere hire of the coachman and the groom. Then there is the levy for the carriage itself, as well as oats and care for the pair of horses that pulls it. The savings will be substantial, and we could afford the maid as well as more of the fripperies that you require."

"You might just as well forgo your sister's Season altogether," Lydia said, her voice rising. "I had hoped her beauty and her Creighton bloodlines might suffice to win her a husband, for all that she has a pittance for a dowry. But, without a carriage of our own, Rebecca, we are as sapphires."

"You mean 'ciphers,' " Rebecca said as her stepmother's intent became clear.

"Indeed, I just said as much," Lydia asserted. "Certainly your sister will not be reckoned a diamond of the first water, as I had hoped."

"It is either the maid or the coach," Rebecca maintained. "We can hardly afford the one, and it is certain that we cannot bear the cost of both." Her eyes swept the bundles on the floor meaningfully. "In any case, unless these things are among the purchases that were planned, I fear that Ellen must return them in the morning."

"I vow I have never seen such a clutchpurse!" Sarah exploded, throwing the dress box to the ground. "I have not the half of what I shall need, yet you insist upon impossible economies. 'Tis not enough that you make yourself into an ugly crow, Becky Creighton, but you would make us all into a raven's flock. And to do without our own carriage? I shall be a veritable laughingstock. It will be your fault if I end my days as a preachy spinster, just like you!" With a final stamp of her feet, she ran off to her room.

"I do my best, Lydia," Rebecca said stiffly, facing her stepmother's accusing eyes.

"I understand, dearest," Lydia said, making a woeful attempt at a smile before following in Sarah's stormy wake.

But from Lydia's teary expression, Rebecca was certain that her father's widow understood nothing at all. This time, her stepmother had been caught out before the bills came to Rebecca's attention. Tomorrow, Lydia would be all penitence, but it would scarcely take another two sunsets before she was off again to Madame Robard's or some other shop where the bargains were beyond her powers of resistance. Then there would be more unexpected demands for payment in the post and yet another woeful scene of remorse and contrite promises, ad infinitum.

Economy.

When pigs might fly.

Rebecca bent to tuck the gown back into its box, rearranging the spill of silk reverently. She removed her spectacles and wiped away hot tears with the back of her hand, wondering why she was wasting her time crying. Tears would solve nothing, and it would not do to stain the gown. Madame Robard would likely refuse to take back her expensive creation if it was the least bit damaged.

Even if Lydia had bargained the modiste down to a Bartholomew Fair price, Robard's gowns cost nearly what it would take to keep a coachman for a year. Foolish Lydia was such a widgeon, but ninnyhammer though she was, she was kind at heart. It was no fault of hers that Rebecca felt more like Lydia's mother than her stepdaughter.

Before she closed the lid, Rebecca's eyes devoured the embroidered bodice, the delicate lace at the neck, memorizing the detail so that she might use it. It was the type of costume that Cathy of Covent Garden might wear, after she sold her soul to her protector for silks and jewels.

Not a preachy spinster.

Not an ugly crow.

"Sarah didn't mean it, Becky." A high, reedy voice came from the landing above. "You know she didn't."

"I know, Harry," Rebecca said, trying to muster a composed expression as her half brother descended the stairs.

Amber eyes, so like her own, stared sympathetically from behind a pair of spectacles.

"I shall give up ices and pastries at Gunthers, if that will help," the ten-year-old offered solemnly.

"Thank you, Harry," she said, softly, "but I hope that will not be necessary."

"And baths, I shall give those up as well, since it must cost money for the fuel to heat all that hot water," he added, a teasing glint in his eye.

"No, Harry, you need not make so terrible a sacrifice," she said, her lips quirking in amusement. Swiftly, she drew him to her in a hug. "Thank you, dear."

"It must be hard," he said, his voice muffled against her. "Like being the only good hitter on the entire cricket team."

"Yes," she agreed, looking down at his solemn face. "It is hard, but it is my duty."

"Why?" he asked.

She was saved from the necessity of an answer by the swift rapping of the brass knocker. From her vantage point on the landing, she could see their gray-haired butler, Goode, shuffle slowly across the entry hall. A gust of wind blew up the stairs, chilling her. Though the front door was out of her view, words drifted up intermittently.

"Mrs. Creighton . . . urgent . . . favor of a rapid reply . . . Earl of Elmont . . ."

Rebecca's heart began to hammer. The Earl of Elmont. Her father's old friend? Surely she had mistaken the name. Ten years . . . the earl had sent a note of condolence, to be sure, when her father had died, but other than that, his lordship had made no attempt to contact the Creightons since . . . Rebecca shook her head, trying to banish the flood of humiliating memories.

"A letter has arrived for Madame, Miss Rebecca," Goode informed her. "Do you know where I might find her?"

"I will bring this to my stepmother," she said, going down the stairs and taking the sealed sheets of vellum from the silver salver in Goode's hands.

"His lordship requests the favor of a speedy reply," Goode said.

"I shall tell her so," Rebecca agreed, turning the letter over in her hand.

"Who is it from, Becky?" Harry asked eagerly. "Shall I bring it to Mama?"

"The Earl of Elmont," Rebecca answered distractedly. There was no doubt now that she might have misheard. Even if she had not recognized the earl's crabbed hand, the distinctive phoenix imprint in the wax was most definitely wrought by Elmont's signet. Heaven knew that she had seen both of them often enough during those heady days over a decade before.

"Ain't he the one that . . ." Harry's voice trailed off as his half sister looked up. He had only once before seen that bleakness in her eyes, just after they found out that Papa had died in a carriage accident on his way to preach in Bath.

"Not the earl," Rebecca said quietly. "His son, Oliver, the Viscount Elmont." She lightly touched the boy's cheek, easily reading his suddenly stricken look. "That water has long gone under the bridge, Harry. It happened before you were born, dear. I was just startled to hear the name after all this time, nothing more."

Harry nodded, accepting her words, though he recognized a brave false front when he heard one.

Her stepmother was just leaving Sarah's room when they came up the stairs.

"A letter, Lydia, from the Earl of Elmont," Rebecca said, handing her the missive.

The older woman's brow arched upward as she quickly broke the seal and scanned the message. One hand flew to her breast as the other clutched the vellum convulsively. "I cannot credit it," she murmured. "I simply cannot credit it!" Once again, she looked down at the paper, carefully tracing the words with her finger as a smile transformed her face. "Our worries are over, Rebecca! Tell Ellen to bring the parcels up and put them away."

"What does he say, Lydia?" Rebecca asked. "Surely, he is not prating about offering me an annuity again? Papa was absolutely against it, and as he said, no amount of money could recompense for Oliver's insult. I will not have it, Lydia! He cannot buy the Creighton honor."

"No, dearest, nothing of the kind," Lydia said, putting a soothing hand on her stepdaughter's shoulder. "There is a letter enclosed here from the Viscount Elmont. Apparently, he feared that you would not accept any direct communication from him."

"If Oliver wishes to express his regrets, you may tell him that it is a full ten years too late."

Lydia fairly trilled with joy. "This is not a simple apology, Rebecca, but far more. From what the earl writes, the viscount is entirely cognizant of the wrong that he has done you. You know full well, dearest, that father and son have been estranged ever since that dreadful day. Well, it would appear that the breach is, at last, being healed. It is as your dear father always said. 'Arrears may endure for a night, but joy cometh in the morning.' "

"I believe the Psalmist said tears, Lydia, tears in the night," Rebecca corrected.

"Indeed, as I am saying, is not poor Sarah weeping over our debts at this very moment?" Lydia asked. "But we need not worry about the duns ever again, dearest. We may keep the carriage and hire as many servants as we may need. Somehow, Lord Elmont is aware how badly we are dipped and is offering us a sum to carry us through until the wedding."

"Wedding?" Rebecca asked. "Who is to be married?"

"Why, you, of course," Lydia replied, puzzled at Rebecca's confusion. "Silly goose, the Viscount Elmont is asking for your hand in marriage."

"Again?" Harry asked, looking up at his sister in puzzlement.

Chapter 2

Michael started up the aisle, trying to find himself some unobtrusive place at the rear of the small church. However, the simply wrought pews were nearly filled, and all the seats near the exit were occupied. Reluctantly, he took one of the few remaining spots against the wall, feeling much like a soldier trapped behind enemy lines.

With rising uneasiness, he surveyed the territory, noting the number of people and pews that cut off any hope of rapid escape. As he craned his neck and looked around, he could see that all of the benches were brimming. Nonetheless, the flow of people did not cease until all the walls and railings were obscured by standees. *Perhaps it would be best to leave?* Michael hesitated. Having been unable to secure leave to attend Oliver's wedding, Michael had never met Miss Creighton. Curiosity prevailed.

Not for the first time, Michael found himself wondering at the Paragon's game. Miss Creighton's moral plays had been tediously staged by schoolgirls in every select seminary between Bristol and Penzance. Nonetheless, since her father's death, she had moved well beyond the sphere of the drawing room religious set. Within the past year her pamphlets had proliferated like penny ballads, and her very name had become a byword for the straight and narrow. To "do the Creighton," was to behave with excruciating propriety.

But as Michael looked around him, he began to question that popular opinion. It was only by chance that he had heard one of the men at Soldier's Sanctuary speaking of her engagement to give an address in Covent Garden. By straying from the relative safety of Mayfair, Miss Creighton was treading dangerous ground.

Though the disturbances that had occurred in London and its environs were almost beneath notice, the unrest simmering beneath the surface in the poorer parts of Town could not be denied. While the cleric in the entry was doing a brisk business peddling Miss Creighton's tracts, on the streets outside there were publications of a more radical kind being hawked.

Indeed, the very mention of her name was enough to make Michael's old friend William Cobbett froth at the mouth. Cobbett found Miss Creighton's prosings more damaging to his radical cause than those of that Clapham saint, Hannah More.

From the samples of the Paragon's work that Michael had read, he had little doubt that jealousy was as much at the root of Cobbett's disdain as any revolutionary zeal. Miss Creighton's writings were far more entertaining than Hannah More's and certainly superior to Cobbett's penny pamphlet ramblings. If the number of tracts sold at the door were any indication, then Miss Creighton's publications were highly profitable as well.

Could that be the reason, then, that she had left Oliver and his offer of marriage twisting in the wind for better than a week now? Surely, Miss Creighton could not intend to reject the son of an earl, one of the wealthiest men in England. Michael's mouth twisted in a cynical smile at the very notion. No, it was undoubtedly some convoluted female notion of sport or revenge. After all, Oliver had once left her waiting at the altar.

But ultimately Michael was certain that the money and title would prevail. With bait like that dangling, she would not resist the lure too long. After all, his erstwhile fiancée, Elizabeth, had succumbed to those self-same temptations without any hesitation, claiming all the while that she loved him. The pang of regret was startling; how was it that those long-ago memories still had the power to cause him pain?

Deliberately, Michael turned his attention to the undercurrents of talk around him. Apprentices and laborers, servants on half holiday, a sprinkling of shopkeepers, all shifted uneasily on the hard wooden pews, tracts clutched in their hands. Even with borrowed feathers, Michael felt much like a peacock among the pigeons. He tugged at the collar of Eager's Sunday best, but there was no relief from the chafing. Resigned to discomfort, Michael examined the tract that he had purchased. The cheap print and poor-quality paper did not bode well for the contents. *John Drinkgin and the Road to Blue Ruin* had the less than encouraging subtitle, "A moral tale about the evils of drunkenness." With a sigh, Michael began to read.

"A good-sized crowd, Miss Creighton," the Reverend Silas Havermill declared as he locked the cash box and set it in the rector's desk. Carefully, he turned the key, making certain the drawer was secure before adjusting his clerical collar.

Rebecca peeked out the door at the sea of faces, trying to keep her hands from trembling. "So many," she whispered, her throat constricting. "There must be well over two hundred people out there."

"At least," Havermill agreed casually.

"I . . . I . . . cannot," Rebecca stammered. "When you told me that I was to address a small church group, I had no idea . . ."

"Come, come, Miss Creighton," Havermill said, his chins wagging in irritation. "Surely, you wish to reach as many poor souls as you may?"

"But so many . . ." she said. "I have difficulty enough speaking before lesser gatherings. Why did you not tell me?"

"Does it truly matter whether you address a drawing room with fifty or a sanctuary of five hundred?" Havermill asked, his tones chiding. "Are the humble poor of Covent Garden any less deserving than the middling classes of Bloomsbury or the exalted rich of Mayfair?"

"It was the outside of enough when you told me that I was not to speak in Bloomsbury as I expected but in Covent Garden," Rebecca said, recovering herself. "If I had realized—"

"—That your words are read in Covent Garden, Miss Creighton?" Havermill cut off her protest smoothly. "What is a mile or two here and there after all? You have become a woman of wide influence. Only recently, His Highness was saying that your pamphlets have helped to keep the populace calm. When the eyes of the people are fixed upon heaven and the rewards of righteousness, they are not so inclined to listen to the urgings of the radicals."

"Lofty commendation from so saintly a man," Rebecca said, her sense of the ridiculous coming to her rescue. *Prinny singing her praises, indeed.* "If His Highness feels that my humble writings help to keep the peace, I suppose it proves that even the devil's disciples have some use for religion."

"Miss Creighton!" Havermill's chins rose in indignation. "We will have to speak of this lamentable tendency toward flippancy. Your dear father—"

"—Enjoyed a bit of fine irony as much as the next man, sir," Rebecca said, pulling her sheets of text from her reticule and jamming her spectacles upon her nose. "Well, Mr. Havermill, it is as you say, why sell fifty pamphlets when you can peddle five hundred? I shall have to make certain that these people get their money's worth."

"You demean yourself and your mission when you speak of mere profit, Miss Creighton. In fact, I have given away more pamphlets than I have sold tonight," Havermill said haughtily. "You know that our object is not lucre, but to improve the general moral climate. Where better than here, where the need is greatest?"

"Yes," Rebecca said, suddenly feeling ashamed. What was she becoming? When had she begun to count pennies

more than souls? She could hear the vicar of the church beginning to introduce her; her stomach tightened into a knot
of anxiety. "You are quite right, Mr. Havermill. Where better than here?"

"Miss Rebecca Creighton!"

At the sound of her name, Rebecca swallowed, trying to
calm the pounding of her heart, telling herself that it was no
different than addressing Lady Shand and her friends. Taking a deep breath, she stepped from the concealing shelter of
the vestry.

Though Oliver had described his former fiancée as a near-
dwarf, Michael realized that his friend had been speaking in
terms of his own proportions. Miss Creighton was not a
pocket-sized woman to be sure; her height was pleasing.
Nonetheless, Michael felt his heart sinking as he assessed
the seeming paucity of her feminine assets. She was not
beautiful, certainly not in a way that would cause a man to
look twice.

Covered in black bombazine from toe to neck, her figure
seemed to be composed entirely of angular lines. Since
every lock was scraped back beneath a somber bonnet, the
color of her hair was uncertain. Her walk was light and
graceful as she mounted the pulpit, but that was scant comfort. Candlelight glinted from the lenses of her spectacles,
and he groaned inwardly as he recalled the foremost argument that he had employed in his attempt to persuade his
friend into a new proposal of marriage.

"She was only seventeen. No doubt she has blossomed."
His reassurances to Oliver echoed mockingly in Michael's
mind. Even thistles bloomed. However, from the look of it,
if there had been any budding, it must have withered with
astonishing swiftness.

Judging from his knowledge of Oliver's predilections in
the muslin ranks, Miss Creighton would not suit his tastes at
all. There did not seem to be much of substance for a man to
cuddle. In fact, there was an air of fragility about her that

was almost otherworldly. Little wonder that the woman had an earthy man like Oliver quaking in his boots. Despicable though it was, Michael began to understand why Oliver had left this unfortunate female literally waiting at the altar.

As the applause faded, Rebecca stared out upon the sea of faces, suddenly conscious of her own inadequacy. By what right did she speak? Was she offering them anything more than feigned emotion in return for their generosity? Was she truly any better than the wretched women she had interviewed in preparation for her next tract?

"Miss Creighton?" The voice of the church's pastor recalled her to the present. Desperately, she recalled her father's advice. *I pick someone at the back of the room, child,* the reverend had told her; *that individual becomes my focus.*

Dark brown eyes met hers, deep and rich as the color of melting chocolate. There was a challenge in his searching look, as if he could somehow see beyond the pretense, into the core of fear and loneliness in the center of her being. *Fraud!* Those eyes seemed to declare. *Charlatan! Do you have anything real to offer? How dare you stand before us?*

She tried to look away, but his gaze was like a vise, holding her, demanding her attention. His weathered face was lean. A nose just short of aquiline dominated the high-boned planes of his cheeks. A chiseled chin boasted the merest suggestion of a cleft.

Not much older than herself, Rebecca suspected, yet there was an air of weary wisdom about him, as if those dark eyes had seen far too much. His ill-fitting garments bespoke an upper servant, yet there was nothing servile or humble in his frank appraisal. It was as if he were judging her. Slowly, the corners of his mouth rose in a sardonic quirk, as if he were finding her wanting and the thought amused him.

Automatically, she straightened, her chin jutting out in defiance. Who was he? By what right did he weigh her with no more than a look and then dismiss her? She compelled herself to seek elsewhere for another locus; the earnest young woman who sat on the edge of her seat? Or perhaps she might concentrate on the slender fellow who had the look of a clerk about him? But try though she might, those chocolate eyes pulled at her like lodestones.

Very well, so be it, Rebecca decided. She would take up his gauntlet. Rebecca removed her reading glasses, setting them on the lectern. Truly, there was no need for the lenses because she had come to know every word of her text as well as her catechism.

Michael watched as Miss Creighton stood for a moment, seemingly uncertain as she set the pages upon the lectern. Then her smile swept the audience, transforming her face from plain to luminous. Hesitant at first, the smile grew slowly, as if she were just recognizing a dear and beloved friend. With a look she touched each and every individual present as if she silently spoke to him or her alone. Then, like the lifting of a curtain, she reached up and put her glasses aside. Suddenly, Michael found himself caught in a molten swirl of amber. Trapped within her eyes, he felt suddenly breathless, powerless.

Michael had half expected the voice to be as harsh as the appearance of the woman, but her soft, lilting strains were as musical as a siren's song, putting him under her spell. Though he was enscorcelled, he could still recognize the strength of her discourse. She spoke persuasively, confidentially, almost as one friend to another. Yet, while her voice was soft, there was no prevarication in her words, no effort to pander and make the harsh more palatable.

Candidly, without any evasion, Miss Creighton spoke about the vice of drunkenness. The sordid picture she painted was as biting as any of Hogarth's caricatures. However, the people whose downfall she described were not cartoon figures, but sisters, brothers, husbands and wives, friends and neighbors. Unbidden, the recollection of Oliver's sodden countenance slipped into Michael's own thoughts. Almost as in a trance, Michael looked around him.

Women wept unashamedly, and the shoulders of the thin man in front of him started to shake with sadness.

As she spoke, her words began to echo in his mind, her soft cadence almost like the saddest of songs, but amidst the ruin and degradation there was a refrain of hope. *Let me show you the way*, those intense doe eyes begged him, *let me show you the way*. What was she, this woman, that she could move him so with only the sound of her voice and a melting glance? How unfortunate that she was not more pleasing to look upon; she could have made a fortune upon the boards and rivaled Sarah Siddons. But for her face, Miss Creighton would have made an excellent actress.

Suddenly, the small church echoed with a thunder of applause. Like a sleeper arising from a vivid dream, Michael shook his head. What in the world had he gotten poor Oliver into? Michael wondered. For the bright-eyed female who bent her head in humble acknowledgment was far more worrisome than the crow he had expected. A crow might be ignored, discounted, but not this woman. At seven and twenty, Miss Rebecca Creighton was clever, lucid, and extremely eloquent. If she had been half so at seventeen, it was little wonder that Oliver had been terrified.

The cleric who had been selling her pamphlets at the door moved up the aisle, passing the collection plate for donations. From the way it drooped in his hand, it was clear that it weighed heavy. Michael slipped a gold crown in among the growing mound of copper and silver as he contemplated his friend's predicament.

The earl had thrown a sop or two to stave off the worst of Oliver's creditors. Nonetheless, the debts would not be completely settled until the notices appeared in the papers. She would accept the offer, Michael vowed with a scowl of determination, and soon. The thought of Oliver exiled to France or Fleet was not to be borne.

*   *   *

Rebecca had been trying to ignore the compelling presence that was drawing her attention across the room. As she smiled and mingled with the audience, she determined to pay him no regard. After all, she was no foolish schoolroom miss, to be dazzled by a handsome face and a pair of broad shoulders. With a pang of that undeniably strange awareness, she knew that he was trying to make his way toward the door, pushing through the crowd like a swimmer fighting the tide. Too late, she realized that the surge of the throng was bearing her directly toward him.

Helplessly, Rebecca struggled against the current of humanity, but it was useless. Just as he reached the aisle, the sea of coarse faces parted and she found herself directly before the dark-haired stranger. He was taller than she had originally thought, rising above her by half a head. Amid the garlic and sweat of the crowd, the smell of the bay rum that he wore was especially distinctive.

Michael forced a smile and nodded. Her lips seemed full, almost sensuous, as she responded in kind, revealing even white teeth. At least she was not a gap-mouthed miss. Cursing under his breath, he frantically searched for a route of quick retreat. But as he started to edge his way toward the door, a beefy hand came down on Miss Creighton's arm.

"Go back to Mayfair where you belong, Miss Hoity-toity!" a burly man demanded. "Wastes good money on those penny preachings o' yours, my woman does. All a man hears these days is 'Miss Creighton says this, Miss Creighton says that.' Won't be ruled by petticoats. Come here with your fine clothes and your full belly and sermonize to us what ain't got nothing and take the few pennies what we got!"

The smell of gin was nearly overpowering, and there was the anger of an enraged bull in the man's rheumy eyes. Michael tried to gauge how best to take him down before that fury exploded.

"And every penny comes hard," Rebecca said, fully understanding the pain in his voice. "Your sweat, your toil, squandered on a bit of paper, one of my tracts, mere words that you can neither eat nor drink."

Michael watched in astonishment. Miss Creighton had to be frightened, but though there was worry in her eyes, her demeanor was calm. Her expression was one of utter sympathy and her soothing flow of commiseration did not falter.

"Aye, you have the right of it, miss," the man said, his grip relaxing slightly. "What's a man the likes o' me to do these days? Served king and country, I did. But what's England done for me, I ask you?"

The crowd murmured sympathetically, and Michael could see the man's confusion. Miss Creighton's unexpected compassion had disarmed him. A few more well chosen words and the bruiser might be persuaded to let her go.

"What has old George done for any of us?" Michael agreed. "But this lady has naught to do with the wrongs we have suffered, my friend. Why not let her—"

"Sedition!" The Reverend Havermill's voice rose shrilly as he elbowed his way through the crowd. "You speak no less than treason, sir. Now unhand Miss Creighton or I shall . . . shall . . ."

"Shall what?" the man mocked, squaring his shoulders and advancing menacingly, pulling Miss Creighton along with him. "What 'shall' you do, little man?"

"I shall call the watch immediately," Havermill blustered, backing away. "That is what I shall do. Someone call the watch!"

"Call the Charleys, would you?" one woman cried indignantly. "Just for a man speakin' his mind? For shame!"

"For shame!" The crowd took up the cry. "For shame! Remember the Corn Laws! For shame when an honest Englishman cannot speak."

From the looks upon their faces, it was clear that the audience's sympathies had shifted entirely. The cry of treason, the threat of the watch had altered the balance to the brink of chaos. All that would be necessary to ignite the powder keg was one more foolish word. It was not long in coming.

"The penalties for sedition are extremely severe!" Havermill exhorted.

While all eyes were focused on the cleric, Michael found his opening. Quickly, he snatched Miss Creighton's hand, taking advantage of the few seconds that surprise had given him. He dragged her toward the entrance.

"Unhand me, sir!" Rebecca demanded as the crowd erupted into a roaring mob. Her bonnet flew from her head. Hands clutched at her shoulder as they struggled toward the entrance, and she heard the sound of ripping fabric, felt the rush of air on her suddenly bare shoulder. But despite her pleas, the stranger's fingers gripped her like a vise, dragging her toward the door.

They spilled out onto the steps. Rebecca stumbled, but her abductor pulled her rapidly upright.

"Fight! Fight!" The call came from unseen throats, both warning and invitation, horror and excitement. Fleeing refugees crossed paths with hopeful spectators hurrying to enjoy what promised to be an impressive show.

"Let me go!" Rebecca ordered again, emphasizing her demand by twisting against his grasp.

"Miss Creighton," Michael said as he pulled the struggling woman into a cul-de-sac, "within the next few minutes, I assure you, this street will be as close to hell as any of your sermons. If you have a particular wish to see the insides of a jail, I will oblige you by leaving you behind. However, I should warn you first that the watch is not known for their mercy or their sense of discrimination, particularly in the event of a riot."

"Riot?" Rebecca echoed, hearing the screams and chaos erupting behind them.

"Aye, riot," Michael said grimly, glancing over his shoulder. Her torn dress drooped precariously low above her breast. Disheveled curls spilled from their anchoring pins, framing her ashen face. "Do you ever read anything beyond those tracts of yours, Miss Creighton? There has been a fear of mob violence for quite some time now and with just cause, for if ever a people had reason to riot, it is England's poor. The price of bread is above their touch, and we export our grain abroad when they cannot feed their children. Is it any wonder that they are at the point of boiling?"

"Violence is not—" Rebecca began.

"I have no intent of stopping now to discuss politics, miss," Michael said, cutting her off abruptly, once more towing her along behind him as they plunged back onto the street, fighting against the crowd. "I assure you that Charley's stick is neither Tory nor Radical, and a bullet will kill you regardless of whether you are high church or Methodist."

"Bullets." Rebecca gasped with indignation. "Surely, you do not think that the forces of law would fire upon an un-armed crowd?"

"It may yet come to that. The powers-that-be are desperately afraid. People and governments do foolish things out of fear," Michael said as they emerged onto a relatively quiet street. Soon, the reason for the lack of traffic became apparent. A solid brick wall loomed at the end of the street. "It appears that we have run down a blind alley. We shall have to turn around and retrace our steps."

Just ahead of them, he heard the sound of running feet. Quickly, he pulled Miss Creighton into the darkness of a doorway, shielding her with his body. "Hush!" he demanded. He felt the quick intake of her breath, a yielding softness. She opened her mouth as if to scream.

There was no time for explanation. Swiftly, Michael put his lips to hers, effectively swallowing the sound. Though he meant only to silence her, her taste was surprisingly sweet. Amid the odors of the street, the delicate scent of roses drifted to his nostrils, and for a brief second he forgot the danger, forgot that this female was destined to be Oliver's, forgot everything but the feel of this woman trembling in his arms.

Rebecca tried to bring up her hands, to fight against this assault, but one wrist was clasped tight, and the other arm was pinned firmly between them. The cry that formed in her throat became a hoarse whimper as he claimed her mouth. She felt his hard, lean body pressing her back against the rough brick of the entry. Footsteps approached them and halted.

Though it was dark, she closed her eyes, trying to keep the creeping terror from possessing her entirely, but the sounds and scents seemed to intensify into an overwhelming welter of sensation. A woman screamed in the distance, and somewhere above, a baby cried. Noxious odors of unnameable detritus were masked by the scent of bay rum. His fingers tangled themselves in her hair, freeing one of her hands to explore, to seek. Deep in the folds of his coat, Rebecca felt the cold, hard comfort of metal. A pistol.

"I'd fancy a bit o' that, myself," a voice sniggered.

"You can wait till I've had mine," Michael said, pulling her against him in a possessive gesture, trying at the same time to shield Miss Creighton from their view. He kept his voice deliberately casual as he estimated his chances against the four shadows that advanced toward them. Even if he was able to reach his pistol and take one down, there were three left. "Hear that the shops are givin' away their wares for free tonight. I'd be up near the church right now, gettin' a bit o' that rum swag myself, if I hadn't already paid this bit o' Haymarket ware."

"An' oo are you callin' 'aymarket ware?" Rebecca replied, quickly taking her cue from him, trying to imagine this nightmare as part of a scene in one of her tracts. *What would Cathy of Covent Garden say?* "Bring me back something pretty, boys, 'cos I'll be here all night."

"And what if we wants it now?" one of them demanded.

Rebecca pulled the pistol from her captor's pocket and leveled it along his shoulder. "One at a time, gents, is my rules. If it's play together you want, there's plenty o' houses here that will oblige you." For emphasis, Rebecca cocked the hammer with a telltale click, fixing her eyes upon each face in turn. "Now go on; come back later and ask for Cathy, Cathy of Covent Garden, or meet my barker now."

Michael held his breath, readying himself to turn and fight, but to his surprise, the men started to laugh.

"Aye, wait for me, Cathy, and I'll bring yer back sommat real big, luvly!" he pledged with a cackle of glee.

"But it won't be pretty," another hooted.

They left with a raucous chorus of ribald promises. Michael waited until the sound of their footsteps faded before stepping back.

"I vow, you amaze me, Miss Creighton, or shall I say 'Cathy?' " he said, letting loose a relieved breath. "How the devil did you come up with that so quickly?"

"Research," she said, backing away from him, the pistol still clutched in her shaking fingers. "I am presently writing a tract about a fallen woman."

Somehow she did not seem so prim and proper now. Her hair had come wholly undone, cascading down her back and framing her piquant face. Beneath the ripped shoulder and bodice of her gown, her skin was as smooth as alabaster. His hands remembered the soft curves beneath that loathsome gown. "*Cathy of Covent Garden*, I take it. I shall look forward to that publication with interest," Michael said, watching her as the moon winked from behind the clouds.

"It is not yet completed," Rebecca said, trying to keep herself from thinking what might have happened. Even now, she could feel the touch of his fingers on her skin. The taste of his lips had not yet faded. What was wrong with her? Why did she suddenly want to fling herself into his arms? Was it fear? And why was he eyeing her in that odd way . . . could it be that he might think her desirable? "In my research I have found that there are many misapprehensions about the state of these poor females."

"Are there, indeed, Miss Creighton? And pray, what misapprehensions are those?" It would seem that the Paragon was a woman, a most unusual woman. Any miss of his acquaintance would have been indulging in a fit of vapors by now.

"There are few who reach the status of a famous courtesan, such as Harriet Wilson," Rebecca said, trying to keep up the flow of words. "It is a miserable life, I am told, full of disease, violence, and unhappiness."

"And have you talked to many . . . er," Michael searched bemusedly for a safe word, scarcely able to credit the topic of conversation, but it was clear that she needed to talk of something, anything. The moon illuminated her blanched face. Her tawny eyes were still wide with fear, her brave words no more than a facade.

"Bits of muslin? Harlots? Which euphemism do you prefer? There are so many," she said, relieved at the sudden anger that sparked within her; far better to be annoyed than to harbor these absurd impulsive feelings. "Yes, I have spoken to a number of those unfortunate women who are now seeking to change their lives. You might be surprised to find how innocently it starts. Very few of them realize the end of the road upon which they travel."

"Even Harriet Wilson began as an innocent," Michael said with a shrug. "You believed their stories, I take it?"

"And you do not, I take it?" Rebecca retorted. "Are you one of those men, sir, who believes that every woman is a Cyprian at heart? That we are all the same in the dark, after all? Is that why you kissed me?"

"A most unusual topic of discussion, Miss Creighton," Michael said, shaking his head in a mixture of amusement and incredulity. "My beliefs about women are not the issue at present. But if you choose to think so ill of me, then I begin to find myself feeling somewhat apprehensive about that loaded pistol in your hand. You had best give it back to me."

"I think not, sir," Rebecca said with a ragged breath, bringing up the weapon. "I have no intention of continuing where we left off."

"Nor do I," Michael said, inexplicably annoyed by her

mistrust, even though he understood her reaction, "much as I might have enjoyed it." Silently, Michael cursed himself for those last few words; it had been entirely the wrong thing to say to a nervous woman with a cocked pistol.

No matter that it had been no less than the truth; he had almost lost himself in that kiss. Perhaps there was hope for Oliver after all. With a bit of instruction and practice, she might even be passable company. He shook his head, alarmed at the wayward direction of his thoughts. "Unfortunately, I had little choice but to kiss you," he said, gentling his tone.

"Indeed," Rebecca said coldly, fighting to keep her hand steady. "And how did you come to that grievous conclusion?"

"You will not deny that you were about to scream, Miss Creighton," Michael explained, trying to match her superficial sangfroid. "In the dark, I had hoped to evade the attention of your would-be swains entirely, but it seems that was not to be. Were it not for your quick thinking, you might have found out far more about the Cathys of this world than your informants had ever told you. Those men were not about to let me stand between them and a bit of fun." He advanced slowly, cautiously, his palm outstretched. "Your clever little farce likely saved our skins. Now, if you will hand me my pistol, we had best be gone."

"Stay back," Rebecca warned, frightened by the look in his eyes. Never in all her life had a man looked at her so. *Much as I might have enjoyed it*—his words took on an ominous note.

"You made Cathy sound extremely enticing, Miss Creighton," Michael said softly. "Even now, your admirers might very well regret the missed opportunity."

A cat yowled, streaking from the alleyway with startling swiftness, causing the pistol to slip from her grip. With a roar of powder and flame, the weapon spat its load. In a cloud of sulfurous smoke she saw her captor fall to the ground.

"I have killed him." Rebecca moaned, kneeling at his side. "Dear merciful heaven, I have killed him."

"Not quite yet, Miss Creighton, though not for want of effort," Michael said, trying to keep a tight rein on his anger as he rolled to a sitting position. "A decade on the Peninsula gave me ample experience in dodging bullets. But it would have served you right if you had been left to fend for yourself. Perhaps you would find that life is not like one of your tracts, where justice invariably triumphs and innocence vanquishes evil."

"I am s-so sorry." Rebecca rose, staring about her in shocked bewilderment.

Her eyes were wide, and she was starting to shake. Michael had seen the signs often enough on the battlefield. He could not afford to have her go into shock now. He came to his feet quickly. "No harm done," he said, keeping his voice firm and bracing, touching her shoulder gently.

"Why has no one come to our aid?" Rebecca asked as he helped her to her feet. "Surely, someone must have heard the gunshot."

"No one wants to be the first to find trouble, Miss Creighton," Michael said, stooping to retrieve the pistol. "In these streets a murdered man is stripped to the bone; not even the clothes on his back remain. Only a fool would rush to be a witness while the pillage is still in progress." He brushed with ineffectual vigor at his borrowed clothing. "Damn! Now I have ruined Eager's new suit! And I had promised him to take extreme care. Devil a bit!"

"I shall reimburse your friend for his suit," Rebecca said, her chin rising in indignation. "There is no need to curse, sir."

"Well, la and gracious dear me, whatever was I thinking of?" Michael said, deliberately nursing her ire; far better anger than paralyzing fear. He took her hand and led her from the alleyway. "If my blasphemies annoy you, Paragon, I would suggest you stop your ears. I doubt I will be 'doing the Creighton' tonight and I am damned sure that I will be overstepping more than a few of your 'thou shalt nots' before I deliver you home to your door. Now we had best make ourselves scarce before your would-be swains come back to take you up on your generous offer, *Cathy*."

Rebecca swallowed as she realized the truth of his words. She was entirely dependent on this stranger. Swiftly, he began to reload his pistol, his movements deft and sure with obvious experience. Then to her surprise, he extended the ready weapon, placing the grip in her hand.

"Here," he said, his tone oddly gruff as he closed her fingers around the butt of the pistol. "Just remember, Paragon, if you choose to point it again, be prepared to use it."

There was something that she could not define in those brown eyes, a wordless plea. He was asking a silent question. Suddenly, she knew the answer.

"You take it," she said, taking his hand at the wrist. Gently, she unfurled his fist and placed the weapon in his palm. "My skills are rather limited, Mr. . . . Mr. . . ." She smiled hesitantly. "I do not even know your name, sir."

"Call me Michael," he said, looking at her upraised face. Why was it that he wanted to gather her close? To kiss the fear away? The danger of the moment perhaps? Without question, that was the reason.

"The keeper of the keys to heaven," she said softly. "Prince of angels."

Michael smiled at the allusions. "I would not rely too much on a name, Miss Creighton. There are not a few people who might tell you that I am in league with Beelzebub himself." He tucked the pistol securely into his belt and led her into the night.

Chapter 3

Though it was early April, the night had grown chilly. The wind cut like a razor as they emerged from the sheltered area between the buildings. Ahead of them, Rebecca heard a strange tinkling sound. Magnified by the walls of brick, the echoes of shattering resounded in the darkness.

"Breaking glass—I was afraid of this," Michael muttered, coming to an abrupt halt at the sound of running feet.

"What is happening?" Rebecca asked, folding her arms tightly about herself. "Why are they shouting?"

"An invitation, Miss Creighton," Michael explained, his mouth tightening into an apprehensive line. "If I calculate our location correctly, there are rows of shops along the next street. It would appear that the riot has begun to spread."

Quickly, he swept her from the center of the street. From the doors and alleyways a torrent of people spilled. Men, women, and children surged into the streets, laughing and shouting as if they were on holiday, headed for the St. Bartholomew Fair. Michael and Rebecca stayed close to the wall until the flood faded to a trickle.

"I thought you were making up a story when you spoke of looting," Rebecca said, her eyes wide with horror.

"Riot and pillage are like fire and smoke—one is rarely unaccompanied by the other," Michael said, frowning as he weighed their prospects. "And this part of Town was waiting tinder. I had hoped to head directly eastward and take the shortest route back to civilization, but that no longer seems like the best of ideas."

"And I am responsible for all this," Rebecca said, shivering. "If not for me . . ."

"No, Miss Creighton," Michael said, putting his hand on her shoulder. The stricken look on her face told him that she honestly believed herself to blame. "You are not at all at fault for the start of this. I have little doubt that you would soon have had that drunkard eating out of your hand, if not for that fool of a clergyman." Reluctantly, he changed their course and turned toward the Thames and one of the roughest parts of London.

"Surely you c-cannot blame Mr. Havermill," Rebecca protested. "He was merely trying to come to my aid. Poor man, I hope that he was not hurt. I should have . . ."

"Done what, Miss Creighton?" Michael questioned in exasperation, wishing he knew some way to assuage her baseless guilt. "There was naught you could have done to prevent something like this from happening tonight. And if it had not occurred at the church this evening, it would surely have started elsewhere, tomorrow. These disturbances have become almost commonplace."

Rebecca shook her head in disbelief. "I had thought that the rumors were hysterical nonsense."

"Do you think that the government has wanted the news to circulate, Miss Creighton?" Michael asked. "The papers have not reported the half of what has been happening. So long as these conflagrations confine themselves to small outlying areas or the poorer sections, they are thought of little consequence. With so many flooding the city in search of work, London has become a virtual powder keg. It is only a matter of time before it explodes in our faces."

"You sound much like M-m-Mr. Cobbett," Rebecca said softly. She smiled at his startled look. "You s-s-see, I do read s-something b-b-beyond my own tracts."

"Damn me, your teeth are chattering." Unthinkingly, he took her hands between his own, chiding himself for a self-centered fool. "Your fingers are like blocks of ice. You must be freezing."

"There was scarcely time to fetch my cloak, as you rec-c-call," Rebecca replied, wondering at her reaction to his touch, a flare of heat that was hardly in proportion to the warmth of his hands. When he let her fingers free, she felt suddenly bereft. But her puzzlement turned swiftly to dismay as he shrugged off his own outer garment. "There is n-n-no need for that, Michael."

"Indeed there is," Michael said, eyeing her with a wicked grin. "Your very proper bombazine has become more than a trifle revealing, and though I fear to say it, Miss Creighton, lest you turn my pistol upon me again, the charms that your modified gown reveals are sufficiently enticing to make any man want to see what else might be hidden beneath. We shall have to find you some decent clothing, or else I may find myself fighting for your virtue."

Rebecca's mouth formed an O of amazement. Never before in her life had any man described her as remotely attractive. Unbidden, the feel of his body against hers came to mind, and she flushed red as she tugged at her torn gown. Desperately, she searched for some reply. "No Spanish c-coin, if you please," she said, primly. "But I c-c-cannot deny that these streets are filled with desperate men tonight." She quivered at the memory of that encounter, those hungry eyes devouring her.

"I will take care of you, Miss Creighton," Michael promised, wondering why she had taken such pains to conceal her every asset, to hide her womanliness beneath those layers of mourning. Once again, he felt a longing to touch that cloud of hair, to feel if it was truly as soft and silken as memory had made it. He contented himself with brushing it lightly as he draped his jacket about her shoulders.

Turning her to face him, Michael tucked the garment beneath her chin, buttoning the front for her almost as if she were a nursling. But she was most definitely not a child, he thought, as the warmth of her breath touched his hands. Though she tried to hide it, those amber eyes showed her thoughts clearly. It was as much fear as cold that was making her quiver.

Fear of him? The thought was oddly disturbing, yet as his fingers reached up to touch her shoulder, he realized that a bit of apprehension might be judicious for them both. "You will get home safely, I swear," he said, with a gentle squeeze of reassurance.

Rebecca snuggled gratefully into the remnants of his warmth. Though he had mentioned that his finery was borrowed, the oddly comforting scents of snuff, bay rum, and macassar oil were clearly Michael's. His light touch was like the seal to his oath, and she felt some of her anxiety slipping away.

Though she did not know how, in less than the space of an hour, she had come to believe in this man, to trust in him. "Thank you, Michael," she said guiltily. His linen shirt and waistcoat could afford him little protection against the chill. "But you must be cold yourself now. We should find a hack immediately."

Michael chuckled, his rich, deep baritone sending a curious warmth through her. "And just what is so funny, pray tell?" Rebecca asked, perplexed at his reaction.

"You might as well wish for the moon as for a hired cab in this part of Town. No driver who values his throat would be so foolish as to venture here at night, especially when there is unrest in the air," Michael explained, pleased to find that Eager's waistcoat was sufficiently loose to provide decent concealment for his pistol. "We had best get started. I suspect we may have something of an adventure ahead of us."

"What of the Opera House?" Rebecca asked, resisting an urge to bend down and rub her aching feet. Her thin-soled footwear was not made for wear on the London streets. "Surely, there are carriages for hire on Bow Street, and that cannot be very far."

"We might as well try to reach Bombay tonight, Paragon," Michael said, shaking his head. "Although I am none too familiar with these streets, I believe that Bow Street lies beyond those shops. We would have to return in the direction we came." Michael stiffened at the unmistakable crack of a gunshot. "Have you ever been in the heart of a melee, Miss Creighton?"

"No," Rebecca said with a negative gesture. "At least never before."

"Those shopkeepers will be defending their homes and livelihoods with everything they can muster," Michael said, looking around, trying to get his bearings in this unfamiliar territory.

There was not even a parish lamp to guide them, only the light of an unreliable moon. One dark street looked very much like another, and a wrong turn could easily get them both killed, or worse in her case. "Sane, ordinary, law-abiding people plunge into lunacy, committing acts beyond their maddest nightmares. All the veneer that we call 'civilization' slips away. And those who tend naturally toward violence . . ." Michael closed his eyes, shuddering involuntarily at the memories of transformed faces, atrocities, men turned into monsters.

All at once, the tentative touch of a hand penetrated the haze of recollection. His eyes flew open again, and she was gazing up at him, the fear gone, replaced by compassion and concern.

"You were a soldier," she said, moved by the vivid pain she had seen in that unguarded second. Within those earthen depths agony rose briefly, then all emotion was buried.

"What gave me away?" Michael said, summoning a rueful grimace.

"Nothing and everything," Rebecca said, trying to give words to her thoughts. "There is something in your bearing, the way that you speak, as if you are accustomed to having your word obeyed. And your countenance . . ."

"Is the mark of Cain visible to your saintly eyes, Miss Creighton?" Michael asked, only half in jest.

"Saintly?" She shook her head. "You are more of a saint

than I, I suspect. You have been tried by fire, tested in the worst hell that mankind can devise . . . and from what little I have seen, you emerged with your humanity. And as for the sign of Cain, I would be frightened indeed if you bore no mark of your experience. If you could pass through such carnage and remain untouched, unmoved, then you would be less of a man."

"But you do not fear me now?" Michael asked in disbelief, his hand covering hers. "I could be dragging you to a brothel, delivering you for sale to slavers, or seeking to deceive you for my own wicked purposes. You have no idea who I am, what I am, yet you have no apprehensions?"

Rebecca met his searching gaze and looked within herself for the truth. "No, Michael, I would be lying if I said that I had no misgivings at all. You are still a stranger. Nonetheless, though I do not know who you are, you have taken me out of harm's way and protected me."

"Perhaps for my own nefarious reasons," he argued. Her hand was so small inside his own; her skin was warmer now. Yet, she could not realize how helpless she was or else she would not be staring at him with such naive trust. "I could be anyone, anything, leading you into the bowels of hell."

"It would seem to me that we have already reached the borders of Gehenna," she said, trying to contain a shudder as a rat sauntered casually across their path. Raucous laughter sounded from a doorway behind them. "Your clothes tell me that you may be a footman or a clerk, but you gave me your coat when I was cold. Though you may think it foolish, I am not afraid of you now."

"You might do better to be wary of me," Michael said.

She shrugged. "Perhaps, but still, I do not suspect you of designs on my person. A man of your looks could do far better than a woman like me, without the risks entailed by abduction."

Though the jest was at her own expense, Michael heard the pang of anguish in those self-deprecating words. Her twist of a smile was rueful, speaking volumes about her feelings of inadequacy. For the first time in his life, Michael wondered what it was to be ill-favored, to endure the sly digs and humiliation in a world where beauty was the main yardstick.

"If you had let those ruffians get a better view of me back there, they might well have gone away laughing at your poor taste in Jezebels. And if you are concocting schemes of white slavery, I would doubt your eyesight. Any price that you might get for me would be hardly worth the trouble," she added, trying to force a chuckle.

How much had that forlorn effort at fun cost her? Michael wondered. She wore the same despairing look that he had seen on any number of women, the ones who sat among the matrons at the edge of the ballroom floor. But had he ever recognized that pasted-on countenance of good humor for what it truly was? Seen the wistful longing behind the smile? What would it be to know himself as the object of raillery or pity? How many woman had he danced with out of politeness or obligation, longing only for the music to end, never seeing the wistful longing behind their facades?

Michael wanted to find some way to comfort her, but could think of nothing that would not be taken as a counterfeit compliment. No, she was not a beauty, and yet, there was something about her that intrigued him as no Incomparable ever had. They trudged together along the moonlit streets in silence. Certainly, he had not experienced this easy companionship, without the need to fill the void with inconsequential chatter. She walked on, without pressing him for the reassurance of words.

At the level of the street, most of the windows were dark. Rebecca stared longingly at the occasional lights above. In their own way, they seemed as distant as the very stars. Within those circles of light were families preparing for sleep, children saying their prayers and being tucked in for the night. She thought of the story that she had promised to Harry, but she would not be home in time to tell it now.

Were they wondering what had happened to her? Had Mr. Havermill returned home without her?

Rebecca stole a glance at her rescuer as she considered her situation. She might try knocking on one of these doors and begging for shelter. But she knew enough to understand that there might well be danger beyond those lit windows. This section of London was rife with flash houses and gambling dens. Every vice known to man could be found beyond these doors if one only knew where to look. Up ahead, she saw the gleam of several splendid equipages.

"We had best skirt this street," Michael said, coming to a complete halt.

"But why?" Rebecca asked, wincing at the very thought of backtracking. Her feet were beginning to ache terribly.

"Up ahead is one of the most popular brothels in all of London," Michael told her, facing her firmly in the opposite direction. "I had not realized that we had reached Drury Lane, but there are several such houses all along here. You would be quite surprised at whom you might meet coming out of these doors. An additional few steps is well worth the risk of avoiding someone who might recognize you."

Flags of color touched Rebecca's cheeks as she realized that Michael was correct. The eminently proper Miss Rebecca Creighton, walking with a stranger in a part of London where no respectable woman would dare to be seen even in daylight—her name would be stewed into scandal broth.

"Well," she said briskly, her feet aching as she matched her pace to his, "at the least we have just proven that you are not shepherding me to a house of ill-repute."

Once again, her reaction surprised him, and his estimation of Oliver's might-be bride went up yet another notch. Loathsome though it was, Michael realized that he had deliberately been seeking to shock her in order to gauge her response. He had not expected humor.

"That still leaves any number of foul objectives, Paragon," Michael said with a chuckle.

"That is the fourth time this evening that you have called me 'Paragon,' " she said, allowing him to tuck her hand beneath his arm. "Why?"

"Are you not the epitome of feminine virtue, Miss Creighton?" Michael asked facetiously. "Dispenser of advice and homilies, model of womanly rectitude?"

"My, my, you have neglected to mention the fact that I have been known to walk across the Thames without aid of a bridge," Rebecca said, pulling her hand away. "And you have quite forgotten my halo."

Michael's right eyebrow elevated at her rejoinder. Apparently, she did not take her image too seriously. Once again, she had defied his expectations. "Have I insulted you, Miss Creighton? If so, I deeply regret my remarks about virtue and moral rectitude. I meant nothing of the kind."

"I was well aware of that, sir. Indeed, your inflection made your sarcastic intent absolutely clear," Rebecca said, warming to her topic. "But I suspect that you did not believe that I would catch your meaning. There are any number of people like you who equate religiosity with gullibility."

"People like me, Miss Creighton?" Michael asked with deliberate dryness. "Do you exclusively mean footmen or clerks who have been former soldiers who go about abducting saints? What of people like you, who make judgments based on the cut of a borrowed suit?"

Miss Creighton laughed. Oliver might change his tune somewhat if he could see the changes that merriment made in her countenance, Michael thought, watching the transformation in silent wonder. Her eyes grew bright and luminous. No longer was the sensual fullness of her lips hidden by that dogged look of eternal solemnity. And the melodic sound of her, the rippling arpeggio of that chuckle played up and down his spine in musical sensuality. Yes, the Paragon would certainly do well to laugh more often.

"You are quite right; we all tend to make assumptions based on superficialities," Rebecca admitted as they halted at the crossroads. "Still, you cannot deny that you have me at something of a disadvantage. You have heard me speak, read my work. All too frequently, someone reads one of my tracts or sees one of my moral plays, and in the wink of an eye they become an expert on Rebecca Creighton."

"And you are forever playing the role of Lucy, in *Lucy's Valuable Lesson*," Michael said, relieved to see a familiar side street just ahead of them. At least they were now bound in the right direction.

"Ah, yes. That vile sin of my youth will haunt me forever, I suspect." Rebecca winced. "I was barely seventeen when I wrote it, not much more than a child, and very, very certain that the world was like one of my father's sermons. Love pure and true was destined to prevail."

"And you found that true love is naught but a tale for children," Michael said.

There was a barely perceptible tightening of his grip, and Rebecca found herself wondering at the source of the sudden bitterness in his voice. "No," she said, trying to explain her meaning, "not quite, but I have found that what I once mistook for true love was little more than a girl's fantasy. That does not necessarily mean that true love is a myth, only that I had made an error in judgment."

"And do you still expect to find true love?" Michael could not help but ask. Perhaps that was why she had not yet accepted Oliver's proposal? Was she foolish enough to whistle away a fortune in hope of some romantic dream?

She shook her head, as if she could not quite trust herself to speak. Once again quiet reigned between them, but this time the lack of speech made Michael uneasy. Moonlight traced a suspicious gleam on her face. Michael lifted his hand, but let it fall back to his side. It was not his place to wipe away her tears. He wished that he could call back the question, for clearly he had touched a raw nerve.

True love? Rebecca mulled over his question as she walked on, trying to forget about the mounting pain of her feet. Was that what she had been wishing for in the sanctuary of her heart, the same fantasy that she had woven for herself at seventeen? Was she cloaking Oliver in shining armor, hoping that he would profess undying devotion?

Rebecca caught a glimpse of herself in a shop window. Her hair straggled down her cheeks in hoyden fashion; her face pale and ghastly in the moonlight, more like the countenance of a crone than a woman of seven-and-twenty. Swathed in Michael's dark jacket, she seemed almost shapeless, like a disembodied head floating in a sea of black. *True love?* How could any man ever want *that*? If she harbored any such nonsensical dreams, it was past time to let go.

Michael had thought that the Paragon was going to let his question pass, and he was surprised when she finally broke the barrier of uncomfortable stillness.

"You asked me about true love? I am beyond the expectation of such miracles," she said. Though her tone was conversational, her eyes held the dying embers of hopes and dreams. "At seven and twenty, I am a spinster, sir, at my last prayers. A woman in my position would be fortunate to get an honorable offer of marriage, much less a pledge of eternal affection. Nonetheless, I have come to believe that true love is only for the very young and the very foolish."

"And what is it you want, if you reject this romantic ideal?" Michael asked, confident of her answer. "In my experience, most females seek first for financial security, physical comfort . . ."

"And have you asked so many females for their hands in marriage that you know the requirements of my sex?" Rebecca countered with a puckish grin.

"Only one, Miss Creighton," Michael replied, endeavoring to match her light tone. "I have toyed with the parson's mousetrap only once, but Elizabeth concluded that the other fellow's purse was far superior to mine. So much for true love."

His countenance could have been carved from stone, and there was no longer any humor lurking in his mockery of a smile. Try as he might to disguise it as banter, his words revealed a bleeding wound. If he had honestly loved this woman, then no amount of time would fully heal that pain.

"If money would turn her away, then she was not your true love," Rebecca concluded, "any more than Oliver was mine."

"You speak from experience, I take it," Michael said, curious to hear her response. "Did you truly love this fellow?"

"I thought that I did," Rebecca said, marveling at her own temerity. Never before had she revealed any of this, not to Lydia, not even to her own father while he lived. Her feelings, her thoughts about Oliver had been locked away for so many years, and now she was opening her heart to a stranger.

"He was very handsome, and I was barely seventeen," Rebecca continued, glancing up at Michael's face. Would he think her a shallow fool? Why did his good opinion suddenly matter? "When he asked for my hand, I scarcely dared to believe my good fortune . . ." Her throat clogged with unshed tears as those memories of overwhelming happiness flooded back. "Even then, I was good at weaving stories. It was very simple to place myself in the role of heroine, to make myself believe that he had seen beyond my face and form into the center of me. Ultimately, what happened was more my fault than his . . ."

Michael felt unexpected annoyance well at her justification of Oliver's actions. "Do you savor the role of martyr, Paragon? I vow, you seem to enjoy bearing the burden of guilt that belongs squarely on the shoulders of others. Ol . . . this damnable rascal who obviously took French leave en route to the altar does not deserve—"

He halted abruptly, aghast as he realized what he had just said. Oliver's future hung in the balance of this woman's yea or nay, not to mention a potential fortune in Michael's own pocket. Yet, try as he might, Michael could not bring himself to take the words back, to let her absolute belief in her own guilt stand unchallenged.

"Indeed, it was literally on the way to the altar," Rebecca

admitted with a strangled sound that was neither a laugh nor a sob. "But I had ignored what should have been quite obvious even to a girl of seventeen. His father had forced him to make the offer of marriage, not any romantic yearning for me. I came to realize that my fiancé saw nothing more than I saw in the mirror—a rather plain young woman with nothing much to recommend her. In the meantime I had created an elaborate daydream based entirely on a handsome face and a polite smile. In truth, Oliver did not really know me, any more than I knew him."

"Such marriages are common enough among the Quality, I am told," Michael said.

"Perhaps he did me a great favor, then, when he jilted me," Rebecca said, musing. "I find myself wondering if it might not be better to lead apes in hell than to live without—"

"True love again, Miss Creighton?"

"No," she said softly. "I would much prefer honor . . . respect. Without those, marriage is nothing more than a quid pro quo, a base transaction that is no less than an act of sanctified prostitution."

"You continue to astound me, Paragon," Michael said, relieved at the opportunity to turn the subject. "You sound almost like Mrs. Godwin."

"Have you actually read her work?" Rebecca questioned, her eyebrows rising in a searching look as she added yet another daub of information to her inner portrait of this man. Not an upper servant, to be sure. But even as she tried to place him in the proper social pigeonhole, she realized that it did not matter.

Michael nodded. "I have, but have you, or do you vilify her based entirely on hearsay, as so many do?"

"No, coward that I am, I have my copy of *The Vindication of the Rights of Women* hidden discreetly away, of course. It would not do for Rebecca Creighton to be seen reading such things," Rebecca admitted. "Nonetheless, though we disagree on many basic ideas, she and I, I cannot deny some of the truths in what she says."

"I would have guessed that you would be of the kind more inclined to hiding away a copy of Byron."

"Byron!" Rebecca said derisively. "A posturing popinjay if ever there was one. No, my tastes are more honest, sir. *A Soldier's Journey* is more to my liking."

"So it would seem that there was a third copy sold," Michael mumbled beneath his breath in utter amazement.

" 'Cross the sere Spanish plain,' still thrills me even though I have read it no less than half a dozen times," Rebecca confessed. "However, Byron's *Corsair* was far better than warm milk in the way of a soporific."

She had read his verse, favored it above Byron's. Oliver's fiancée was clearly a woman of superior taste. Michael would have questioned her further, but a sudden movement in the shadows caught his eyes. The moon was playing hide-and-seek between the cover of the clouds; except for an occasional passerby, the flow of people had almost ceased. With a cautioning pressure, he touched Miss Creighton's arm even as his other hand sought the butt of his pistol.

"Lookin' for company?"

Rebecca judged that the garishly painted girl who stepped from the alleyway could have been no more than thirteen. Her tawdry gown concealed nothing, and the desperation in her gaunt face sent Rebecca's hand seeking for her reticule, but the bag was long gone.

Before Michael could stop her, she had gone to the girl.

"What is your name, child?" Rebecca asked.

"What der yer want it t'be?" the child asked, her eyes ancient and canny.

"Rebecca!" She felt Michael's hand upon her shoulder, drawing her away. Hastily, she pulled her last penny from her pocket and pressed it into the girl's filthy hand.

"What der yer want?" the girl asked suspiciously. "This ain't enough fer two."

"Go home," Rebecca told her. "Go home, child."

"Ooh, hoo, rich that is." The girl began to laugh. " 'Home,' says she."

The child's mocking laughter followed them down the street as they hurried away.

Michael whirled her to face him. Her look of honest bafflement made him want to shake her. "Never do that again." The words came slowly and deliberately from between clenched teeth.

"She is no more than a baby," Rebecca whispered, blinking her eyes against the sudden sting of tears.

"She never was a baby," Michael told her. "And somewhere nearby there is doubtless some man who will take that coin you have given her along with every other penny she earns tonight. You have certainly done her no good, and your foolish gesture brands us as easy marks, strangers to these streets."

Rebecca shook her head in dismay.

"Do you know how many fools die each night, lured by dollymops like her, or are robbed and beaten within an inch of their lives?" Michael continued relentlessly.

"Merciful heaven."

"Perhaps your heaven, Miss Creighton; mine has never been so." His gaze swept their surroundings, searching for signs of confederates. With any luck at all, all the flash in Covent Garden had gone to join the looter's fest. Still, they could not afford to be careless.

"We have entered a battlefield, Paragon, and we are surrounded by the enemy," Michael explained, making no effort to soften his words. "Give way to those do-good impulses of yours again, and you may well find just how harsh reality may be." A thousand nightmarish possibilities made his gut wrench. He had to make her understand her danger. "Do you have any conception of what they would do to you, Miss Creighton? There is no room here for mercy, for weakness. Do not stray from my side again, because I am your only defense tonight." Her eyes widened into pools of terror, and he knew that he had succeeded in making his point.

"I understand," Rebecca said, trying to blink back the

tears that threatened. Wordlessly, he pulled her to him. She
leaned into his warmth, gathering strength from the steady
beat of his heart. For a moment, she dared to pretend that
they were more than two strangers thrown together by cir-
cumstance. He was her champion, the knight who would defend her to the death.

Rebecca looked up at the harsh planes of his face, silvered
with moonlight, and though his eyes were still narrow with
agitation, she felt strangely comforted. She knew now that
the anger was all for her sake, for her own protection.

His fingers rose to her cheek, brushing the ridge below
her eyes lightly in a gentle caress, a gesture that held more
pity than passion. Suddenly, Rebecca wished with all her
heart that she had been given the gift of beauty, so that this
man could look upon her face and feel desire. Though she
knew it was sinful, she wanted more than succor, more than
a touch that would suit a frightened child.

Her body began to tremble, and she found herself holding
her breath, waiting for something unknown. His chocolate
eyes began to change, to darken. She felt his fingers cupping
her chin, tipping her face upward. There was puzzlement in
his gaze, as if he could not quite understand what was happening.

Those tawny eyes swirled, wide and luminous. He could
feel the tickle of her breath, tantalizing against his fingers.
Bathed in the mercury glow of the moon, her skin was like
fine porcelain, delicate and fragile. But most beguiling of all
was that look of innocent trust in her eyes.

No woman had ever gazed at him with such utter confidence, a belief that bordered perilously on worship. She
could not know how she tempted him, how close he was to
taking advantage of that peculiar allure of virtue. *And she is
Ollie's,* Michael reminded himself. *Ollie's woman.*

"Ah, Paragon," he whispered, forcing himself to take a
step back. "You are most fortunate that I still have some
semblance of honor."

His withdrawal was like a slap in the face, bringing her

abruptly back to reality. Shame crept across her cheeks, and she turned her face away, grateful for the shield of night.

What was happening? She had taken a simple embrace of solace and nearly turned it into something sordid. Rebecca bowed her head, knowing that she had all but asked him outright to kiss her, flaunted herself, behaved like the most brazen of hussies. It would appear that the Minerva Press novels that she secretly devoured were taking their toll.

Lucky, indeed, that her looks had served to shield her virtue when her own sense of decency had failed. Still, as they walked on, Rebecca wondered why she was damning Michael for his sense of honor.

Chapter 4

In the nursery at Cavendish Square, Lydia pulled up her son's bedcovers and gently kissed him upon the forehead. "Sleep well, Harry, dear," she said, picking up the snuffer and reaching for the candle.

"Becky promised me a story before bed," Harry protested as his mother bent to put out the candle. "She said that she would be home in plenty of time."

Lydia frowned. "She and the Reverend Havermill must have been delayed. Perhaps she will tell you two stories tomorrow."

"May I stay up and wait until she comes?" Harry asked.

"You may not stay up," Lydia told him. "But if you would like, *I* will tell you a story."

"Two stories tomorrow," Harry decided, snuggling into the pillows. "Tell Becky when she comes home."

"I shall," Lydia said. The chimes of the hall clock echoed up the stairs as the hour was struck.

Rebecca and Michael had nearly reached the Strand when he noticed that Miss Creighton had begun to limp. In truth, though they were hand in hand, he had barely looked at her, fearing that he would see contempt in those golden eyes. It was no less than he deserved after his disgraceful behavior. He had come perilously close to kissing her.

Now, once again, he had good reason to curse himself for an unmindful boor. The light shoes that she wore were little better than household slippers, designed for no heavier use than the walk between a carriage and a hostess's door. She might as well have been barefoot for all the protection that those thin soles gave her, yet she had not complained or made him slow his pace.

"Sometimes, Miss Creighton, there is a thin line between courage and stupidity," Michael said with a sigh, guiding her to a vacant stone stair. "Why did you not tell me that your feet were bothering you?"

Rebecca shrugged. "What could you have done about it?" she asked, trying to summon a smile as he sat her down. "As you say, there are no cabs to be had. Indeed, I have not seen so much as a dray on the streets tonight. You cannot carry me on your shoulders, so there is naught to do but walk. It would serve no purpose to complain."

"I could have slowed the pace," Michael said, kneeling before her. "And I know of a few tricks that might help. Unfortunately, the boots that were supplied to our soldiers were often not of the best. Would you let me see what I can do?"

Rebecca nodded uncertainly, knowing that this was not the time for missishness. Even so, as he unwound the ribbons that bound her shoes at the ankle and instep, it felt like an unspeakable intimacy. Her thin cotton stockings were almost no barrier as he touched the sole of her foot. Despite her determination, she winced as his fingers brushed across a bruise.

"Damn, there is a nasty cut on your heel, Miss Creighton," Michael said, annoyed once more at his own thoughtlessness.

"I shall endeavor not to slow us down," Rebecca promised. "But there is no need to curse at me, though I understand your vexation."

"I am not swearing at you, Paragon," Michael said, gently massaging her instep. "It is myself that I blame, for not foreseeing this."

"Now who is taking up a burden of undeserved guilt?" Rebecca asked, abandoning herself to the momentary pleasure of his touch. His hands were working magic, caressing away the soreness. In a few minutes she feared that he would have her purring like a tabby. She closed her eyes as he set down one foot and began on the other, savoring the gentle pressure of his fingers as the throbbing ache began to disappear.

Her head was thrown back, and her hair cascaded down behind in a wild curtain of chestnut. With her lips slightly parted and her eyes closed in the throes of sensation, Michael's mind began to paint other pictures, to wander in directions that were wholly out of bounds. He concentrated on her poor, bruised feet, trying to keep his hands from straying above those neatly turned ankles, all the while wondering if her legs were equally shapely.

She gave a soft moan, of pain or delight, he could not say. A strange form of insanity had descended upon him, his world narrowing to a few inches of cotton-clad skin and the woman who was responding to his touch.

A window opened above them. "Ay now, there'll be none o' that on my steps! Take yer fancy-piece to yer own dossing-ken!" a blowzy woman shouted, shaking her fist.

"You mistake the situation completely, madame," Rebecca said, quickly snatching up her shoes. "I was just resting my feet."

"Aye, ducky, he was workin' his way up to the *rest,* to be sure. And *rest* like that will have you a bun in the oven before you can tie your shoes up!" She laughed coarsely at her own witticism. "Move on with you, before I send my man out to help you along!"

Rebecca tied her ribbons hastily, feeling her face flushing once more. "Horrid, vulgar woman," she said as Michael helped her to her feet. "Let us leave here at once." To her dismay, the moment that she put her full weight on the ground, the pain returned. Rebecca bit her lip as the woman's imprecations faded behind them.

"This will not do, Paragon," Michael said, draping her arm over his shoulder. "You cannot go on like this for too much longer."

"Perhaps if I wrap it with a bit of my petticoat?" Rebecca asked hopefully. "It is only a small cut, after all, and it does not hurt all that terribly."

"You are not much of a liar," Michael said, seeing the shadows of pain in her eyes.

"That has always been one of my worst failings," Rebecca said, trying to concentrate on putting one foot before the other. "The ability to lie judiciously is an indispensable asset which I, to my everlasting despair, have never been able to develop. Unfortunately, I have found that I am only capable of deceiving myself."

"And are you telling yourself now that you are not in pain?" Michael asked, his eyes lighting on a familiar landmark.

The Tudor gables and Venetian windows of Newcastle Street were a welcome sight. Nonetheless, the opportunity that had abruptly presented itself was the height of impropriety. Indeed, it would make the rest of the evening seem like a study in circumspect behavior. Though Miss Creighton limped on with valiant determination, it was clear that she could not go on much longer as she was. He studied her surreptitiously, trying to find a way to delicately broach the subject.

As they made their slow progress up the street, Michael decided that the best course was to stay mum until the last minute. After all, there was no telling if his former mistress had found a more fashionable residence in the months since he had last visited her. From the hordes of swains that surrounded Eve Norton in the Green Room at Drury Lane, it had only seemed a matter of time before some protector would establish her in some cozy nest. However, Michael decided that if she chanced to be at home on Newcastle Street, then the rules of polite society might be damned. The game had changed, and tonight the devil held the reins.

Rebecca stumbled, crying out as she felt herself falling, but strong hands encircled her, lifted her.

"It would seem that even my capacity for self-deception has its limits," she admitted, looking up at Michael in dismay. "I cannot expect you to haul me about London like some ponderous bit of baggage. Perhaps we might find someplace where you could leave me, Michael. Is there some inn nearby with a private room that we might hire? I will give you my address, and then my stepmother could send our carriage back for me. You would be well rewarded for your trouble, I assure you."

He bit back a sharp retort to her promise of payment; the wisdom of his decision was now clear. There was no choice for it, they would have to seek refuge at Eve Norton's home. "In fact, Miss Creighton, I may have just the safe harbor that you require. But I warn you, Eve is an old friend of mine, and I will not tolerate any insult to her, is that clear?"

"Eminently, sir."

Her curt nod of agreement held a silent rebuke, and the questions in her eyes remained unasked. She pulled away from him, asserting her independence, taking an unaided step forward. Michael caught her as her legs crumpled beneath her, swinging her up in his arms. "I would have done this long ago had I known that there was so little substance beneath those yards of black bombazine, Paragon."

"There is not much to me, Michael," she whispered, trying to hold back the tears of pain and humiliation.

"On the contrary, Miss Creighton," he said, watching the moisture seep from beneath her closed lids. "There is far more to you than meets the eye. I apologize for my harshness; it is just that Eve is . . . was . . ."

"Searching for a euphemism again, are you?" Rebecca asked wearily. "Shall we choose 'loose woman' this time? Do you think that I am blind, that I do not see what is around us, Michael? The women lounging in the windows, displaying themselves like so many haunches of meat? I realize that these men and women who are holding hands and laughing so loudly are not married."

"They are too damned happy with each other? Was that the clue that gave it away?" Michael asked, trying to coax a reaction from her, but she did not even venture a smile.

Rebecca rested her head against his shoulder, desperately trying to stop the flow of tears. It was not so much that he was taking her to his paramour's home, she told herself, but that he thought her stupid enough to be rude. Stupid, silly, and now a burden to boot. Michael's coat flopped over her fingers. And ridiculous, she added another deficiency to her list. Insufficient that she was going to be in his mistress's debt, but Rebecca knew that she looked like something the cat had dragged in.

Starched lace curtains still hung in the bow windows, and Michael took a relieved breath. Eve had not changed venues yet. The combination of privacy and lace-filtered moonlight had always been her hallmark. A light was shining in the window, like a beacon amid the shoals. On the front door a brass knocker in a stylized shape suggestive of a bare female leg shone bright. Michael rapped at the door.

"*Bonne nuit,* Celeste, is Eve at home?" Michael asked as the door swung open.

"*Oui,* monsieur," the servant said, her initial hostility changing into a smile as she recognized him. "Madame will be most pleased, monsieur."

"She will indeed!" A voice called from within. "Michael, is that you?"

Rebecca closed her eyes tighter, not wishing to see if Eve's face matched the deep, throaty texture of her speech.

Michael carried his burden into the entry. "Indeed it is I, Evie, bringing trouble to your doorstep, I fear."

"Another of your strays, Michael?" Eve asked. "Bring her up to the spare room, poor thing. I'll see what we can find in the kitchen."

Poor thing . . . as if she were a wounded sparrow. "Do you often plague this poor woman with the results of your knight errantry?" Rebecca asked, opening her eyes.

"Still with us, Paragon?" Michael said, barely masking his relief. She had been so still, so listless. Now there was a flash in her eyes once more. Shocking to find that he preferred that combative spark to dull compliance. Once again, her expression was an open page, easily read as she took in her surroundings.

The entry of Eve's home was simply furnished, but the

sparse pieces achieved an elegance that any stylish hostess might envy. The ormolu clock and console table rivaled anything that Rebecca had seen in the most prestigious establishments in Mayfair.

"Were you expecting velvet and cavorting nudes, Miss Creighton?" Michael asked in amusement as he carried her up the broad staircase.

"I suppose that I may look upon this as research," Rebecca observed dryly. "I see that you can find your way without direction."

"I would never have suspected you of jealousy," Michael said, pushing open the door to Eve's spare bedroom.

"You flatter yourself, sir," Rebecca retorted, trying to look about her without being too obviously curious.

"If I do not, no one will," Michael said, depositing her gently upon the bed. Her hair fanned out on the pillow, surrounding her like a soft cloud. He let his hand linger beneath her, feeling her weight, getting another impression of the firm flesh beneath those stiff layers of crepe and petticoat. He forced himself to let go, to keep his fingers from reaching up to touch that delicate face. "Luckily, this is the room without the fresco of nymphs and satyrs, though I must say, I do miss the mirror on the ceiling."

"Why on earth would anyone put a mirror in so odd a location?" Rebecca asked.

"Have you become a corrupter of innocents now, Michael?"

Rebecca looked up and felt her throat tighten. Eve was the most exquisite woman that she had ever seen. An aureole of guinea-bright blond hair framed a perfect heart-shaped face. Her figure was beautifully proportioned, and her green eyes gave her the appearance of a wood nymph. She moved across the room with floating grace, giving Michael a smile that held both unabashed affection and amusement. Setting the tray that she carried on a small table, she crossed the room toward him.

"I would have to be old Nick himself to sully this paragon of virtue," Michael said with an answering grin. He kissed Eve lightly on the cheek. "Actually we did meet in church."

Rebecca turned her face away, disturbed by the casual display of affection. Although her knowledge about such matters was paltry, it was obvious from the other woman's expression that Michael had been more to Eve than a friend.

"You, Michael? In a church?" Eve chuckled. "A nunnery perhaps, but never a church."

Michael smiled uneasily at the warm reference, hoping that Miss Creighton would miss the meaning entirely. "I . . . uh . . . Miss . . . Miss . . ."

"I take it that she is a lady of Quality. Under the circumstances, perhaps we should dispense with names," Eve suggested, eyeing Rebecca speculatively. She had rarely heard Michael at a loss for words and never had she witnessed him put to the blush. A flush was creeping up his neck and painting his stubbled cheeks . . . most interesting.

"You are the soul of discretion, Eve," Michael said, hastily redirecting the conversation. "We soon found ourselves in the midst of what promised to be a rather nasty situation."

"A riot, actually," Rebecca explained, finding her voice again. She would prove to Michael that she was capable of minding her manners, no matter what the circumstances. "Michael came to my rescue. He was trying to get me home, but I did not realize that I would need stout boots when I dressed for the evening."

"She could not walk any farther, Eve," Michael said. "When I realized that you were nearby—"

Eve rejected any further explanation with an impatient wave of her hand. "Let me have a look at those feet. Tell Celeste to bring up some hot water and my ointments immediately."

To Rebecca's surprise, Michael turned and left without any further comment.

"Sometimes I think that he ought to be horsewhipped. He should have seen that these shoes were not worth spit," Eve said, gently easing off Rebecca's slippers. "Can you loosen the stockings for me, miss?"

Rebecca was surprised to see uncertainty in the older

woman's face, an expression that she could not quite read. As Eve avoided her eyes, the curious thought occurred that this poised creature might actually be nervous of her. "Call me Rebecca," Rebecca said, fumbling for the stays, but the sleeves of Michael's jacket got in the way. She slid the garment off.

"I'm Eve, then," Eve said, her lips easing into a smile as her hand went to the tear at Rebecca's shoulder. "You have the beginnings of a bruise there. Looks like things got rough."

"Yes," Rebecca agreed with a shudder. "They did indeed. Though you ought not to blame Michael for the state of my feet. Most men do not get past my neck before they start to look elsewhere."

Eve's lip curled as she rolled down Rebecca's stockings. "You could be pretty enough," she said, disturbed by the younger woman's dismal estimation of herself. "With the proper clothes, your hair dressed well, a bit of help with what nature has already given you."

"You are very kind to say so, Eve, but . . ." Rebecca began.

"No 'say so' kindness about it," Eve said as she slipped the stockings off and examined Rebecca's bare feet. "You have a shapely leg, and by my guess, the rest of you must be in proportion beneath that sack that you wear."

"I am in mourning," Rebecca said.

"Might as well be buried yourself," Eve said, shaking her head. "You have fine skin, but black makes you look sickly."

"Whites and pinks are no better," Rebecca said with a sigh. "My stepmother tried, believe me; she nearly put us all in Fleet so that she could launch me in the height of style. But though no expense was spared, my Season was still an unmitigated disaster."

"I suppose that I should be grateful," Eve said with a snort. "If all the women of the *ton* were suddenly granted good taste, there would be less need for women like me. Someone of your coloring needs bright hues. Green for instance." She opened the connecting door and hurried into the room beyond, returning with an emerald dress. "You can wear this home," Eve told her, fanning the skirt across the bed.

"I could not take it," Rebecca said with a sigh, touching the folds reverently. The silk shimmered beneath her hand.

"I was going to discard it, in any case. The neckline is far too demure for my tastes. Take it," she commanded. "You cannot go abroad in what you are wearing now, not unless you wish to continue wearing Michael's coat."

"No, I suppose not," Rebecca said, folding Michael's garment carefully. "I would be thankful for the loan of your dress, Eve, though I doubt it will be any improvement."

"Not a loan, a gift," Eve said, draping the dress over a Chippendale chair in the corner of the room. "If not to you, then to Michael."

"For Michael, then," Rebecca agreed.

"He's a good man, is Michael," Eve said, noting the look on the younger woman's face, the change in her voice when she said his name, "the type who would give the shirt off his back to a friend."

"Or his jacket to an absolute stranger," Rebecca said, brushing some dust off the sleeve.

For a fleeting moment, the girl's soul was in her eyes, and Eve wondered if she ought to say more. If Rebecca had only just met him, then there might be no real reason for concern. Yet, Michael was so easy to love. Of all people, Eve knew that extremely well. Rebecca continued to caress the fabric absently, but with the hand of a lover, almost as if Michael himself were wearing it. Eve made a decision. A few words would cost her nothing.

"He's the kind of man who would give anything except his heart, my dear," Eve said softly. "Certainly not to a woman like me."

Rebecca looked up, meeting the older woman's sad jewel green eyes.

"And I doubt that he would even give it to a woman like you," Eve concluded, touching Rebecca's cheek lightly. "Michael would never mean to hurt you, but he couldn't help it, any more than you could keep yourself from falling in love with him."

"But I am not in love with him! We only met this evening. I do not even know his last name," Rebecca said in astonishment. "I know that he could do far better than a woman of my looks."

"No harm done then," Eve said with a shrug, turning her attention to Rebecca's feet. Perhaps she had misread the signs. She certainly hoped so, but the girl's final comment seemed especially telling. "Not too bad. A few bruises and a small cut. A wash and a bandage, and you should be right as a trivet."

"That is good news to hear. We should have had you in Spain, Eve," Michael said pushing the door open as he carried a basin full of steaming water into the room. Celeste followed, carrying a basket of jars and bottles. "Even if you failed to cure them, at least they would have died happy."

Rebecca scrambled to cover her legs. "A gentleman would have knocked."

"A gentleman would not be pressed into duty as a water bearer," Michael said, trying to stifle the memory of those shapely limbs as he set the bowl on the nightstand. "Shall I wash your poor feet, Paragon? A very Biblical thing to do, if I might say so."

"You may not. Get out of here, you wretched creature," Eve said, giving him a playful shove toward the door. "Go down to the kitchen and make yourself useful. I am sure that Rebecca must be famished after her ordeal."

Just as Michael was about to step out into the hall, a hollow knock reverberated through the house. "Expecting someone?" he asked with a frown.

Eve shook her head, worry knitting her brow. "Not tonight," she said. "Celeste, see who is at the door."

They waited in silence as the maid scurried to do Eve's bidding. In a few minutes Celeste returned with a sealed note.

Eve broke the wafer and scanned the lines anxiously. "Wyecliff. Apparently there are several disturbances abroad tonight. His lordship would like to take his dinner with me after the theater and stay the night, rather than risk returning to Mayfair." She looked at Michael and Rebecca with regret in her eyes.

"Lord Wyecliff?" Rebecca asked in disbelief. "Why he is a deacon . . . he is . . ." She felt both pairs of eyes upon her. "He is most vociferous in his moral stance," she finished lamely.

"And a married man," Michael added impishly. "You are a charitable woman, Eve, to be sharing this burden with Lady Wyecliff. She has no idea of the debt that she—"

"Hush, Michael," Eve demanded, "can you not see that you are embarrassing the child? She is as bright as a beet! *I* am expected to be without shame, but *you* ought to know better. Now leave us alone so that I can take care of Rebecca before Wyecliff comes."

Michael frowned. "I had hoped to leave Rebecca here while I found a carriage."

"I could try to hide you." Eve considered the possibility. "But it is too much of a risk. What would happen if she is somehow discovered here, Michael?"

His frown was all the answer she needed. "I thought as much," she said. "I do not require a name to know a lady when I see one. You will have to be gone before Wyecliff arrives."

"How long?" Michael asked.

"We have no more than an hour, I would say, until the opera is at an end," Eve said, calculating quickly. "No telling how long Wyecliff's footman dallied before he got here."

"Perhaps Lord Wyecliff would loan us his carriage?" Rebecca suggested.

Michael and Eve turned in unison, looking at her in amazement. Eve smiled sadly. "Ah, child, how simple everything seems to the innocent. Bad enough that you are alone in Michael's company, but I am certain that he will contrive some story. However, if your connection with me is ever found out, your reputation will be in tatters. You would be utterly ruined, Rebecca, a pariah."

"She is quite right, Paragon," Michael said. "We cannot take the chance. I fear that we will have to patch you up as best as we can, then go on our way."

*   *   *

Eve eased a pair of boots over Rebecca's bandaged feet. "How do they feel?" she asked as Rebecca stood and took a few steps. "Are they too snug? Even though my feet are somewhat larger than yours, those dressings take up the extra space."

"Perfect," Rebecca said, wiggling her toes gingerly. "You are a veritable magician, Eve. And that ointment of yours is truly wondrous. I can scarcely feel the cut anymore. If you could send me the receipt when I return your . . ."

"I told you, child, there can be no communication between us, for your own sake. Keep or discard what I give you, as you will, but do not continue to prattle about sending me back my things. You would put yourself at risk," Eve scolded as she picked up a black capuchin cloak from the chair and handed it to Rebecca.

"This is not the first stare of fashion," Eve said, "but it is warm. And do not tell me that you cannot take it." She put a cautioning finger to Rebecca's lips. "You would not begrudge a Cyprian a token act of kindness; I could certainly use any credit that I can get with heaven."

"Thank you, Eve," Rebecca said, taking the older woman's hand. "I will remember you in my prayers."

"And will you pray for me as well, Paragon?" Michael asked, halting as he came through the open door.

"Do you wish me to?" Rebecca asked, perturbed by the strange look on his face. His brown eyes were wide and his mouth almost agape. "Eve insisted that I take her dress. Are you angry?"

Eve stifled a giggle. Michael's dumbfounded expression was definitely worth the price of a pair of nearly new boots, an old cloak, and a dress she would never deign to wear. As the silence lengthened, she wondered if the chit might have a chance after all.

What on earth had Eve done to the Paragon? Michael thought. Her brown hair was knotted once more, but a myriad of tiny ringlets curled, bordering her face in a merry profusion.

Though the emerald dress hung a trifle loosely, the clever drape of the fabric contrived to be revealing while still being entirely within the bounds of decorum. As she walked toward him, the gown gave teasing hints of a lithe, womanly shape beneath its folds. The bright color made her skin appear lucent, almost radiant in the candlelight. Her fingers twined and untwined in palpable anxiety as she awaited his answer.

"No, Paragon, I am not at all angry," Michael said at last, his throat feeling oddly rusty. *Merely stunned,* he added silently.

"Does it look well?" Rebecca asked, wishing the question unasked as soon as it was out. He would be kind, of course; that was his way.

There was no art in her query, none of the usual questing for compliments. The Paragon did not know that she had been utterly transformed. Oliver would be absolutely delighted, Michael thought as his fists clenched unconsciously at his side. "You would do well to put on that cloak that you hold," Michael said, thinking of the type of traffic that was common upon the Strand. Damn Eve for making the job of getting Miss Creighton home intact all the more difficult. "I shall meet you downstairs."

Michael turned, determined to ignore the disappointed expression on Miss Creighton's face. If she was seeking approval, she might soon get more masculine attention than she had ever hoped for. He could only pray that the cloak would conceal most of Eve's artifices.

"He is angry at me," Rebecca said, shaking out the monkish cloak and draping it around her shoulders. Her fingers fumbled with the closures. "He did not like it."

"I rather suspect he liked it all too well," Eve said, deftly taking over the job. With a pat on Rebecca's cheek, she pulled the hood into place. "No, child, he is not angry at you, only at himself." Eve regarded the young woman thoughtfully. "He was badly hurt when we first met."

"Elizabeth?"

"He mentioned her to you, did he?" Eve asked in surprise.

"Yes, Elizabeth was her name. That bitch didn't have much joy of the old man that she took in Michael's place, I'll tell you that." Though she did not say it outright, Eve's inflection made it clear that she had made her own highly personal comparison. "But Michael might be ready . . ." Eve said pensively, "he just might."

"Ready for what?" Rebecca asked as they went out the door.

"Ready to care again," Eve said with a smile that was somehow forlorn despite its brightness.

Michael heaved a silent sigh of relief as Miss Creighton came down the stairs. The billowing folds of the cloak amply hid the Paragon's newfound charms, and the hood concealed her face in its shadowed depths. Nonetheless, he could not help but think of the picture that she had presented upstairs. As she reached his side, he was almost tempted to demand that she remove the garment, to determine that what he had seen was not some figment of his warped imagination.

"Celeste has packed you some food," Eve said, putting a parcel in Michael's hands. From the street they heard the clatter of a carriage.

"That must be Wyecliff," Michael said. "We shall make our exit through the kitchen door." He pecked Eve hastily on the cheek. "My thanks, Eve, for everything."

"And mine," Rebecca said, taking Eve's hand and clasping it in acknowledgment.

"Remember what I said, child," Eve said, squeezing Rebecca's hand in return.

"I shall," Rebecca promised, looking back over her shoulder as Michael grabbed her hand and hurried her out the door.

Eve straightened her shoulders and touched her hair into place as she heard the kitchen door slam closed. "G-dspeed, Michael," she whispered, pasting on a smile. "And heaven help you both."

Chapter 5

Sarah stared out the window of the library, looking out onto the darkened square. Every whinny of horses, every rattle of wheels caused her to press her face to the glass, but none of them stopped.

"Is that Rebecca at last?" Lydia said as a carriage clattered across the cobblestones. "Cook has been asking for her for this hour past. She was supposed to review the menus for the week."

"Ellen said that Lady Brand's footman came by our kitchen," Sarah said, her blue eyes murky with worry. "They have only just got home. There is rioting in Covent Garden, he says."

"Well, that explains matters," Lydia said cheerfully. "No doubt traffic has been disrupted all over Town. Mr. Havermill will take good care of her."

"But riots, Lydia!" Sarah said.

"In Covent Garden," Lydia said, putting an encouraging hand on her stepdaughter's shoulder. "She is nowhere near there."

"Michael, what in the world are you doing?" Rebecca whispered as they circled back toward the front of Eve's house.

"I mean to have a word or two with Wyecliff's coachman," Michael said. "From his master's note, it would appear that some of the thoroughfares are blocked. It might be best to know which ones we ought to bypass." He tucked the package of food that Eve had given them under one arm and offered her the other. They started sauntering casually toward the waiting carriage. All at once Michael began to smile broadly.

"What is it?" Rebecca whispered.

"It just occurred to me that I ought not to have rejected your excellent idea out of hand," Michael said. "Say nothing—let me do the talking."

"Simple enough," Rebecca agreed with a nod. "Since I have not the vaguest notion of what you are talking about."

Just when she thought that they would bypass Lord Wyecliff's carriage entirely, he pulled the watch from his pocket. "Wouldn't know the time, would you?" he asked.

The coachman shook his head. "Opera's done with, half hour or more, I'd say."

Michael shook the timepiece angrily. "Damned thing is broken again. I should have been on my way back to Mayfair nearly an hour ago."

"Well, good luck to you," the coachman said with a short laugh. "Oxford Street is altogether closed."

"Never say so," Michael said, feigning astonishment. "A fire?"

"Riots," the coachman said, warming to his subject. "Wouldn't try Piccadilly neither. Lord Wodesby's coachman said that way ain't safe. They overturned a dray, and there's fires set. Last I heard, those what were determined t' go back tonight were going up Tottenham all the way to Marylebone and then doubling back through Mayfair."

"Is that the way you plan to return?" Michael asked.

"Me?" the coachman snorted, bobbing his head toward Eve's house. "I'll be stabling the horses out back and waiting in the kitchen till morning, that's what I'll be doing."

"Well, good night to you then, and thanks for the advice," Michael said as he stowed his watch in his pocket.

Once more, he offered his escort to Rebecca. She was just reaching up to take his arm when Michael looked back and eyed the coachman thoughtfully as if an idea were suddenly presenting itself.

"It just occurred to me that you might be just the man we need. How would you like to earn a quid while you wait?" Michael asked. "My lady friend and I need to get to Mayfair. You could be back here before your master drinks his coffee and kisses his bit o' muslin good-bye. You will be a quid richer and no one the wiser."

"Ain't gonna risk a run for Mayfair tonight," the coachman said, evaluating Michael's ill-fitting suit dubiously. "You and your ladybird want to get there, you'll have to use shank's mare."

"Two quid," Michael offered, digging into his purse and pulling out the sovereigns.

The coachman hesitated at the golden gleam. "Ain't worth my job," he said adamantly, as if trying to convince himself. "If we gets in the middle and sommat happens to the horses or to his lordship's carriage, then there'll be the devil to pay and it's 'out the door, Harry' with no reference for yours truly."

"I understand completely," Michael said, thinking quickly. From the set of the man's jaw, it was unlikely that raising the price would change his mind, but what of a change in direction? "Well, sweetheart, it looks like you will not be able to see my apartments tonight after all. Shall I take you back to your place then?"

Rebecca took her cue from his eyes and nodded.

"Well, I thank you for the warnings," Michael said, inclining his head in a gesture of farewell. Once more he offered his arm, and they took a step or two when he bent toward her. "Pretend that you are whispering to me, Paragon."

Obediently, she moved her head closer. "I haven't the foggiest notion of what you are doing," she said softly.

"Just follow my lead, Miss Creighton—follow where I lead." Michael turned around once again just as the coachman was gathering up the reins to lead the horses around the back. "You wouldn't be interested in taking us up to Threadneedle Street, would you? It seems that the lady has no wish to walk, even though it is not that far."

"Threadneedle, eh?" The coachman scratched his head and considered. "Ain't heard of no trouble up that way. How much?"

"A quid," Michael said.

"Dunno." The coachman's voice became wheedling. "What if there's problems."

"Then you let us down and turn around," Michael said.

" 'Twas two quid before!" the coachman began.

"If it's t'be two quid, we walk, and I'll have me one o' them," Rebecca said, seething. *Two sovereigns, indeed, for a distance that could not be beyond a mile or two.*

Michael shrugged. "You heard the lady. One sovereign or we hoof."

"Follow me," the coachman said grudgingly. "One quid to Threadneedle it is, but any sign of trouble we turn tail."

When they rounded the corner, the coachman opened the door. "Get in with yer, and keep yer boots off the velvet." He held out his palm. "Payment in full."

Michael held the coin just above the coachman's open fist, meeting his eyes. "Oh, by the by, just so you do not worry, I have absolutely no intention of mentioning this to Lord Wyecliff, not unless you attempt to cheat us, that is. A dishonest man, for instance, might take the money and try to force us out or even be so foolish as to call the Watch. But you have an honest face."

The coachman paled at the mention of his master's name. "Kind of you to say so, sir."

"It would pain me deeply to have to knock on Eve Norton's door and disturb their little tête-à-tête. I suspect that it would make Horace furious," Michael said, flipping the coin in his hand. He could see the realization that this ill-dressed stranger really did know Lord Wyecliff flitting across the servant's face.

"Rely on me, sir. I'll get yer to Threadneedle safe and sound," the coachman said, touching his forelock.

"Good man," Michael said, pressing the coin into his hand. "See that you do."

"How did you guess that he was planning to cheat us?" Rebecca asked, pulling her hood back as the coach started down toward the Strand.

"I did not know it," Michael said, leaning back against the rich velvet squabs. The clean lines of her profile were limned with moonlight, and the dark cowl of the cloak accentuated the long column of her throat.

He had never been of the mind to write poems about eyes and lips, and his verse had never celebrated the curve of a cheek, the graceful wave of a hand. Yet those were the words that were whispering in his head, twisting their way through his heart. "Sometimes one has to rely on instinct, Paragon. Any man who would consent to risk his employer's equipage might very well be disposed to fleecing a flat if he could."

Rebecca's hand flew to her mouth as a horrible thought occurred to her. "What have we done? We have suborned Lord Wyecliff's employee, caused him to misuse that which does not belong to him!"

"And saved ourselves a quid in the bargain, thanks to you," Michael said. "You were magnificent, Paragon. Or was it Cathy of Covent Garden that I heard back there?"

"If the truth be told, I begin to find myself wondering who I am tonight," Rebecca said, warmed by his praise, despite her bafflement.

What they had just done was wrong, dishonest. What in the world was happening to her? The approval in Michael's eyes made her feel almost proud for her part in the farce. "I am saying things, doing things of which I would never have thought myself capable."

"Still guilty over old Wyecliff's carriage?" Michael asked. "If he had stayed at home where he belonged, this equipage would be snug in his stables."

"One sin cannot possibly justify another," Rebecca said, trying to rouse her sense of moral indignation, but somehow, she could not feel the sense of remorse that she knew was proper.

"Would you rather I tell Master Coachman to halt and we will use shank's mare the rest of the way to Whitechapel?" Michael asked with an edge of irritation. "If it will satisfy your delicate moral sensibilities, I am certain that he would be more than willing to oblige us, though this was, after all, your suggestion."

"I suggested nothing of the sort!" Rebecca said indignantly.

"I noticed that you did not protest at the thought of riding," Michael snapped back.

Rebecca sighed. "I did not mean to anger you, Michael," she said wearily, cupping her face in her hands.

"And I ought not to have ranted at you," Michael apologized, his tones softening. "Poor Paragon—to have thrown your lot in with a man whose sense of right and wrong are somewhat muddled. It has been a long evening, Miss Creighton, and we are even farther from home than when we began."

"Life seemed very simple when I left Cavendish Square this evening," she said, rubbing her eyes like a weary child. "I did not expect to be speaking at Covent Garden, you know. I am certain that my stepmother would not have approved had she known. Mr. Havermill was entirely wrong to make us both think otherwise."

"The cleric with the foolish tongue?" Michael asked.

"He is not usually so, really," Rebecca said, feeling obligated to come to her benefactor's defense. "Mr. Havermill has been very kind to us since Papa died. It was he who introduced me to London Society. He was the one who persuaded me that there might be people interested in paying for my tracts. Though the income is small, it has allowed us to survive."

Though the income is small . . . Michael found himself wondering just how small. If the number of Rebecca Creighton's pamphlets that he had seen in the streets were any indication, those tracts were bringing someone a bloody fortune. Obviously, that someone was not Miss Creighton. "And Mr. Havermill handles all the details?" Michael asked.

"Oh, yes!" Rebecca said enthusiastically. "He schedules all of my engagements to speak and arranges for the publication and sale of my tracts. My stepmother, Lydia, convinced me that it would not do at all for me to take care of it myself, you see. She feared that it would smack of trade. It is a great deal of trouble for poor Mr. Havermill to manage it all for the small remuneration he allows himself. I do not know what we would do without him."

"Hmm." Michael did not know either, but he was definitely beginning to wonder.

"I do hope that he was not injured," she murmured, peering out the window into the darkness. "He must be mad with worry for me."

"Indeed, he must," Michael agreed, especially if his newfound suspicions were true. Equally disturbing was the possibility that Havermill might be the reason that Miss Creighton had left Oliver to play a waiting game. "He must love you very much," Michael said, waiting for her reaction.

Her gurgle of laughter was unexpected. "*Love me? Silas Havermill?* If anything, he is sorely vexed with me of late. He had not even bothered to read my last pamphlet prior to handing it to the printer. When Lady Shand informed him that I had criticized the enclosure laws in "A Common Matter," he was absolutely mortified. I have not had my ears blistered so since I used my father's vestments to play at blind man's bluff." Her humorous look faded quickly. "No . . ." Rebecca said wistfully. "There is no one in love with me, not even the man who has asked for my hand."

"You have an offer of marriage?" Michael asked, trying to draw her out.

"Unbelievable, is it not?" Yearning turned to desolation as she gave a short answering nod. "That a woman like me should receive so excellent an offer? He has wealth, position, his looks are those of a Greek god . . . yet . . ."

"Yet . . ." Michael echoed, hoping to finally resolve the question that had driven him to come hear Miss Creighton speak tonight. Why had she failed to jump at the chance of leg-shackling herself to a future earl?

"I hesitate . . . though his offer of marriage seems a godsend, I have not given an answer," Rebecca said, her hands unconsciously pleating the fabric of her cloak. "I find myself wondering why he would want me. Why after all these years . . . ? They tell me it should not matter, yet it does."

"They?"

"My stepmother, my sister." Her agony and confusion were almost palpable, yet she tried to take refuge behind a facade of humor. "It seems as if the only one who is not plaguing me is Harry, my younger brother. He even offered to give up Gunther's ices if it would help the family finances."

"A noble young man," Michael said, beginning to recognize that the situation was far more complex than an offer and an answer.

"Yes, Harry is a fine little fellow," Rebecca said, making a lopsided effort at a smile. "He deserves far more than I have been able to provide for him. They all do. Sarah should enjoy her Season without being forced to count every groat. Lydia ought to have the wherewithal to buy her fans and folderols without having to sneak behind my back. If I accept that offer of marriage, all that would be possible."

"And what of you, Paragon?" Michael asked. "What do you deserve?"

"I?" Rebecca asked, not quite understanding what he was getting at.

"You," Michael repeated, watching the play of emotions on her face as she considered what seemed to be a novel concept to her. "What of you? It seems to me that you have played Atlas for a long time, supporting your entire family's world upon your shoulders. Is there nothing that you want for yourself?"

Rebecca thought for a moment. "To write what I wish, to

say the truth as I see it, without worry of whom I might offend."

"And nothing more?" he asked, one eyebrow rising quizzically.

"What is the use of craving for what I shall never have?" she asked, trying to keep the welling bitterness from her voice. "A partner? A companion?"

"And you do not think that Ol . . . this man who has asked for your hand might fill those roles for you?" Michael questioned, looking out the window as they passed Fleet Prison, the shadowed structure reminding him of just what was at stake. He attempted to persuade himself that it was possible for her to be happy as Oliver's wife.

Oliver would make a liberal husband, the type who would not hold the reins too tightly. Doubtless, he would even be kind to her, in his own offhand way. But when Michael tried to envision his bluff friend in the part of the Paragon's soul mate, he could not. Michael shook his head. It was none of his concern.

"I do not truly know Oliver," she whispered. "I realize now that I never really did. It is so selfish of me, to cry off for foolish reasons, but I cannot bring myself to say yes."

"Ah, Paragon," Michael said, sliding over to her side of the carriage. He told himself that it was the scent from Eve's clothing that was making his heart pound a tattoo, but he knew himself for a liar. "I do not believe that you could be selfish—you do not know how."

"I am so confused, so very confused," she said, regarding him in bewilderment. *And you are the principal part of that confusion,* she added silently. *Why does your nearness make me breathless? Why do I want you to come closer when I should be telling you to move away?*

"It is all so very perplexing, life in the real world," Michael said, his fingers rising almost of their own volition. He was not even aware that he was touching her until he felt the delicate texture of skin to skin. " 'Needs must,' my dear, 'needs must.' "

" 'And the devil drives,' " Rebecca concluded the phrase, trying to quell this sudden longing, enjoining herself to edge away, turn her head. A word from her, a hand held out to stop him, and he would go no further. There was a question in his eyes, and she knew what her answer ought to be. But the word "no" had disappeared from her vocabulary. In fact, she could find no words at all amid the silence of anticipation.

"Yes, Paragon, the devil drives, indeed," Michael said, as his lips came down upon hers. He had not planned to kiss her, but when they touched, the contact had seemed necessary, almost inevitable. Michael told himself that he meant only to console, but the warmth of solace was somehow transformed into a burning need, gentle communion spiraled into driving desire. One hand slipped up to her hair, burying his fingers in silken softness, the other drew her closer to him.

He did not really want her, she told herself. She understood that he could not possibly feel anything for her. Yet, even so, she wanted to taste him, to savor his lips on hers. Her conscience relentlessly cried warning, but she gave it no heed as her arms twined around him. *Tomorrow,* she promised herself, *I will repent tomorrow, but just tonight let me dream.* Recklessly, she abandoned herself to his kiss.

Michael felt the last vestiges of her resistance melting in his arms. As her hands pulled him closer, he knew that he could cross any boundary, and she would not rebuff him. His hands slid down her neck as the cloak began to slip from her shoulders to reveal a neat row of pearl buttons that he knew could easily be undone with one hand. All of Eve's gowns were made that way.

But she was not Eve.

Even as all of his senses soared, that knowledge began to stem the swell of his tide of emotions. Tendrils of unwelcome thought crept in, gnawing through the edges of passion.

The Paragon was meant to be another man's wife, his best

friend's wife. He had already stolen her first passionate kiss, and he knew that it would be a crime beyond pardon to take any more from her. If she ever found out who he was, his relationship to Oliver Rowley, she would surely despise him. Perhaps he already had passed beyond forgiveness.

But it was not entirely for Oliver's sake that Michael finally forced himself to retreat. If he went any further beyond the pale of propriety, the Paragon would never blame him. Though he had only known her for the space of a few hours, he was certain that she would place the burden of guilt on her own shoulders. He would have to end it here, have to let her go before he could not stop himself.

She moaned softly as he broke away. Michael cradled her head upon his shoulder, calming himself, trying to be content to simply hold her as the carriage wended its way through the streets of London. Slowly, he stroked the curls back from her forehead. Those luminous amber eyes opened, filled with questions and innocent wonder. Her fingers rose languidly to brush his unshaven cheek. *When the ride ends,* he promised himself, *when we get to Threadneedle Street, I will let her go.*

As the carriage swayed, his body rocked against hers, and she savored each sensation, his fingers on her skin, his warmth. But as she looked up at him, she saw that his expression was troubled, distant, closed.

"Do not condemn yourself, Michael," Rebecca said, choosing each word with care. "I certainly do not. I know this means nothing to you."

He opened his mouth as if to protest, but she put a hushing finger to his lips. "You have no need to lie to spare my feelings. I am not the sort of woman you would favor. We are two people thrown together by strange circumstances; the danger that we have faced, mere proximity weaves its own peculiar spell."

She hesitated, gathering up her courage. "I wanted you to kiss me," she said, as if confessing a vile crime. "And I want you to kiss me again because . . ." Her voice trailed off, and she turned her face to the darkness of the carriage. "Because I suspect that even if I choose to marry, I will still be alone . . . but at least I will confront all those empty tomorrows with a memory. Let me deceive myself, just for tonight. Just for tonight, I will pretend that you . . . care for me."

Her eyes glistened as she faced him once more; all that arid future reflected in those tawny shadows.

"You do not know what you ask, Rebecca," Michael said, his voice husky with emotion. He was tempted, sorely tempted to do as she asked, but he was not certain that he could stop at a mere kiss. "This is no child's game we play here. Tomorrow will come, and we will have to live with the choices we make tonight. I may not be a Clapham saint, but I have my own faith, my own honor. You may well come to hate me, but not because I took a rake's advantage of your innocence."

She tried to look away, to hide her humiliation, but Michael would not let her. He cupped her chin between his palms.

"Look at me, Rebecca," he demanded, trying to ease the naked shame that burned upon her face. "I do care for you, or else that emerald gown would have been lying on the floor since Fleet Street. If I had no real regard for you, I would be taking everything that you have to offer and more . . . and more." His eyes swept her body, and he took a ragged breath. "It is not because I do not want you, Rebecca Creighton. At this moment, I find that I desire you more than anyone that I have ever wanted in my life."

"You must think me no better than I should be—a tease," Rebecca whispered, feeling the bitterness of shame rising up in her throat. "A desperate spinster, a fraud."

"I see a woman, Rebecca," he said, trying to make her believe that he spoke the truth. "A woman of valor, who has not yet realized that her worth is beyond pearls." He smiled at her look of surprise. "My apologies to Ecclesiastes. You see, the devil does quote scripture to make his points. You esteem yourself too little, but I cannot." His fingers brushed her kiss-stung lips in regret. "I cannot count you so cheap, Miss Creighton."

Miss Creighton . . . the distance in that formal address was almost physical. As he moved back to the other side of the carriage, Rebecca felt the ache of desolation. No matter what pretty and kind words wrapped the package, the box was empty. Michael did not want her, and though she had known it all along, that did not soothe the hurt.

She huddled in the corner of the carriage, staring unseeing at the unfamiliar streets. For the first time since Michael had snatched her hand in the church, she felt entirely alone. Strange, until tonight, Rebecca had never realized just how forlorn she was.

Michael watched her as the parade of emotions slipped across her countenance. She had not believed him. How could she, when she did not believe in herself? But he did not dare try to comfort her, not until he could pinpoint the reason for his appalling lack of restraint. Though he would not have admitted it aloud, much of what she had said was true. The Paragon was wholly unlike any woman that he had ever known.

It was somewhat disconcerting to realize that all his liaisons, apart from Elizabeth, had been little more than friendly transactions. And Elizabeth, too, he thought ruefully, had been bartering herself, even though he had not realized it at the time. Quid pro quo had been his motto. He had never dallied with innocents. Until now.

His rebuff was no more than she had deserved. In fact, she ought to be down on her knees, thanking heaven for his rejection. Carefully, she adjusted the cowl of her cloak, grateful for the shelter of its shadowed depths. Shred by shred, Rebecca gathered up the tattered remains of her self-respect, praying for the strength to overcome this weakness, seeking the courage to get her through this night.

Rebecca straightened, forcing herself to face him. She had no right to encumber him with the consequences of her wounded pride. His rejection had shattered her, but Rebecca vowed that he would never know it. After all, she had brought about her own dishonor. More unnerving, still, was this unexpected streak of recklessness within her, as if she were a stranger to herself.

Desperately, she sought for some commonplace, a means of breaking the increasingly uncomfortable silence. A discussion of the weather? Her hand chanced to brush against Celeste's parcel. *Food!*

"Are you hungry, Michael?" she asked in what she hoped were normal tones.

Hungry, yes that was one word for it, but it was clear that she meant another form of appetite. "I am famished," Michael said, seizing upon the excuse for mundane conversation. "What did Celeste throw together for us? Ah! Bless her French heart, croissants!"

"We had best be careful not to be sloppy about this," Rebecca said, looking at the crumbly pastry warily. As she took one in her hand, she tried to keep herself from trembling. She forced herself to take a bite, chew, then reminded herself to swallow even though the flaky roll had all the savor of ash. Like a clockwork doll, she forced herself through the simple repetitive motions. Bite. Chew. Swallow. Bite. Chew. Swallow.

"Yes, Mother, I shall be careful of the upholstery," Michael agreed, biting into the pastry with a show of enthusiasm, devouring it entirely even though it tasted like sand in his craw. Miss Creighton ate with the same dogged determination. So long as they chewed, the discomfort of speech was unnecessary.

Chapter 6

A battered hackney carriage pulled up to the steps of the home on Cavendish Square. Silas Havermill had barely put his foot upon the bottom marble step when the front door was flung wide, spilling light into the empty street. Lydia stood aghast. The clergyman's collar was hanging awry at his neck. One sleeve was half torn from the shoulder, while the other was entirely gone. The orbit of his left eye was turning color, and the eye itself was swollen shut. His lower lip puffed out precariously.

"Where is Rebecca?" Lydia asked as the hackney drew away.

"You mean that she has not yet come home?" Havermill asked, his hand upon the railing.

Sarah barely caught her stepmother as she fell into a swoon.

Rebecca and Michael were polishing off the final chicken leg when the carriage drew to a halt.

"Threadneedle," the coachman called from the box. "Make it sharp now, I'd best be getting back to Newcastle Street."

"Well, it would appear that a sovereign is not sufficient to get him down to open the door for us," Michael said, swinging down from the cab and offering Rebecca his hand.

"Here, take this first," Rebecca said, handing him the cloth with the chicken bones. "I will not leave a mess behind."

"Hurry up, hurry up," the coachman shouted, "ain't got all night, y'know."

Michael helped Rebecca down and looked around him, his expression hardening. "Well, this is a fine hullo; this is not Threadneedle, my man."

"That way," said the coachman, pointing ahead. "Won't go no farther than this. The drive took too long as is, what with the traffic with everyone trying to get round the mess in the city! His lordship might even get a notion to try and make it home."

"To Lady Wyecliff, not bloody likely," Michael said.

"Ain't going no farther. Now close the door, or get in and come back the way you came. All be the same to me," the coachman said, shaking his fist.

"Very well," Michael said, taking hold of the door handle as he shook open the cloth of chicken bones, scattering them all over the interior of the coach. With a flourish he slammed the door shut.

"Michael!" Rebecca exclaimed as the carriage rattled off. "What will Lord Wyecliff say?"

"I am certain Master Coachman will come up with some interesting excuse," Michael said, looking around him and getting his bearings. "Cheapside, I think. Threadneedle is not far off, but I should have been paying more attention to the road."

"We were both a trifle distracted," Rebecca said, feeling herself growing warm beneath his amused scrutiny.

"Aye, 'a trifle distracted,' a neat way of putting it," Michael said, putting his hand out. "Pax, Miss Creighton?" he asked. "We cannot continue walking upon eggshells the rest of the journey. Might you extend your talents at self-deception to me, do you think? Would it be possible to pretend that I was not a lecherous brute who took unfair advantage?"

"You are not a brute, Michael, and if anyone was acting in an unseemly—"

"Hush, Paragon," Michael said. "It is unbecoming for a

saint to chastise a sinner for penitence. Now do not contradict me. If you would prefer a different phraseology, you might try 'bawdy beast' or perhaps 'sensual savage,' or even 'lustful libertine.' I particularly like that last one—rolls off your tongue with all those 'l's. I was a lustful, lascivious, licentious, lewd, libertine."

It was impossible to keep her face straight; Rebecca could not stifle her smile, not with Michael declaiming, his hand raised as if he were exhorting the rabble to the barricades. "You have entirely forgotten lecherous, you know," she said.

"Lecherous," Michael said, effecting a leering sneer and cocking his eyebrow in his most villainous fashion. "How could I have neglected to mention it?" All at once, he became serious. "Can you forget and forgive, Paragon?"

"Very well. I forgive you, Michael," Rebecca told him. *But I shall never forget,* she added silently. *I will remember tonight always.* "If you will tell me where we are going."

"I was wondering when you might get round to asking," Michael said with a relieved grin. "We are going to visit a friend of mine."

Miss Creighton frowned, saying nothing, though her disapproval was patent. Michael could almost read her thoughts.

"Not another Eve, Paragon," he said, "though I must admit that they are certainly not the type of people whom you would meet in the normal scheme of things."

"Strange, how appealing the 'normal scheme of things' has suddenly become," Rebecca remarked dryly. "In the course of these past few hours, I have suddenly come to value that which is dull and boring."

Her wistful smile tugged at Michael's heart, but he could not allow himself to comfort her, not yet, not while the memory of her touch was still so fresh in his mind. "Well, at least we have not too far a walk from here," Michael said, determined to distract himself from his own wayward thoughts. "The DeSilvas' home is just off of Bishopsgate."

"DeSilva . . . ?" Rebecca searched her mind, trying to recollect why the name was somehow familiar. But she had little leisure to ponder. Michael was hurrying her along, past the streets with the telltale names of Bread Street and Iron-mongers Lane. Though she had occasionally visited Cheap-side Market during the daylight hours, the shuttered shops and stalls gave it an oddly sinister aspect. Still, it was comforting to see well-known landmarks, places that she had visited under normal circumstances.

But as if to remind her that their circumstances were not at all within the realm of the norm, an eerie howl split the night.

"What was that?" Rebecca whispered, peering into the darkness.

Michael put up a cautioning hand. "Nothing good, I fear."

A dark apparition erupted from the alleyway ahead. At first, Michael thought it was another particularly large cat, but as it pelted toward them, Michael realized that the creature was definitely canine. Before he could react, it had skittered to a panting halt behind the shelter of Rebecca's skirts. The animal looked up at him in an appeal of almost human desperation, its eyes wide with fright.

"Poor little mite," Rebecca said bending down. "Look at him, Michael, you can count every rib. He appears to be a terrier of some kind."

"Of some kind," Michael agreed, keeping his gaze fixed on the entry to the alley. "Stay sharp, Paragon. I have my own corollary to Newton's rules, to whit, every reaction has some proportionate action at its root. This animal is quivering like a dropped aspic; I suspect that we may be about to discover the source of its fear."

Rebecca heard footsteps echoing in the darkness.

"When I find you, you mangy little piece o' . . ." A bruiser ran into the streets, the cudgel in his hands emphasizing the implicit threat. "Where are you, you bloody—?" His question ended in mid-bellow as he caught sight of his quarry.

Michael's hand tightened around his own stick as the dog edged between himself and Rebecca as if claiming sanctuary. He could feel every bone in its emaciated body knocking against his calf.

"Yours?" Michael asked, seizing the initiative.

"Aye!" the man shouted. "And he ain't worth the blunt I paid for him, I'll tell you. 'Prime goods,' says he, 'champeen stock out o' Samson,' says he. But tonight when it's my blunt on the table, the cur's tail goes twixt his legs. Scrambles clean out o' the pit and out the door. An all of them laffin' at me fit to bust!"

Michael was hard pressed not to laugh himself. To mistake this pitiful creature for the kin of the celebrated ratting terrier, Samson, would require an uncommonly high degree of stupidity. "I can see how you might have thought that," Michael lied, looking down at the animal with a studied air. "Same noble brow, same dark patches round the eyes—yes, indeed, he has Samson's look about him."

The brute stopped, his mouth gaping in awe. "You've seen Samson fight, then?" he asked.

Michael nodded. "Took down eighty-nine rats one night down at the Westminster pit, an awesome sight to behold, my friend, an awesome sight. I would have purchased this dog myself, just on the chance that he might be Samson's get. What did you pay for him?"

The ruffian's eyes narrowed in calculation. "Gave two bob for him," he said slowly.

"Two shillings." Michael gave a sage nod. "That would have been a bargain for a ratter if the dog had any bottom to him. Maybe if you fed him up a bit . . ."

"Michael, surely you cannot be thinking of turning the creature back to this . . . this . . ." Rebecca searched for a sufficiently derogatory term as she bent to put a protective hand on the dog. It snuggled closer to her, whining softly.

"This animal's *owner*," Michael reminded her with a cautioning stare. He locked eyes with the dog's master in a look of mutual commiseration. "Women."

The bruiser gave him a gap-toothed grin, acknowledging fraternity in the eternal war against abiding female ignorance. "Don't understand naught, do they?" he asked, making it clear that no answer was required.

Michael shrugged. "Looks like my lady is taken with him. Give you a tanner for him."

"Sixpence for Samson's get!" the bruiser roared. "An insult that is!"

"Suit yourself," Michael said, drawing Rebecca up forcefully.

"But Michael . . ." Rebecca protested. "He intends to beat this poor beast."

" 'Tis his money, his property," Michael said, warning her with a tightened grip. "Now if it were me, I would rather have a tanner in my pocket than a carcass that is worth nothing either alive or dead, but it is his affair, not mine."

The dog's owner stepped forward, and the animal skittered back behind Rebecca's skirts with a yelp. Michael gave a derogatory snort. "A tanner is probably too much for this coward. Leave it be."

Michael pulled at her elbow, almost dragging her forcibly as the dog clung to her shadow.

"Six and three!" the bruiser countered as they started to leave.

"He will sell the dog to us for nine pence," Rebecca said, digging in her heels.

"Do you think I have cloth ears, woman?" Michael asked, his brow furrowing in irritation. "Nine pence for a quaking ball of fur and bone? I would do better throwing my money down a well and making a wish upon it!" He took her by the wrists, staring at her as if enraged by her defiance.

"A tanner, you said . . ." the dog's owner reminded him almost timidly.

"I did, didn't I?" Michael said from between gritted teeth. "A woman often makes a man say and do foolish things."

"Aye, that's the truth," the bruiser agreed. "Still, when a man's given his word in fair bargain . . ."

Michael sighed as he dug in his pocket. He pulled out the silver coin with a show of reluctance, looking daggers at Rebecca as he placed it into the man's open palm. The dog whined, burrowing further into the haven of Rebecca's skirts.

"Take 'im then," the ruffian said with a triumphant grin, his fist closing around the money. "And good luck to you!"

As the dog's former owner disappeared back into the darkness, Rebecca pulled out of Michael's hold. "How could you?" she asked, furious.

"I should have started at tuppence," Michael said, keeping his eye on the alleyway until he was certain that the bruiser had not changed his mind and decided to keep both the animal and the money. "But if he was stupid enough to believe this sorry beast to be one of Samson's offspring and worth two bob, so small an offer would most certainly have sent him into a fury."

"You would have given this poor creature back into his hands!" Rebecca accused, bending down to soothe the trembling canine. "And for a difference of a few pence."

"Do you think so?" Michael said, his speech turning cool. "How free you have become with my money, Miss Creighton."

"I have offered reimbursement," Rebecca said, her voice trembling.

"Indeed, noblesse oblige; shall we now add a cur at sixpence to the price of Eager's ruined suit and a sovereign for a carriage ride? A most expensive night it has been." Michael tugged his forelock mockingly. "Should I have offered him the only other coin in my possession then, milady? I can assure you that he would not have been able to make change for a sovereign. What do you think our chances would have been had he gotten a glimpse of that gold? You could bet that he would not have hesitated to try that cudgel of his to get it from us, and I would have been left with little choice but to fight him."

He eyed her, his voice scathing. "Or would you have preferred that we come to blows? After all, any man who would beat a dumb creature deserves no less than a facer." The dog whimpered, cringing at his tone, retreating toward Rebecca.

Michael bent at the knees, extending his open hand. The dog peered up at him, sniffing tentatively. "Those ribs are not the result of one missed meal," he said, deliberately making his tones soothing, coaxing, as the dog edged closer. "And most of those scars on his coat are long healed; not the consequences of rat bites, I guarantee you, though they might well have deceived our foolish friend—yes, indeed." He spoke quietly, like a nanny to a shy nursling. "Do you scent the chicken, little one? Had I known, I would have saved you a piece. Yes, indeed. I would have saved some for you."

The dog smelled his hand, ready to retreat in an instant. The pink tip of his tongue flicked out, lightly tasting, then licking. Michael laughed softly. "Sorry, old man, but a lick of the finger is all that I can give you for now." He tousled the dog's head softly as he rose. "What shall we name you, hmmm? Our friend must have been three sheets to the wind to believe that you are a son of the famous Samson."

"How do you know?" Rebecca asked, disconcerted by the sudden change in his demeanor, slowly realizing, to her chagrin, that Michael's actions had been nothing more than an act. Belatedly, she understood that Michael would never have allowed any harm to come to the animal. His manner had become almost childish, the classic captivation of a little boy with a new puppy.

"He is most definitely not a full-bred terrier from the look of him; far too meek and mild. A true ratter would be as likely to take your finger off at the bone as lick it," Michael told her offhandedly, before addressing himself to the dog once more. "What shall we name you, little fellow . . . ? I have it! Maximillian!"

"A rather pretentious appellation," Rebecca ventured.

"On the contrary, Miss Creighton, 'tis just the ticket," Michael said, straightening. "There is nothing like a high-flown name to give a bit of countenance, and our diminutive coward here needs all the flummery that we can muster."

"But Maximillian?" Rebecca said, warmed beyond all reason by his use of "our" and "we."

"After the ruler of Bavaria," Michael explained. "Stuck to Napoleon until Leipzig, then turned coat in order to retain his kingdom. A wise coward if ever there was one. If one is doomed to be a chicken-heart, then prudence is a highly desirable attribute. And now that we have christened him, I think that we ought to walk on."

"But what shall we do about Max?" Rebecca asked, noting that the dog had already begun to frisk around them in circles.

"For shame, Paragon," Michael said. "Such familiarities! Maximillian, if you please, lest you reduce his consequence even before he has any. Why only earlier this evening, he was the son of the mighty Samson. Now he is merely a cur of uncertain lineage. Just think how he must feel." Michael loosened the knot of his neckcloth.

"Did you really see this notorious dog, or were you just telling a tale?" Rebecca asked, watching in fascination as he unwound the length of snowy cloth.

"I? A falsehood? You wound me," Michael said, sarcasm rife in his tone. "As a matter of fact, a friend of mine did insist that my life would be incomplete unless I saw the great Samson fight." He smiled faintly as he recollected the night that Oliver had hauled him up from Oxford, contending that Michael would be a dolt to miss one of the canine wonders of the world. Absently, he put the corner of the linen to his teeth, starting a rip along the length of the fabric. He knotted the two ends of the halved cravat together and bent to loop the makeshift leash around the newly christened animal's neck.

"And was your life made complete?" Rebecca asked as they started to walk once more.

Michael's eyes grew distant, and the corner of his lip twisted upward as he reminisced. "I still remember the excitement of the ring, the air of anticipation, young bloods mixing with all manner of men from all walks of life. There are few places on earth that are more egalitarian than the sporting ring or the battlefield, it seems to me," he said. "Unfortunately, I was foolish enough to eat a good meal, for by the time that Samson had done his third rodent in, it was out the door and in the gutter for me."

"And your friend?" she asked.

"Stayed until the eighty-ninth rat had gone to its Maker," Michael said, certain that her horrified expression was caused by his admission of cravenness. Why had he been so foolish as to tell her of his reaction? But there was no help for it, and besides, it was no matter what she thought of him. "My friend had a good laugh at my expense. He had no problems at all with keeping his food in his stomach. You think it unmanly of me, I suppose."

"Not you," Rebecca said, shaking her head in disgust at the picture he had conjured. "Not you, Michael. 'Tis the thought of a group of grown men gathering for the sole purpose of watching other creatures tear each other to shreds that galls me. It is your friend's reaction that appalls, not yours."

It is your friend's reaction that appalls . . . yet another black ball in Oliver's box. Maximillian surged forward, and Michael yanked back in reaction, angered not just at the cur but at Oliver, at a Providence that forced people into awkward situations.

Maximillian slipped loose, and Michael knelt down to retie the knot, attempting to persuade himself that the frank distaste evident in Miss Creighton's kindled eyes and pursed lips were of no real import. There are many marriages that succeed despite differences, Michael reminded himself.

"Is that your friend's neckcloth?" she asked, trying to break the lengthening silence.

"Luckily, it is one of my own," Michael said abruptly. "And do not inquire as to its cost, if you please, or add it to your reckoning of the evening's expense."

Rebecca thought that she understood the reason for his gruff reply; she had, after all, impugned his integrity. "I owe you an apology, Michael," she said. "I did not think of the consequences if you had not bargained with Maximillian's master. You might have been forced to come to blows or even use your pistol."

"I prefer not to fight if I can avoid it, Paragon," Michael said, rising and walking forward to test his makeshift leash. A slight tug and the dog scampered at his heels. "At the risk of you believing me as fainthearted as our Maximillian, I think it a prudent policy never to antagonize those individuals whose wrists are wider in span than my thighs."

Rebecca smiled, glad of his bantering return. "No, I could never think of you as a coward, not when you have braved my wrath." Cautiously, she extended her hand. "You cried pax before. Now it is my turn to tender apologies. It is a grievous fault, to stand in judgment without just cause, especially when I owe you so much. I am sorry that I doubted you."

"You should doubt me," Michael said, shaking his head at her gesture of confidence. "You seem the type of person who trusts too easily." He slid his palm beneath hers and enfolded her hand, savoring her warmth, her simple belief in him even as he felt compelled to give her warning. "Withhold your faith, Paragon, or else you will soon find it broken, along with your heart."

"Do you use Elizabeth as your yardstick?" Rebecca asked, knowing as she spoke that she was treading on dangerous ground.

His grip tightened, and his liquid brown eyes hardened at the mention of the name. "You just begged my pardon for jumping to conclusions," he said stiffly. "Yet, you do so again; my past is none of your concern. You know nothing of Elizabeth."

"Little more than you yourself have told me," Rebecca admitted, purposefully omitting Eve's disclosures. "I know that you cared for her and that she betrayed your trust." She plunged on, despite the noticeable tightening of his expression. "If you spend your life trusting in nothing, in no one, it is true that you may never be deceived, but you will never find true friendship, or real love either."

Her amber eyes were wide with concern. Even in the midst of his irritation at her gall, Michael found himself moved by her earnest assertions. Why, he wondered, why would she risk offending a stranger who had her utterly in his power? But more puzzling still was his growing conviction that she actually did care about his happiness. "You are a fool, Miss Creighton, a gullible, naive fool," he said, telling himself that she needed the warning.

She swallowed the hurt, but she surprised herself with her bold reply. "There is no sin in being a fool."

"If so, you ought to be glad of it, else you would be condemned to eternal damnation," Michael said, taking an exasperated breath. "You cannot claim to know me, yet you are entirely too free with your trust and your advice."

"As for my trust, then I may well be wool-headed," Rebecca said, seeking to explain something that she did not wholly understand herself. "And as for the advice, perhaps I give it *because* I do not know you. I cannot judge your past, only here, only now. I have nothing to gain or lose by saying what I feel is the truth."

"And pray, what is the truth?" he said, trying and failing to keep his tone light and bantering.

"You are a good man," she said, gathering her courage in the face of his patent disapproval, "but you are unhappy, and I think that you are as lonely in your own way as I am."

"You are lonely?" Michael questioned sarcastically. "I had thought that faith and trust were sure antidotes to that disease."

"Not a cure," she said, attempting to explain her meaning and contain her pain in the face of his mockery. "We are not all destined to receive the blessings of home and hearth, of family and bosom companionship. For those of us who live with disappointment, our faith helps us to endure, to make what we can of life's ordeals. But a man like you . . . a man like you has blessings waiting outside the door, if only you would open it."

" 'A man like me,' " he repeated. How was it that she had seen into the depths of dark emptiness that swirled at the center of his being? By what right did she presume to tell him that happiness could be so easily achieved? "I am not one of your hymn singers. So do not attempt to rewrite my life into one of your damned pamphlets with their ever-so-happy endings. Honest Jack always wins in the end, does he not in a Rebecca Creighton tract? Well, I am not one of your penny pamphlet heroes, miss. Moreover, I am quite satisfied with my life. Indeed, I am currently the happiest of men."

"Are you?" Rebecca asked, the question rife with disbelief.

"Why would you doubt it?" Michael asked, unable to contain himself. "I can easily direct you to a dozen people who will assure you that I care only for yours truly."

Maximillian whined, sensing tension in the air. Rebecca knelt down to touch the animal with soothing strokes, glad of the distraction. "And I am sure that there are many more who would tell me the opposite."

"How can you be so certain?" Michael exploded. "Why do you try to make me into a damned saint? Perhaps I am an evil man rejoicing in my wickedness, who is even now planning to ruin you after lulling you into a false sense of security."

"Well, if you are, you are certainly taking a great deal of time and trouble about it," Rebecca retorted. "You have already spent far more than I would fetch, I assure you. No, you will have to try much harder if you wish to convince me of your wickedness."

"You are entirely ignorant of my character!"

"I think not," she said, looking up, compelling herself to meet his eyes. "I believe that you are basically a kind man, however much you might deny it."

The candid faith in her gaze somehow goaded him and

loosened all holds on his tongue. No woman had ever looked at him with such utter confidence. If only she knew just how much he wanted to touch her, to explore the dangerous sensuality that was waiting beyond that innocent trust. "Do you think that what occurred in the carriage has any meaning beyond a man and a woman alone in the dark? Do you truly believe that I care for you, Paragon?"

"Yes, or else I would still be in Covent Garden," she said softly, hoping that the sudden sting in her eyes would not turn to tears. "You care for me, but not any more than you would care for Maximillian or any of the other strays that Eve mentioned. But, do not fear, I have no expectations." She forced herself to lift her chin and willed herself to smile.

He would have been no less shamed had he actually struck her a blow. Her quiet acceptance was almost as much of a rebuke as the haunted look in her eyes. In a way, he was worse than the beast who had sought to beat his dog. Although that had been an unequal contest, at least there was a savage honesty in that brutal exchange. But there was nothing at all that was honest about his feelings at this moment. He wanted to shout at her, to use every oath in his considerable vocabulary of blasphemy, to shock her until she would loathe him. Surely, loathing would be preferred to quiet endurance.

More confusing still was this nearly overpowering urge to sweep her into his arms, to admit to something rich and strange that was battering at the long-closed door that she had alluded to. Yet, Michael knew that he could not afford to acknowledge the truth in her words. If he dared to seek beyond that door, it would be no blessing, but a curse, a betrayal.

Though he told himself that he cared for his friend's sake, that current matters would be no different if she had been an ape-leader, the prosy spinster of Oliver's nightmares, Michael was aware that such assertions were the products of a growing desperation.

Her upturned face was a temptation that he was obliged to

resist. Another kiss would give the lie to all of his cruel de-
nials, but it would be no kindness to surrender to this mad
need, to show her that his interest was becoming exceed-
ingly personal in nature, much more so than either comfort
or conduct would properly allow. It was better to leave those
wounds bleeding rather than risk destroying her with a temporary cure.

"We had best hurry on," he said, unexpected tightness in
his throat causing him to sound brusque.

Rebecca nodded, searching for a banal reply. "Yes, of
course, it is rather late. My family must be frantic."

Michael held back a groan as he perceived yet another un-
foreseen complication. In all likelihood, the Creightons
would be in a high state of anxiety. He could not very well
appear at the doorstep on Cavendish Square in the wee
hours of the morning with the Paragon in tow.

Though the Fairgrove fortune was as a drop in the bucket
compared to the Rowley hoard, and his baronetcy was but a
bauble compared to Oliver's eventual earldom, Michael had
no illusions as to whose neck would wind up in the parson's
noose should the circumstances of this night become known.
Without marriage, Oliver's choices would once more be
fixed between Fleet or France. Michael would have to watch
his step carefully to avoid complicating this deuced tangle
even more so.

The dome of St. Paul's loomed on the hill as they made
their way up Poultry Lane to Threadneedle Street.

"Oh, my!" Rebecca exclaimed as they emerged at the true
heart of the City. The imposing facade of the Bank of England was glorious, its marble columns and arches silvering
in the moonlight.

"Impressive, is it not?" Michael said, staring for a second
at England's temple of high finance, before moving on. "It
would appear that the riots must have been confined to a
small area. I see that there are no horse or foot guards posted
to protect the bullion in the vaults. If the authorities feared a
repeat performance of the Gordon or the Corn Law Riots,

the usual six o'clock detachment would surely have remained to stand sentry."

"You seem rather familiar with the routine," Rebecca observed.

"Mayhap I am an aspiring felon," Michael said as they walked swiftly up Threadneedle Street, "or even a would-be grave robber seeking to unearth the corpse of the seven-foot clerk who is reputedly buried in one of the courtyards. Or even worse, I might have the dastardly soul of a Cit, Miss Creighton."

"I shudder at the thought," she said with a chuckle.

"Indeed, you should," Michael said. "All of the Quality should tremble, because for all that they might wish to deny it, 'tis in the hands of the Cits that England's true might gathers. And there is more power in the house that Edward Jarman built than in all of Whitehall," Michael added, nodding toward the Royal Exchange just across the way at the intersection of Cornhill and Threadneedle. "Much as the *ton* deceives itself, we would still be a lonely island of farmers and shepherds without the financial power that resides in these piles of stone."

"Perhaps," Rebecca admitted, "but a very wise man once asked, 'If a sparrow cannot fall to the ground without His notice, is it probable that an empire can rise without His aid?' "

"The psalms of David?" Michael asked, trying to place the phrase.

"Benjamin Franklin," Rebecca informed him, delighting in his startled look, her eyes twinkling with mischief, "a student of human nature, like the psalmist, though I am told that Franklin was less than pious. Cobbett is not the only other writer that I have read, beyond myself and the Bible."

Michael gave a whoop of relieved laughter, pleased that the tension between them had dissipated once more. "You will never forgive me for that remark, will you?" he asked, stooping to adjust Maximillian's temporary tether, making certain that the loop had not tightened to the choking point before they moved along again. "You continue to astound me, Paragon."

"Only because your expectations have been so abominably dismal," Rebecca observed. She tried not to wince as her soles began to ache once again.

"Your feet?" he asked, coming to a halt.

"Far better than they were before," Rebecca said.

"I see, so that furrow in your brow and the biting of your lip are of absolutely no significance whatsoever?" Michael asked. "I vow that I have never met a saint who makes so free with the truth."

"I take it then you have met a great many individuals of a religious persuasion," Rebecca replied, matching his sarcasm. "The church bells have just finished tolling, Michael. I know what the hour is. I would as lief reach home before the sun comes up, even if I have to limp to the door."

The sheer hopelessness in her expression strangled the mocking reply in his throat. "Lean on me then, Paragon," he said, shifting Maximillian's leash to his other hand. "We have just a bit further afoot, and then I hope that we may ride the rest of the way."

At the end of Threadneedle they turned onto Bishopsgate. "In Tudor times these were the homes of wealthy merchants," Michael said, seeking to distract her. "Have you ever heard of Nathaniel Bentley?"

A negative shake of her head bade him continue.

"He was better known as Dirty Dick. His house is on Bishopsgate, about number 200, if I recall. 'Tis said that his fiancée died on the eve of his wedding. Bentley's broken heart apparently affected his attic, for he sealed up the dining room with the wedding feast left on the table."

"Never say so," Rebecca said, determined that he would not have to carry her.

" 'Pon my honor, it is no less than the truth." Michael slipped his arm around her waist to take more of her weight as he continued the tale. "He stuck his spoon in the wall a few years ago. Lived like a veritable swine; allowed his house to dilapidate into a ruin; but upon his death it was found that he was worth a fortune. Have you ever heard of anything so foolish?"

"How very sad," Rebecca said under her breath. "I suspected that if I had turned up my toes on my wedding day, Oliver would have danced for sheer joy. Why in the world has he asked me again, I wonder?"

Michael caught her whisper and cursed his choice of topic. Yet again he changed the subject, pretending that he had heard nothing. "Just a little farther," he said encouragingly, "just past St. Helen's Court and we are there."

The facade of the DeSilva home was modest. Even the brass knocker on the door was unadorned, devoid of the usual artful carvings that characterized the homes of the well-to-do. There was nothing that would set the home apart, save a scrolled case of silver adorning the right doorpost. Michael rapped at the brass plate. "I feel guilty waking them at this hour."

"How curious," Rebecca said, reaching up to trace the Hebrew letters on the case, "*Shin, Daled, Yud,* one of the sacred names in the Bible. What is it, I wonder?"

"Isaac calls it a *mezuzah,*" Michael said. "It contains parchments with biblical texts to bring blessings upon the house. It surprises me that you can read it, yet not know what it is."

"Yet another surprise that is no surprise at all when one looks beyond the surface," Rebecca said. "My father felt that you could not get the entire meaning of the divine texts unless you read them in their original language. I must admit, though, that I barely got beyond the rudiments. Is your friend Mr. DeSilva of the Hebrew faith?"

She could feel him stiffen at the question. "No, Michael, I beg you, please do not even ask what is on the tip of your tongue," Rebecca said with sudden weariness, leaving the support of his arm to lean against the lintel. "How foolish you must think me, if you have even half a notion that I might disgrace you with rudeness to a son of Abraham."

She had read his intent exactly, but before Michael could offer an apology, the door opened. Instead of the disgruntled footman that Michael had expected, Isaac DeSilva himself stood in the entry. An elaborately stitched white garment flowed around him, unlike any night robe that Michael had ever seen. The skullcap perched on his gray head was white instead of his customary black head covering.

"Michael?" the elderly man's face changed from inquiry to concern as he took in his young friend's bedraggled state.

"I am sorry to disturb your family at this late hour, Reb Isaac," Michael said, using the familiar honorific. "I know that it is Friday night, your Sabbath. Please forgive me for bringing you to the door in your nightclothes."

DeSilva smiled. "It is no nightdress, Michael, but a *kittel,* a special raiment that is worn on certain occasions," he explained, opening the door wide. "And you need have no fear that you have troubled our sleep. On a normal Sabbath night I would be long abed. However, this evening we are also celebrating the first night of Passover. Families, such as mine, who still cling to the old ways, tell the miraculous tale of the Exodus from Egypt far into the early hours of the morning."

He looked like a painting by Rembrandt, one of the patriarchs of old with a flowing white beard and wise, kindly eyes. *"Shalom Aleichem,"* Rebecca said, rendering the guttural "ch" in the salutation of peace with an accuracy that would have made her father proud. "We apologize for disturbing your festivities, sir, but Michael felt that you might be able to help us."

"Brucha Haba'ah!" Reb Isaac greeted her with the customary blessing, his piercing blue eyes filling with questions as he turned back to Michael. "Have you decided to make a career of rescuing Hebrew maidens, dear boy?" he asked, ushering them in.

Maximillian barked, then backed away warily as Michael helped Rebecca into the entry. The old man accorded the canine and his cravat leash an amused glance. "And stray dogs as well?"

"Aye, stray dogs and damsels in distress. However, this time the object of my gallantry is not of your faith," Michael said.

"It is! It is!" A little boy came running into the entry, his face alight with rapture. "I knew that I heard a dog. May I pet it, Uncle Michael?"

"Why not take him down to the kitchen, little Michael?" Michael suggested. "He is rather hungry."

"May I, Grandfather?" the child asked, looking toward DeSilva for permission.

The old man nodded.

Rebecca watched with trepidation as the boy took the leash from Michael's hand. Since his rescue, the dog had not strayed two steps from his savior's trouser legs. However, the cur trotted off happily with barely a backward glance.

"What did I tell you, Paragon, a Maximillian if ever there was one," Michael said. "He knows where the jampot is."

How in the world had Michael known her very thoughts? It was uncanny and entirely disconcerting.

"Your namesake is growing," DeSilva observed proudly. "My daughter, Esther, and her husband have come to be with us for the holiday. They will be most pleased to see you again. How fortuitous that you have come tonight. Always, at the Passover table, we have places set for strangers, as it is written 'all who are in need, come and celebrate.' "

"We cannot stay overly long, Reb Isaac," Michael said regretfully. "In fact, I must get this lady back to Mayfair as soon as possible, and I must ask your help to do it." He gave a rueful grin. "It is a long story, Reb Isaac, a very long story."

"Tonight is the very night for long stories," DeSilva said, his hoary eyebrows arching in curiosity.

Chapter 7

Lydia paced the library, going to the window for what must have been the thousandth time. "I am going to send for the Runners," she declared, her brow furrowed with worry. "I cannot think why I did not do so the instant that you returned without Rebecca!"

Silas Havermill tugged uncomfortably at his collar. "I beg you, Mrs. Creighton, think of the possible scandal if you report Miss Creighton abroad alone in London."

"Indeed!" she said, her eyes flashing with fury. "I do not know what you were thinking of, to abandon her while half of the City is in a state of riot!"

"I was injured coming to her defense," Havermill moaned, holding a raw steak to his bruised eye. "By the time that I had struggled to my feet, she was gone. Had the rector not given his assurance that he saw her leave the church uninjured, I would be combing the streets for her myself," he said, neglecting to mention that the worthy had also witnessed the poor girl being dragged along like a fish hooked upon the line. "No doubt she is merely finding it difficult to find transportation back home."

"Indeed!" Lydia said icily, reaching for the bellpull to summon the footman. "You found your way back well enough, Mr. Havermill."

"Surely, madame, you do not think that anyone would harm Miss Creighton," Havermill protested. "She is not—"

"Pretty?" Lydia said. "If you think a plain face ample protection against harm when chaos is reigning, then you are a

blasted fool! I am sending to Bow Street, and there is not a
word you can say to stop me!"

Rebecca sighed as she finished the last spoonful of soup.
The clink of silver on fine china punctuated the flow of conversation as Michael explained the difficulties of her situation to their host and his family. She bit into a crispy wafer
of matzo, the unleavened bread of the Exodus.

"A remarkable adventure," DeSilva said as Michael concluded a carefully edited version of their tale.

"You must have been terrified," DeSilva's daughter, Esther, remarked with a shudder. "To be caught like that in the
middle of chaos."

Her husband, Aaron, put a comforting arm on her shoulder. "My wife still awakens sometimes at night, screaming,
Michael, even though it happened many years ago," he said.
"Each time I look at my son I am filled with gratitude to
you."

"One does not forget such an experience easily," said De-
Silva, reaching out to squeeze his daughter's hand. "Heaven
alone knows what might have happened if you had not come
to her rescue, Michael. I still cannot forgive myself for allowing my pregnant daughter to travel back to her home in
the company carriage with only a maid and a footman for
protection. I should have known that there would be trouble."

"You cannot continue to castigate yourself, Papa," Esther
said. "Who could have thought that there would be such un-
just hatred directed against our people. And for what? They
were rioting over the rising price of theater tickets!"

"If Michael had not drawn his pistol and defended you
against the mob after the servants ran off . . ." DeSilva
shook his head with an inarticulate choke.

"It is a debt that we shall never be able to repay," Mrs.
DeSilva said, her eyes glistening in the candlelight. "Tell us
what we may do for you, Michael, and it will be done."

Rebecca observed that Michael's face had turned to the

color of a ripe beet. From what she had gathered it was apparent that Michael had rescued DeSilva's daughter from the mob during the uproar several years before when Drury Lane had increased its charges. Rebecca had wondered at the ready reception accorded to a pair of shabby wayfarers at their front door. "Uncle Michael's" close connection with the DeSilva family was entirely comprehensible if he had rescued Esther from the Old Price rioters.

"You understand why I have not divulged the young lady's name," Michael said, striving to quell his embarrassment. "It is not lack of trust, I assure you, but the fewer who know—"

DeSilva put up his hands, gesturing for Michael to cease. "It is not necessary to justify your actions to me, my friend. We know well enough the fragility of a reputation. It is simply a question of what we can do to restore her to her family without rousing too many questions." He stroked his beard in thought.

"If she was taken home in your carriage?" Michael suggested.

"Were this any other night, it could be done," DeSilva said, his voice tinged with sincere regret. "Unfortunately, all of our servants have been given their leave during our holiday. For generations, it has been a DeSilva tradition on Passover to take care of our own needs; a remnant from the days of the Spanish Inquisition when my ancestors had to hide our faith from outsiders."

"Then what would you propose?" Michael asked.

"I could send over to Nathan's home in New Court and ask if he might have a carriage available. Insofar as I know, his servants might be available to return the young lady to her home," DeSilva mused. "But as you say, the fewer who are involved . . ."

Michael gave a negative shake of his head. "I could vouch for Nathan's discretion, but I do not know how tight-lipped his servants might be."

"Surely, Michael would be welcome to help himself to

anything in the stables," Esther suggested. "Although it might be difficult to hitch up the coach, there are several smaller carriages that would not require too much effort."

"Just the thing!" Michael agreed. "It would certainly not be the first time that I have acted as a stable boy."

"By all means, use whatever you need for as long as you require it," DeSilva said, rising and brushing the crumbs from the kittel's folds. "I will show you to the stables."

"Finish your biscuit, Paragon, and I shall have our conveyance ready in a trice," Michael told her as he rose from the table.

He was as good as his word. The ormolu clock on the mantel had barely struck the hour when he helped her down the stairs and into the DeSilva's cabriolet.

"I am not an invalid," she protested as Michael tucked the carriage blanket around her and drew up the carriage's leather bonnet. "There is neither a cloud in the sky nor the slightest chance of rain."

"The less that may be seen of you, Paragon, the better," Michael explained as he placed Maximillian at her feet. "If I could put a veil over your face, believe me, I would."

"A church, a Passover feast, and now you would veil me like a Mohammedan!" Rebecca chuckled. "I wonder what is next?"

"Home, I hope," Michael said, climbing up on the box beside her and taking the reins. They waved farewell to the DeSilva family, who had gathered on the stairs.

"Home," Rebecca repeated as the cabriolet started back toward Bishopsgate. Somehow the thought of returning to Cavendish Square had precious little savor. The moon was full, and the sky was sprinkled with a myriad of stars. If only this ride could last forever . . . Rebecca gave herself a mental shake. Without doubt, her family was worried to death. Had she become so selfish in the space of a few hours that she would not consider their anxiety? Yet she did not wish this adventure to end.

Even through the robe, she felt his nearness, the hard

muscle of his thigh jostling against her as they turned back onto Threadneedle Street. To her disappointment, he distanced himself immediately.

"We would be best advised to take a roundabout route, Miss Creighton," Michael said, taking refuge in polite conversation as sudden heat seared him.

"Are you angry at me, Michael?" Rebecca asked.

"Of course not, why do you ask?" Michael said, keeping his eyes peeled for the landmarks that Isaac had described that would take them past the London Wall and up toward Aldersgate Street. "I am merely trying to concentrate; a wrong turn could easily land us in the slums of Seven Dials or the stews of Clerkenwell."

"Whenever you are out of charity with me, I become 'Miss Creighton,' " she explained. "However, when you are at ease with me, I am the 'Paragon.' "

"Perhaps I have become entirely too much at ease with you, Miss Creighton, if you can read my cards with such facility," Michael speculated. " 'Tis a poor gamester who tips his hand."

"Is this a game then that you play, Michael?" she asked softly.

"I never play games that I have no hope of winning," Michael said, his lips twisting into something less than a grimace as another turn brought her body up against his. As they traveled down the deserted streets, Michael began to comprehend that his choice of the cabriolet had been a serious error. Though it would have taken more time to prepare the DeSilva town carriage for travel, at least she would have ridden inside while he drove from the box. Every jolt became a study in suffering, and sudden turns were a form of exquisite torture.

Rebecca ached as she moved to the corner of her seat. He did not wish to touch her, even by accident. She fixed her gaze upon the moonlit streets, but even the panorama of the dome of St. Paul's had little appeal. "I find myself wondering why you bothered to come hear me in the first place?"

Michael hesitated. "Mostly curiosity," he said finally, at-tempting as much as possible to stick to the truth.

"Or fate," Rebecca said, winning a startled look from him. "Mr. DeSilva's daughter made me realize just how much I owe you. The horror on her face as she recollected her ordeal." Despite the warmth of her cloak, Rebecca shiv-ered. "I wonder what might have happened had you not been there tonight."

"I am beginning to suspect that you might have been bet-ter off without me," Michael said. "You are farther away from home than you began and I . . ." He let his voice trail off, afraid of giving expression to sentiments that were best left unsaid. His eyes met hers, an error that he should have avoided. There he found the mirror image of his own pain, the likeness of his own yearning. Loneliness and the bitter knowledge of barriers, real and imagined, kept longing pent and desire under close guard.

Rebecca looked away as she spoke. " 'Might have been' is the most useless of all phrases, in my opinion, giving rise to foolish speculation and regret. We cannot change history to suit ourselves."

"You are much wiser than I am, Paragon," Michael said, his lips crooking in a sad smile. "I am beginning to believe that I have built much of my life upon might have beens." *And tonight will become yet another of those what ifs,* he added silently.

"Better a 'might have been' than a 'never was,' " Rebecca commented. "All my life I have done as others have ex-pected, with never so much as an odd kick in my gallop to fulfill their wishes. And now . . ."

"Now?" He could not help but echo.

She knew that it was better left unvoiced, yet she spoke. "Now I, too, have a 'might have been' to dwell upon. I will remember tonight, even though I shall likely never see you again, Michael."

If there was to be any chance of her prediction coming to pass, Michael realized that there was little choice but to leave Town entirely. Even when the Top Ten Thousand packed the city for the spring marriage mart that was known as the Season, the habitués of the *ton* comprised a very small circle.

Unless he intended to live the life of a hermit in London, he knew that it would only be a matter of time before he came face-to-face with her at some rout or ball, or met her strolling down Bond Street upon Oliver's arm. Somehow the thought was not to be borne.

"No," Michael vowed for his own sake as much as for hers. "You shall not see me again, Paragon."

His tone bordered upon irritation, and Rebecca cursed her foolish tongue. He had made his feelings more than clear, yet she persisted in making him feel uncomfortable in her presence. What in the world had happened to her common sense? Apparently, she had none where this man was concerned.

As the carriage wheels racketed along the rutted roads, she continued to question what was happening. Within the space of a few hours, her world had gone topsy-turvy. She should be grateful that she had been guided into the care of a man who had a code of honor, who hesitated to take advantage of her unprotected state. Yet, such appreciative acknowledgment was not at all an accurate description of her feelings.

There was grief in the decline of her shoulders, and though her face was hidden by the monkish hood, he knew that he would see the new hurt that he had inflicted reflected in her eyes. Once again, he declined to make any apologies, telling himself that the warmth in her voice was nothing more than natural thankfulness, that she had no concept of how her touch affected him. And if, by chance, there was something more growing in her heart, that it was best uprooted now, before it had a chance to blossom.

"Devil take it!" he cursed as the carriage rounded the bend and he apprehended that there was no egress. "We shall have to turn it round." He peered over his shoulder, trying to see behind them, but the bonnet blocked his line of sight. "The street is too narrow to attempt this entirely blind. If I alight to direct you, could you take the reins?"

Rebecca shook her head. "My father never thought it proper for a female to drive."

"Well, since you are no Letty Lade, there is nothing for it but to fold back the hood," Michael said, setting the reins on the dash and turning about on the seat. "On your side of the interior, you will find a latch similar to the one here, Miss Creighton. Do just as I do to set the frame free."

As Rebecca sought for the release, Maximillian jumped to his feet and began barking furiously.

Michael whirled to find himself facing the muzzle of a pistol.

"Get out," the ruffian demanded. "I've a fancy for a carriage ride t'night."

"Do as he says, Paragon," Michael said calmly. "We will give you no trouble if you give us none."

"The mort rides with me, t'keep yer from playin' the 'eero," the man told him, his eyes raking Rebecca with unmistakable intent. "I'll set her down in a ways."

"No," Rebecca said, moving closer to Michael. "There is no need to take me with you."

Maximillian bared his teeth and growled with an unexpected show of ferocity.

" 'Old th' dog, and shut 'im up, or I'll be wringing 'is neck," the ruffian threatened.

"I would like to see you try," Michael said, trying to prolong the conversation as he estimated his chances of reaching his pistol; none to nil. The Paragon huddled closer to him, her eyes wide, but there was something beyond fear in those amber depths. Her fingers crept under his jacket. As her intent became apparent, his heart leaped with hope and admiration.

Michael leaned closer, trying to narrow the span to the other side of his waist where his gun waited uselessly. Surprise was their only advantage. Though Michael had never thought of himself as a particularly religious man, he began a silent prayer as her hand groped for the butt of his pistol. Aloud, he continued to distract the enemy. "This fellow here is of champion stock, a son of the famous ratter Samson. Just try and touch him and see how many of your fingers are left to you."

"Samson's son, eh?" the footpad asked dubiously, peering at the snarling animal.

"Can you not see it?" Michael asked as he felt the Paragon easing the pistol from beneath his belt. Slowly, he began to bend forward as if to show the dog's high points, misdirecting the brigand's attention and giving her a clear field. "Look at that noble muzzle! His pedigree is unquestionable when you examine the strength in his jaw, the power of his shoulder! Worth every penny of two hundred pounds, he is."

He raised his voice, hoping to mask the telltale click as she cocked the hammer. One shot was all they had. At worst it would serve as a distraction, and he prepared to launch himself at their assailant the instant she fired.

The pistol exploded in a flash of fire and smoke. Michael hurled himself at the footpad, bringing him down to the cobblestones with a thud. Maximillian jumped from the cabriolet with a snarl.

Rebecca dropped the weapon from her suddenly nerveless fingers. The horses panicked at the loud noise, and Rebecca lunged for the reins, pulling at them frantically in a desperate attempt to keep the startled horses under control. Luckily, the end of the street itself effectively penned them in. The cabriolet came to a halt, moving little more than a few feet before the animals realized that there was no place to go.

The two men rolled in the street, fighting for control as Maximillian yapped and danced around them seeking for an opening. When Michael raised his head, the dog found his opportunity, charging ferociously into the gap.

"Keep 'im away!" the footpad wailed, bringing up his

arms to shield his throat and face as Maximillian's snapping jaws went for his neck. "Keep the bloody 'ound away."

"Hold him, Maximillian," Michael commanded as if the cur were accustomed to doing so all the time. To Michael's surprise, the canine went about his business with relish, snarling at the cringing brigand's least movement with a delight that was almost human in its glee. Satisfied that their prisoner was well and truly cowed, Michael went to the horses' heads, calming the frightened animals.

"Well done, Paragon," Michael said, looking up toward her, but she made no reply. Her face was deathly pale, horror shadowing her eyes as she stared down at the prostrate bandit. With the horses settled and the brigand at bay, Michael gently pried her white-knuckled fingers from the reins. He brought her hand to his lips. " 'Tis all over, love," he told her softly, reaching up to caress her cheek. "There is nothing more to fear."

"I think I have shot him," she said, her voice trembling. "I have shot him, Michael."

"Aye, the bitch shot me!" the bandit whined. "Nailed me on me arm, she did. Ball went right through me!"

With Maximillian's teeth snapping at the jugular, Michael knelt by their assailant and saw a dark patch spreading slowly just above his elbow. Michael pulled up the sleeve. From all appearances, the perforation was minor, little more than a graze and barely bleeding. Picking up the brigand's weapon, he went back to the cabriolet and retrieved his own pistol from the floorboard, where it had fallen.

"Bleedin' t'death, I am. 'Tis murder, cruel murder, I say," the man whined, one hand coming up to shield his face as Maximillian lunged.

"He might die," Rebecca whispered, terrified. "And I would have killed him."

"No, Miss Creighton," Michael said, swiftly loading his pistol. "He would have brought about his own demise." He checked the other weapon as well and tucked it into his belt.

"And though I confess that you would have done the world a service by ridding it of this bit of filth, 'tis clear that the thought of his death would trouble you. Unfortunately, I suspect he will live to plague other unwary travelers."

He cocked the pistol and whistled. Maximillian's ears pricked up to attention, and he looked at Michael in canine inquiry. "Come, boy," he coaxed.

For a moment it appeared that the dog would disobey. He bared his teeth and snarled one last time in a final show of ferocity before coming reluctantly to heel.

"Good boy, Maximillian," Michael said encouragingly, squatting to pet the animal as he kept his pistol trained on the fallen criminal. "You are worth every penny we paid!"

"Me lifeblood is spillin', miss," the brigand wailed, "an' 'imself is playin' wiv 'is dog. No 'eart, miss, 'ee ain't go no 'eart."

"You tell her nothing she does not already know," Michael said, accepting a lick upon the hand from Maximillian before rising. "Get yourself up!" he commanded.

"I'm wounded," the bandit protested with a groan, but he rose, clutching at his arm.

"Were it left to me, you miserable bastard, there would be one vermin less to plague innocent travelers," Michael said, his voice as cold as his eyes. "However, for the lady's sake, I will offer you a choice. I could take you up and deliver you to the ministering hands of the Charleys, but it would require far more time than I would wish to waste to remit you to the watch and lay charges. The only alternative that I see, other than dispatching you to your Maker for judgment, would be to leave you to your own devices."

The bandit's expression clouded.

"He says that he will let you go if you are well enough to manage on your own," Rebecca explained. "But you must swear to me that you will be worthy of mercy and turn yourself to the straight path."

Michael could hear the tremor in her words, yet she

looked the brigand straight in the eye with a glare that would put fear in the soul of the most hard-hearted sinner.

"Aye, miss, swear it, I do," he agreed hastily, promptly turning tail and stumbling off into the darkness with Maximillian's barks echoing in his ears.

"A rainbow promise if ever there was one," Michael muttered as he deposited the dog into the seat. Hastily, he flipped back the bonnet. "His vow will fade and be forgotten as soon as the mist clears, Miss Creighton."

"So, I am become Miss Creighton once more," Rebecca said, her voice sinking into a near incoherence as she slumped back into her seat. "I had to try, Michael."

"I know," Michael said, jumping up on the box and grabbing the reins. Skillfully, he turned the vehicle in the narrow street. "Ah, Paragon, if only the world were like one of your pamphlets, where penitence is swift and certain. But people do not learn their lessons so readily. It will take more than a wounded shoulder to put the fear of God into the likes of him."

"Doubtless you are right," she whispered, "but what if he dies because of what I have done? If there is remorse in his breast . . ."

"He will not die," Michael reassured her with absolute certainty, "certainly not from the trifling wound that you inflicted. He will be back waylaying the citizenry before the middle of the week, never you fear."

"A comforting thought," Rebecca said as the beat of her heart began to slow to a normal pace. "Perhaps we should have brought him before the watch?"

"Too complicated," Michael replied. "There would have been no means of keeping your name out of it if we had chosen to lay charges. I hope that if we get you home before dawn, we may be able to avoid a full-blown scandal. We shall have to formulate a story."

"Why not simply tell the truth?" she asked. She was weary, so very weary. Everything was beginning to seem distant, as if she were viewing the world through a filmy haze. Her shoulder was beginning to throb; no wonder that, when the horses' terrified thrashing against the reins had nearly yanked her arm from its socket.

But what frightened her most was this odd sense of satisfaction. It was one thing to point a pistol and pray that she would not have to use it, but quite another to actually shoot a man. She might well have killed him. Yet the look of admiration on Michael's face, his cry of *Well done, Paragon* made her feel almost exultant, as if she had done something extraordinarily wonderful.

"There is nothing at all simple about the truth," Michael said, slowing the cabriolet. "Can you imagine what would be said, Paragon, if you gave a full and true account of what has happened tonight? What the tongues of the *ton* would make of it? No matter how pure your reputation, no matter that you have been entirely without blame in this incident, you would be utterly ruined, my dear, entirely destroyed."

Rebecca closed her eyes. The implications of tonight's adventure had always been lurking in the back of her mind, but his stark statement clarified the full potential for disaster. "My sister," she whispered. "If word should get out . . . her Season . . . What would happen to Sarah?" She began to shudder.

"And what of you?" Michael asked, wanting to shake her. "Can you never think of yourself? What of your life? Your future?"

"My future . . ." she echoed with a short, humorless laugh. Despite herself, a single tear seeped from beneath a closed lid. "To be the maiden aunt, I suppose, to care for Sarah's children and some day, Harry's. To hover at the edge of their lives and pray that it is sufficient to keep my heart from growing cold and empty."

"You have a suitor," he reminded himself as much as her. "You have an opportunity to make a life for yourself; you would want for nothing."

"How would you know that?" she asked, drawing upon her newfound strength. Why was it that even a stranger felt that he had the right to determine what might be right for her? She was capable of making her own choices. "How would you know that I would want for nothing?"

Michael scrambled, trying to recollect just what she had mentioned regarding Oliver's position in life, but that was not her meaning.

"How do you know what I need?" Rebecca whispered. "Perhaps it would be better to stay with the life that I know, rather than risk everything on a man who has already proven once that he cares not at all."

He could hardly deny her fears. "Marriage is always a throw of the dice," Michael began slowly. "Even though you might believe you know people, know them to the depths of their hearts, such notions are little more than comforting self-delusions."

"Elizabeth," she said softly.

"Yes, Elizabeth," Michael agreed, realizing that it was the first time in years that he had been able to say the name with a smile upon his face. "I created an image inside my heart, a chimera that had no more substance than ether."

"She was a fool," Rebecca said.

"Kind of you to say so," Michael said, reaching to squeeze her hand. "But I was more the fool than she ever was. My friends tried to warn me. All about me was evidence that my fantasies were wholly my own fabrications, yet I chose to ignore them because I was like Pygmalion, smitten with my own creation. But unlike Galatea, Elizabeth was already made of flesh and blood with her own wishes, her own desires."

Her fingers were chill. "Then tell me, pray, what is the answer?" Rebecca asked, shivering at his touch. "If we cannot trust in the facades that others present, how can we make any reasonable decision at all? Is everything to be left to chance?"

"I think the clues are always there, if we would but bother to seek for them," Michael said, halting the carriage to regard her uneasily. Her cheeks were still devoid of color, and

she was quivering like a leaf. "But most of us do not go beyond the face, the form. We assume that the vessel is repre-
sentative of the contents. Yet sometimes the most
unassuming packages contain untold treasures." He reached
up and brushed the hair from her face.

She smiled weakly. "Now it is you who are being kind."

"No," Michael said hoarsely. "I offer no counterfeit coin
when I say that you are the most remarkable woman that I
have ever met. You have the courage of a lioness and a heart
that is large enough to contain everyone but yourself. There
is beauty in you, Rebecca Creighton, but it is a splendor that
unfolds slowly, petal by petal, moment by moment, until
you virtually take a man's breath away."

She tried to shake her head in denial, but he would not
allow it. He cupped her chin in his hands, forcing her to look
into his eyes, to see that he was saying no less than the truth.

"In all honor I can offer you nothing but words, Paragon.
But take them as the only gift I can give. And if . . ." He
forced the words from his throat. "When you marry, do not
ever think that your husband has made himself a bad bargain. He was an idiot to abandon you the first time. Seldom
is a man offered such riches a second time around."

"Michael, I wish—"

He put a hushing finger to her lips. If she gave voice to
what her eyes were saying, Michael knew that they would
both regret it.

"You are a person of faith, Paragon. Surely you believe
that a Higher Power sees to the ordering of all things," he
said. "What is meant to be, will be."

"Why am I not comforted?" Rebecca asked, grasping his
hand. "All of my life, I have found consolation for the
emptiness, the disappointments, but now . . ." She shook her
head mutely.

"You will find balm in Gilead," Michael promised her,
twisting the words of Jeremiah, the prophet. "Hold fast, my
love. Search deep within yourself, and you will find it, be-

lieve me. Tonight will be as a nightmare, and once it passes, you will find your solace."

"No, not a nightmare," she said, leaning her head against his shoulder, seeking his warmth, his strength, taking the phrase "my love" and storing it in the deeper chambers of her heart, even though she knew it meant nothing.

He gathered her close to him. "I should not hold you, Paragon. I should not want you like this, but Heaven help me, because I cannot help myself." He groaned as his mouth came down upon hers.

Longing. More eloquently than any words, his kiss spoke of pent-up desire, raging through her like a fire until she felt as if she would be wholly consumed by the touch of him, the rough feel of his fingers on her skin. But even as his caress possessed her, Rebecca felt a strange new sense of herself, a glory in the knowledge that this man truly desired her.

His words echoed in her mind, and she dared to let herself believe that they might be true, that she might be worthy of his admiration. His kiss transformed her, momentarily burning away all apprehensions and fears, tempering the molten doubt within her into steely certainty. She loved him. And though she might never see him again, she would take the memory of this night with her and carry it for the rest of her days.

She knew now that she could not marry Oliver. The Creightons had managed thus far without the Earl of Elmont's lucre. Strangely enough, she was beginning to believe that they might somehow contrive for the future. She had gathered strength from Michael's words and even more from his touch. He believed in her; perhaps she could believe in herself. Her arms went about Michael's neck, pulling him closer, letting him know all that she could not say, all of her love and her gratitude. She offered him the gift of her self, without reserve or hesitation.

Her kiss still held all the awkwardness of inexperience, the charm of a woman who had not yet learned how to lie with her body. Invisible barriers seemed to vanish, the gates thrown wide, inviting Michael to explore and to take. Though he tried to hold fast to the anchors of friendship, of honor, Michael found himself swept into a storm of sensation, a maelstrom of emotion. Though the tentative sweetness of her embrace could not match the sensual expertise of an Eve, he was moved by the bittersweet knowledge that he had found that which he had been unknowingly seeking all of his life.

Never had he given credit to the notion of instantaneous love, but though he tried to convince himself that his feelings were merely the immediacy of desire, the ardor of the moment, deep within he knew that this was far more than the shallow throes of a passing passion. That realization shook him to his core, held him back at the brink of surrender. She offered herself wholly, without reservation. Yet to accept that gift, offered in trust and innocence, would be the ultimate betrayal.

Gently, he held her at arm's length, looking deeply into her eyes, wishing that he could not see her heart trapped in that liquid amber. He could not reveal that his heart, too, was imprisoned, vainly trying to escape. To do so would be nothing less than cruelty.

"We must go home," he said at last.

Rebecca discerned a wealth of unspoken meaning, confirmation, regret, and ultimately, rejection. "Yes," she agreed, moving as far away from him as she could. "We must go home."

Chapter 8

Lydia paced the entry of Cavendish Square. "Where is the footman with the Runners?" she asked.

"I did warn you that Bow Street is almost at the center of the disturbances," Havermill pointed out officiously. "It is highly unlikely that your man has gotten through."

"How dare you place her in the midst of danger?" Lydia asked, seething. "To bring her to address a Covent Garden crowd when there have been rumors of unrest floating about for months! It is beyond belief!"

"Miss Creighton had expressed an anxiety about income, Mrs. Creighton," Havermill said, wringing his hands. "I felt that this would be an opportunity to expand her audience, to put new souls on the paths to righteousness."

"Spare me your prating, Mr. Havermill," Lydia said, seating herself wearily upon the petitioner's bench in the corner.

"I would not dismiss such addresses in the future, Mrs. Creighton," Havermill said earnestly. "Our audience was surprisingly generous. Quite a number of tracts were purchased."

"Really," Lydia said, her head in her hands. "This is of absolutely no interest to me."

"Of course, just so. I would have expected no less of Arthur Creighton's wife. It is the souls that concern you, of course, which is well and good, especially since a heavenly reward is all that we shall reap for tonight's work," Havermill said. "The money is gone, and I fear that this evening's collection was not the only loss."

"Whatever do you mean, Havermill?" Lydia asked, looking up incredulously.

Michael halted the cabriolet before the ramshackle building on Marylebone Street and sat for a moment, loath to move. The Paragon had finally fallen asleep, lulled by the motion of the carriage. He had shifted her, cradling her head upon his shoulder, but now their journey had come to an end.

"Michael?" Rebecca's eyes opened, and she found herself drowning in Michael's stare. His look was tender, unguarded, and she felt her heart begin to hammer as he bent toward her.

Ollie's, Ollie's woman, he nearly chanted the words aloud to himself as he resisted the impulse to kiss her once again. Instead, he touched his lips gently to her forehead. "Not home yet, Miss Creighton, but close. It would be too much of a risk to take you any farther myself."

He leaped from the carriage and pounded at the knocker of the door as Maximillian frisked about his heels. The doorman's surly snarl turned into surprise.

"Major? It must be three of the morning."

"I am well aware of the time, Eager. Has that devil Boyce come in with his hackney yet?" Michael asked.

"Aye, I think so. Came in early. There were few enough fares about tonight, what with the troubles," Eager said, rubbing the sleep away with his fist, his eyes widening as he saw the major's state. "Cor! Will you look at my suit? My new suit! Said you would treat it like a bishop's mantle, and now look at it!"

"The worshipers got a trifle rowdy, I fear," Michael said, impatiently. "Now, wake Boyce up immediately and rouse Nell."

"I dunno, sir," Eager said, shaking his head. "Mrs. Doughty won't take kindly to being shaken from her bed at this hour, especially by the likes of me. Knock me on the noggin with her frying pan, she would, if I as much set foot over her threshold. Hoity-toity, is our Missus Cook and thinks herself well above a simple—"

"Turned you down, has she?" Michael said with an amused smile. "Keep an eye on the carriage then, and I shall beard the lioness in her den myself," Michael said. "We have no time to waste."

"Nell ain't got no beard," Eager grumbled as he stumbled out to take the reins. "My suit, my beautiful new suit what Nell ain't even seen yet. And here I was set to ask her out for a walk Sunday, and now I ain't got nothin' fit to wear."

"I am sincerely sorry about your clothing, Mr. Eager, but there was no help for it," Rebecca said. "You shall be wholly recompensed, I assure you."

"Beg pardon, miss," Eager said, looking up, startled. "Didn't see you with the hood and the dark and all. Don't mistake me, I know that the major's the type o' man who will make it good, to be sure."

"It is my fault entirely," Rebecca said, "and if anyone ought to be paying the shot, it is I. I shall send the money directly to you, Mr. Eager, if you can tell me your address."

"Soldier's Sanctuary at Marylebone," Eager told her gratefully. "All the address that you would need."

" 'Tis all arranged," Michael said, emerging from the building with a satisfied look, Maximillian trotting at his heels. "Boyce is going to harness up his hackney. Mrs. Doughty is dressing and giving your jacket a quick brushing. Listen well, Paragon, to what I have contrived. With any luck at all, we may yet be able to keep your reputation intact. But above all, do not try to find me, Paragon. Think of tonight as a dream, nothing more than a passing dream."

There was no need to sound the knocker. Goode opened the door before Rebecca could even lift her hand to touch the brass.

"Rebecca, dearest!" Lydia said, sweeping her stepdaughter into her arms, tears streaming down her cheeks. "We were so worried about you."

"She thought you would be, m'um," Mrs. Doughty said, brandishing her umbrella like a scepter of respectability.

Eager stepped forward and tugged his forelock. "That's why me and the missus brought her back soon as we was able." He put his arm around Nell Doughty, ignoring the likelihood of future retribution as he threw himself into his role with relish. "Found Miss Creighton outside the church we did and took her under our wing when all hell broke loose, begging your pardon m'um. Told Miss Creighton that we would bring her home in the morning, but naught would do until we found a hackney and brought her home."

"Everyone has been very kind to me," Rebecca said, determined as much as possible to stick to the truth. Though she disliked the Banbury tale that Michael had concocted, she had been forced to admit that it would serve her far better than the facts.

"If I may be so bold as to express that it is good to see you home safe, miss," Goode said, his voice cracking with emotion.

Rebecca took off her cloak and handed it to the butler. "I am very happy to be home, Goode."

"Rebecca!" Sarah launched herself at her sister with a howl. "Where ever have you been? And where ever did you get that dress? It is far nicer than anything you own. I vow, I would not have thought that such bold colors would suit you, but you look far better than you did when you left here."

Rebecca smiled; trust Sarah to notice the clothes. She had forgotten that she was wearing Eve's gown.

"Yes, Miss Creighton," Havermill asked, descending the stairs. "You look quite different. What has happened to your own garments?"

"They were damaged beyond repair in the hullabaloo, Mr. Havermill. Is it not fortunate that Mr. and Mrs. Eager have a daughter who is near to my size?" Rebecca said, surprised that the lie came so easily.

"Yes, our dearest . . ." Mrs. Doughty fumbled.

"Susan," supplied Eager.

"Claire," Mrs. Doughty said simultaneously.

"Susan Claire," Rebecca said, "and a most charming young girl she is. It is a shame that the hour was so late, else she would have accompanied us, I am sure."

Havermill scrutinized them closely, scenting an odd smell about this business. He turned to the Eagers. "Do you live close by the church?" he asked.

"South," Eager said.

"East," said Mrs. Doughty.

"Just south and a little bit east of the church," Rebecca intervened. "And it will take them some time to get home. I would like to thank you both once again and give my regards to Susan Claire."

"Who?" Mrs. Doughty asked.

"Our lovely daughter," Eager said with a nervous laugh. "It's right you are, miss. We've a long way home, and the hackney is waiting."

"Surely, we can give you something for your trouble?" Lydia said.

"Well now . . ." Eager began.

Nell Doughty struck his back with the flat of her hand. "*He* wouldn't hear of it!" she said, putting a distinct emphasis on the word "he." "And he will hear of it," she added under her breath, "if you should take a blessed penny."

"Perhaps some food and drink," Lydia offered.

"It's back home and to bed with us," Mrs. Doughty declared, fixing Eager with a basilisk stare.

"When you put it that way, love"—Eager grinned—"it's out the door for me! Farewell, Miss Creighton, all!" He doffed his cap and put his arm out to Mrs. Doughty.

"Give my fond regards," Rebecca said softly.

"Aye, miss, I will," Mrs. Doughty said, taking her true meaning from the look in her eyes. The poor lamb seemed almost about to weep. "I'll bring back your wishes."

"Vulgar people," Havermill said with a derisive sniff as the door closed behind them.

"Those vulgar people, as you name them, have saved Rebecca from disgrace!" Lydia turned on him, enraged. "Yet you dared to return here alone, your purse empty . . ."

"I was robbed," Havermill protested. "None of this was any fault of mine. When I rose from the floor, my purse was gone and my roll of soft missing."

"And tonight's proceeds . . . ?" Rebecca questioned weakly.

"Were that all that was lost, dearest," Lydia said, her eyes ablaze. "Mr. Havermill also had in his possession the full quarterly payment from the publisher of your tracts. Apparently, the reverend was foolish enough to carry about the notes on his person."

"But we were counting upon that money for Sarah," Rebecca said in a whisper.

"Pooh," Sarah said, her lip quivering. "What does it matter, as long as you are home safe? We were so afraid, Becky!" She folded her sister in her arms and began to cry.

"Have you come to tell me my story?" Harry asked, standing upon the landing in his nightgown, blinking half asleep at the assembly below. "And why is there a lady outside hitting a man over the head with her umbrella?"

Rebecca smiled as she stood on tiptoe to kiss Sarah lightly upon the cheek. "I do not know the answer to your last question, Harry, but in answer to the first, I will give you two tales tomorrow."

She looked around at the faces of her family. Without the quarterly payment, Sarah's Season was over before it had begun. Soon the duns would be at their door, making threats of Fleet and demanding payment. *And what of you, Paragon?* Michael's words whispered in her head. What would she be if she stood by and let them all sink into misery? There was a solution if she had the courage to take it. "I will send a footman round to Oliver's lodgings tomorrow with a note, Lydia. We will accept his offer."

"Are you certain, Rebecca?" Lydia asked. "Are you absolutely certain? Tonight I made a promise to myself that if you just came home safe, I would not say another word about it."

"What other choice is there?" Rebecca touched her step-mother's shoulder, meeting the older woman's guilty gaze with equanimity. "The money that we had depended upon to take us through the Season is gone. Oliver's father was gen-erous enough to offer us a sum that would carry us in com-fort to the wedding, for he knows well enough what dire straits we were in."

"What are you speaking of?" Havermill asked. "Has someone already made your sister an offer of marriage?"

"Not my sister, Mr. Havermill," Rebecca said with an ex-hausted sigh. "It is I who is to be the bride. The Viscount El-mont has proffered his hand, and I have decided to accept." Though she ached with despair, she could not help but smile as the reverend was rendered utterly confounded. Never be-fore had she seen Mr. Havermill at a loss for words. Unfor-tunately, the respite did not last for long.

"You cannot marry the viscount!" Havermill rumbled.

"Cannot?" Lydia repeated. "How can you say so? Indeed, she can and she will, sir. I find your remarks insulting to the extreme! The Creighton bloodlines are older than Elmont's own."

"What would your beloved father say, Miss Creighton?" Havermill asked. "The viscount publicly humiliated you!"

Rebecca looked at him, startled. "You have heard of it? But it was in the country and more than ten years ago . . ."

Havermill's lips thinned into a condescending smile. "You have become a renowned personage, Miss Creighton, and both your friends and your enemies have made them-selves quite familiar with your history. Moreover, the Earl of Elmont's son is well known in London."

"Is he, indeed?" Rebecca asked.

"I would not sully your ears with gossip, Miss Creighton," Havermill said, his tones righteous. "But you would do well to remember that *On Common Ground* has earned you any number of enemies. Your ill-advised words tonight can only make the situation worse. There are many ears listening for words of sedition."

"You go too far, Mr. Havermill," Rebecca said, warning implicit in her cool tones.

Havermill ignored her. "Time and again I have told you, Miss Creighton, your tract about the Enclosure Acts has been viewed as nothing less than an affront by many who once were your admirers. I can barely forgive myself for passing it on to the printer before giving it a thorough reading. Unfortunately, far too many copies were sold before I became aware of its lamentable message."

"Should I have been silent then?" Rebecca said, her eyes glowing with sudden ferocity. "Shall I not speak of landlords who drive honest men into starvation when they enclose land that was once used by all?"

"Your father would not have thought it fitting for a female to speak of such things, much less write of them," Havermill said with a huff. "Since his unfortunate death, I have endeavored to guide you as he would have wished. When you came to London, I introduced you to the cream of Society, and they have embraced you."

"And I am grateful, sir, for your kindness," Rebecca said, relenting.

"Are you, indeed?" Havermill asked, disparagingly. "Of late, you have disregarded my advice entirely; you insult the very members of the *ton* who were once your most ardent admirers."

"I have told no untruths." Rebecca could not help but defend herself.

"But there are some truths that are best unspoken," Havermill persisted. "You cannot afford to ignore your foes, Miss Creighton, for in these perilous times any careless word may cause disaster."

"I do not see how this has any bearing on Rebecca's betrothal," Lydia interjected.

"Your stepdaughter has trod on too many toes," Havermill pronounced pompously. "However, even those who scorn her more unfortunate writings cannot fault her for the viscount's behavior. At present, all sympathy lies with her as the injured party. However—he paused significantly—"if she accepts this offer, she will appear in a less favorable light. There will be those who will see her as grasping for the material things of the world. Your father would not have—"

"How absurd!" Lydia said in annoyance. "You will cease to speak of my late husband's 'would nots' in this matter, Mr. Havermill. I knew his mind quite well in this. My dear Arthur wanted this marriage above all things, and Rebecca knows it, too. The Earl of Elmont was Arthur's dearest friend since the days when they were both studying at Oxford. This match was planned from the cradle, and the disaffection between the earl and his son plagued my late husband no end. I am quite certain that Arthur would be most gratified that they shall finally be reconciled."

"And what of his daughter's happiness, Mrs. Creighton?" Havermill asked, his booming question reverberating in their ears.

"To give up public speaking," Rebecca mused. "To write without fear of whom I might offend, to please only myself. Yes, I do believe I might define that as a form of happiness."

"Have you given no thought of the manner of man to whom you are pledging yourself?" Havermill demanded, his chins quivering in outrage. "A sot given to the worship of Bacchus and Jezebel?"

"I had thought, Mr. Havermill, that you would not sully my ears," Rebecca said, feigning disinterest.

"Is his reputation truly so base?" Lydia asked, her concern roused. "Men are prone to such follies, nonetheless if you know of anything that puts him beyond the pale, I would hear of it."

"He consorts with evil companions, Mrs. Creighton," Havermill said, learning forward and lowering his voice. "A baronet by the name of Fairgrove is his bosom friend."

"I have heard mention of this Fairgrove fellow somewhere," Lydia said thoughtfully. "Is he of the Cornwall Fairgroves?"

"The very same!" Havermill nodded eagerly. "An odd kick to the gallop, every last one of that family. A havey-cavey lot. Word was that the Fairgroves were on more than a nodding acquaintance with the Gentlemen."

"Well, of course they would be," Lydia said in puzzlement. "Odd as the Fairgroves may be, their bloodlines are unexceptionable."

"Mr. Havermill means that they were reputed to be involved with smugglers, Lydia," Rebecca explained uneasily.

Havermill nodded, his eyes glittering. "The viscount's friend is said to be something of a radical, a friend of 'Orator' Hunt," he said with a sneer. "Moreover, Fairgrove is thick with cent-percenters, I'm told. I have little doubt that it is he has encouraged Rowley in his losses."

"You mean that Oliver is under the hatches?" Rebecca asked.

"So it is said," Havermill agreed. "Rumor has it that barely three weeks ago he ran from the Albany in the dead of night to evade his creditors."

"Indeed," Rebecca said. Three weeks since Oliver had fled from the duns, and less than two weeks later he had proposed marriage. She could scarcely believe that the close timing of the two events was a coincidence. "I must thank you for helping to clarify matters."

"Then you have reconsidered your ill-advised decision," Havermill said, his expression brightening. "Though I am not a well-to-do man, if it is solely a matter of a temporary shortage of funds, I am certain that I can loan you sufficient to tide you over. You know what they say, marry in haste—"

"—Makes waste," Lydia finished. "If Oliver is a wastrel and a scoundrel, perhaps we should accept Mr. Havermill's loan, Rebecca."

"A very kind offer," Rebecca said, tapping her chin in thought as the pieces of the puzzle slowly began to assemble themselves in her mind. "Unfortunately, I cannot possibly impose upon you, sir. You have been more than generous."

"You must not marry the viscount, Miss Creighton," Havermill said, his voice shaking in frustration.

"Unfortunately, Mr. Havermill," she replied with a sad smile, "I fear that I must."

Maximillian jumped eagerly at the sound of the hackney carriage drawing to a halt on Marylebone Street. Michael stayed behind his desk, staring at the ledgers for Soldier's Sanctuary, knowing that he ought to be in a state of ecstasy. The neat rows of figures were finally close to achieving a balance. Income from the various enterprises started by the veterans, such as Boyce's cab and Randolph's woodshop, were already paying their way, and other planned undertakings showed exceptional promise.

Yet, Michael could not keep his mind upon his calculations. It might take fifty pounds to start Eager in the business of mixing fine tobaccos, or it might take five hundred. At the moment it made no difference. He closed his eyes, remembering the Paragon's forlorn smile as she had waved her farewell. He had not dared to kiss her, to touch her, for fear that he would never let her leave. The hardest thing that he had ever done in his life was to bring her here to Marylebone knowing that if he had appeared at Cavendish Square himself, he would have been sending announcements to the papers this very morning.

Waiting in the entry, the pup began to frisk in delighted anticipation, but as Maximillian watched in bewilderment, the front door clicked shut again. She had not come. Michael reached down to stroke the disappointed dog, feeling the full measure of pain along with the dumb animal. "She is not coming back," he said softly. "Not now, not ever. We will never see her again."

"She's home safe, Major!" Eager declared, snapping a smart salute as he came to halt before Michael's desk.

Michael returned the salute. "Well done, Eager. Nell." He nodded to Mrs. Doughty in approval. "Was our story accepted?"

Mrs. Doughty flushed. "I hope so, sir, for the lamb's sake. Everyone seemed to swallow whatever we dished up, except for that parson—what was his name, Haversack or Havacare?"

"Havermill?" Michael suggested, the quill snapping in his hand.

"Aye, that was it," Eager agreed. "Havermill it was. Looked like his lips and eye said a 'howdydo' to a clenched fist, they did. Limped a bit, too, if my peepers did not mistake me."

"I suddenly begin to find myself believing in divine providence," Michael said, his fingers forming a steeple as he considered their report. "So Havermill was suspicious."

"And it was all my fault," Mrs. Doughty said, her lip aquiver. "Me saying one thing and you another. If only I had let you do the talking, Eager."

"There, there, Nell," Eager said with a comforting pat on her broad shoulder. "You did the best you could on short notice and no script to speak of. Siddons couldn't have done better, I say. And Miss Creighton had a ready word, so it went well enough in the end."

"I dunno," Mrs. Doughty said with a doubtful shake of her head. "I didn't like his looks, I'll tell you. Reminded me of the lizards from the days when I followed the drum in Spain with Sergeant Doughty, rest his soul. Havermill's got the coldest eyes I ever seen, Major, colder than you would see on a creature crawlin' out from beneath a rock."

"Looked at us as if we came from dirt, too," Eager agreed. "But it seemed as if the cove with the collar wanted to believe what we said."

"He would. From what I suspect, Miss Creighton is his bread and butter," Michael said with a satisfied nod. "Thank you both for your help, and Eager"—he pulled the last sovereign from his pocket, flipping it into the air—"for your suit."

"Weren't worth all that much, Major," Eager protested as he caught it.

"A bonus for a job well done," Michael said. "And there will be something extra for you, too, Nell."

"No need, Major, after what you done for me when the sergeant died," Nell demurred. "Were it not for you, sir, it would have been the streets for the likes of me."

Michael waved his hands. "I shall brook no insubordination here!" he barked, his sharp tone undercut by a half smile.

"Aye, Major, as you wish; but begging your pardon, Miss Creighton might need a word of warning. Collar or cravat, I'd watch my back against that Havermill fellow," Eager said.

"I shall convey your warnings to Miss Creighton's fiancé," Michael said with a nod of dismissal.

"So that's the way of it." Mrs. Doughty gave a cluck of sympathy as she went back to her kitchen. "Poor Major Fairgrove. Ain't it the saddest thing you ever did hear?"

"What is it you're saying, Nell?" Eager asked, confused by the sudden glimmer of tears in her eyes. "No need to cry. You did the best you could by Miss Creighton and the major knows it."

"Are your eyes made of buttons?" Mrs. Doughty asked, punching Eager in the arm for emphasis. "The major is in love with Miss Creighton."

"Is he?" Eager asked. "How do you know it?"

"Didn't you see the way he looked at her when he handed her into the carriage? How his hand held on just a bit too long? How he was touching her with his eyes?"

"Nope," Eager admitted.

"Men!" Mrs. Doughty said the word as if it were an epithet. She put the kettle on the hearth with a clang. "He loves her, make no mistake of it, though he might not know it yet."

"How can you love someone and not even know it?" Eager asked.

She shot him a fulminating look as she got out the tin of tea.

"Besides, she's set to marry someone else," Eager added.

"Sometimes, Eager, I wonder if your brains were in your left arm," Mrs. Doughty said with a sigh.

Rebecca stood at her bedroom window, watching the dawn come up over Cavendish Square. Hers was the least desirable of the sleeping chambers, subject to noise and the hubbub that rose from the street below. Yet, she had always favored the view of the square.

When her father's living had been in the country and the family would occasionally come up to Town, she would spend hours looking at the houses, thinking of the people who had once lived in them. Princess Amelia, the daughter of the second George, had once made her home on the square. Horatio Nelson had lived here when he was but a captain. Yet, this morning she could find no joy in the vista. Somewhere, beyond her sight, was Michael.

Do not try to find me, Paragon. The words whispered in her mind. *Think of tonight as a dream, nothing more than a passing dream.*

A dream, yet it seemed to her that nothing in her life had ever been half so real. She gathered the silken softness of Eve's gown into her fist, clutching it as the sun rose, half hoping that it would disappear, like the fairy-spun dresses in the children's tales.

If it had all been the fabrication of her imagination, then the pain in her heart might fade as well. But the morning light began to grow, and with it the realization that the night was truly over. All the wishes in the world would not change that ultimate tormenting reality. The cyprian's dress, cloak, and boots remained, but of Michael she had no token, nothing at all, save the memories of his touch, his kiss. Perhaps it was just as well. She remembered Dirty Dick of Bishopsgate, living forever in a moldering memory of what would never be. Michael had adjured her to look to the future, to build a life for herself.

Rebecca sat at the delicate escritoire in the corner of her room and sharpened the nib of her pen. As she wrote, she realized that Michael had given her far more than mere memories. Oliver would have her in the end, but she was no longer a green girl, nor would she be content with the crumbs that he might deign to hand her. This time she would dictate her own terms.

The dark-paneled rooms of White's club were nearly empty. At this early hour the young sprigs were still snoring away the night's revels, and save the occasional rustle of a freshly ironed newspaper, silence ruled the room. Michael put his hand into his pocket, seeking the note to assure himself that he had read Oliver's scrawl correctly. Perhaps his sleep-starved eyes had mistaken the time. Ten o'clock in the morning was the cock's crow as far as Oliver was usually concerned.

There were but two pieces of paper in his pocket. One was Oliver's scratch, which did state ten quite clearly. The second was a scrap of vellum. Gently, Michael smoothed the paper open.

While there was no need to scan his work again, Michael read the fair copy beneath his breath. Never had he written anything of the kind, verse more befitting a besotted schoolboy than a poet. If the Paragon could but see it, she would likely laugh at the puerile outpourings that made Byron seem almost a cold fish. He had half hoped that the act of setting his heart onto paper would purge him, but his emotions remained in turmoil.

"Hullo, Michael," Oliver called, as if he had just spotted the fox on the hunt.

Hoary brows beetled in disapproval as the habitués of the club emerged from behind their morning newspapers to

scowl and shake their heads at the rag-mannered insolence
of the younger generation.

Oliver grabbed his friend by the elbow, barely giving
Michael enough time to snatch up his papers. "Shall we
have a bite to eat?" Michael asked, appalled to find himself
being propelled toward the bow window facing Bond Street
and into the chair that was the exclusive property of George
Brummel.

"The Beau ain't here," Oliver said, gesturing toward the
seat as he grinned at his friend's dismayed expression.

"True enough," Michael said, settling back uneasily.
"Still it seems near unto sacrilege."

"Heard a rumor that he's under the hatches," Oliver said
with a snort. "Not surprising, considering his remark about
Prinny's girth. Asks Alvanley, bold as brass, 'Who is your
fat friend?' Man's tongue is like a garrote. Wouldn't be
much of a loss to England if he had to cross the Channel."

"Be glad you will not have to join him if he does, Ollie,"
Michael said, staring out the window into the thickening
fog. He had watched the dawn come up bright, but now the
carriages passed to and fro in the mizzle, fading into the
cloudy curtain like hulking will-o'-the-wisps.

"Might yet want to make the run to Dover," Oliver said,
dismay passing across his amiable expression like a shadow.
"Got word from Miss Creighton this morning."

Could she have actually shown Oliver the door? Michael
knew that it was wrong to feel hopeful. "You cannot mean
that she has turned you down entirely?"

"No, the news ain't that good!" Oliver said, his forlorn
cast quickly transforming into a glare of fury as he pulled
some sheets of vellum from his waistcoat and unfolded them
with an angry crackle. "The parson is still on call, be sure of
that, and I have her permission to send the notices to the
paper. But my lady now informs me that she has heard 'ill
rumors of my character.' She sets conditions. Here! Read!"
He shoved the note into Michael's hand.

Michael scanned the elegant handwriting quickly, his

heart sinking as he scanned the words, ". . . require you to make your offer of marriage in person." He had expected no less, encouraged her to take her chance, yet he could not help but feel a stab of disappointment.

But the balance of her note was an unexpected facer. No flowery phrases and trite sentiments for the Paragon. He could almost hear her voice as she set down her list of conditions. Michael wanted to rise up and yell, "Brava," and he found himself hard pressed to keep from laughing at his friend's expression of choleric outrage. "It appears that the lady wants you to serve as an escort to her and her sister. Apparently, it is the younger Miss Creighton's Season, and your company would lend the girl some countenance."

"Not only am I to partner the woman, but I am to serve as an escort to the infantry!" Oliver said "escort" as if it were a blasphemous obscenity. "Wishes me to take them to Almack's, to escort them to parties and routs. To . . . to . . ."

"I believe the exact phrase that she used was to 'squire her in the manner customary to a lady of her station,' " Michael quoted. "She wishes to acquaint herself with your true character."

Oliver snatched the papers back from Michael's hand, unknowingly taking Michael's poem as well. Indignantly, the viscount stuffed them back into his pocket. "Won't!" he ranted, sticking out his chin like a pugnacious child. "I won't gad about London like . . . like . . . like—"

"A gentleman seeking a lady's hand?" Michael supplied. "It would seem a reasonable request."

"Aye, it would to you," Oliver said belligerently. "You get your shekels as soon as the notice hits the papers."

Michael rose swiftly, his fists tightening at his side. "If you wish to imply that I do this for the money, then I can only suppose that the quantities of gin that you have been drinking have begun to effect what little intellect you have left," he said, his words assuming the halting beat of barely contained anger. "Believe me, if I thought that money could repay the debt between us, your vowels would be ashes, and I would sign over all else that I own immediately."

"Didn't mean no harm by it," Oliver said with the air of a recalcitrant little boy. "I know that the silver don't signify for you, Michael. But I am doomed to be a tenant for life with this . . . this . . ."

"You may insult me with impunity, but do not dare to slur the lady, Oliver Rowley," Michael said in a harsh whisper, "unless you wish grass for breakfast."

Oliver's eyes went wide. "Meant nothing by it," he said.

"If it is your wish to toss the coin between preceding Brummel to France or laying your lot with our friends who dwell in Fleet, I cannot stop you; but Miss Creighton does not deserve your abuse."

Oliver viewed his friend in utter stupefaction. "Don't fathom it at all. Only a few days ago you were cracking wise about her yourself, and now you threaten me with pistols at dawn."

Michael shook his head at his own stupidity. There was nothing for it now but admit that he had met her. "I disguised myself and attended one of her lectures, wholly unbeknownst to her. You are a lucky man, Ollie, a very lucky man."

"You have seen her?" Oliver asked excitedly, his puzzlement forgotten. "What does she look like? Did the years improve her at all?"

Michael's jaw nearly dropped in astonishment. "You have not even bothered to meet with her?" he asked, his words dripping disbelief. "How in the devil did you propose marriage?"

"Sent her a note," Oliver mumbled, staring down at his Hessians.

"And you have paid no calls?" Michael asked contemptuously.

Oliver's abashed look quickly confirmed the negative.

"No wonder the lady is uncertain of your integrity. If you are curious about Miss Creighton, you may damn well make the effort to find out for yourself!" Michael said, turning away, but Oliver's hand grasped his shoulder.

"Didn't mean to offend." Oliver's words came in a near whisper. "Never had to pay my addresses to a proper female before. Plenty of lightskirts, know how to deal with them well enough, but she's a lady, Michael, and a saint at that. What do I do? I am supposed to call upon her this afternoon, and I haven't the foggiest notion of how to go on. What will I say?"

Michael turned back, seeing the honest confusion in Oliver's eyes. "Come to breakfast, Ollie," he said with a resigned sigh. "And I shall give you a lesson on how to woo a Paragon."

"Why not come pay the call with me?" Oliver suggested. "Your nose is forever in some book or other. You will know just what to say to her."

"It is not I who will be wedding her, my friend," Michael said, not quite succeeding in keeping the regret from his voice. "I will be spending the next few days wrapping up my affairs here in Town. Soldier's Sanctuary seems to be running smoothly, and it will not need anything more than my occasional cursory attention, but I have had urgent word from my steward," he lied. "The estate that my grandmother left me is in dire need of attention. By the week's end, I plan to be rusticating in Kent."

Chapter 9

The afternoon sunshine streamed through the library window as Goode set the tray of wine and cakes on the small table near the settee. The silver tray gleamed, and the sparkling crystal decanter shattered the rays of light into all the colors of the rainbow. Despite the short notice, every bit of the house on Cavendish Square that could be scoured, polished, or scrubbed had been subjected to rigorous hands in expectation of the Elmont visit.

"One would think Farmer George himself was coming to call," Rebecca grumbled as Sarah pinned her sister's curls into place.

"Opportunity is coming knocking," Lydia said as she swept into the room. "There is no use greeting it in hobble-de-hoy fashion. You look lovely, dearest."

"Maybe Oliver will not come," Rebecca said, trying to keep the hope from her voice. "He has a history of simply not showing, as you well know."

"Nonsense, dearest, his reply was all that is amiable," Lydia said, tweaking a fold of Rebecca's skirt into place. "Did I not say that Robard gown would be just perfect, Sarah? It looks as if it were made for her."

"I recall Papa reading to me once that the heathens used to sacrifice to their gods by throwing virgins into volcanoes," Rebecca commented under her breath. "I suppose that they were well dressed, too."

"I still think the color she wore last night became her better, Lydia," Sarah commented, oblivious to her sister's grumblings. "That emerald was just the thing for her."

Someone of your coloring needs bright hues. Green for instance. Unbidden, Eve's advice resonated in Rebecca's mind like the echo of a long-forgotten dream. Rebecca sat in a chair, dressed like a child's china doll, waiting for history to repeat itself. She held her breath as the knock finally came, but it was not Oliver who appeared in the open door.

"Mr. Havermill!" Rebecca exclaimed in surprise.

"I am sorry, miss," Goode said, panting as he followed upon Mr. Havermill's heels. "I tried to explain to the reverend that—"

"This could not wait upon ceremony, Miss Creighton," Mr. Havermill said, grasping Rebecca's hand. "I cannot allow you to sacrifice yourself upon the altar of that son of Belial."

"Really, sir," Lydia said. "This is the outside of enough. We have already heard your objections. Rebecca's mind is entirely made up and we are expecting the viscount shortly. You are decidedly *de trip.*"

"*De trop,* Lydia," Rebecca said.

"*De trip, de trop,* it is all a horse of the same color," Lydia said. "You must leave, Mr. Havermill, immediately."

To Rebecca's dismay, Havermill dropped to one knee. "Marry me instead, Miss Creighton. I have long admired your . . . your . . ."

"If you have admired it for so long, I wonder that you cannot name it," Rebecca said acerbically, trying to disengage her fingers from his sweaty palm.

"Physical beauty means little to me, and I care not that you are long on the shelf," Havermill declared. "What I value is the beauty of your soul, Miss Creighton, your fine sensibility, your . . . your . . ."

"Ah, there we are again, Mr. Havermill, stuck upon that ephemeral nameless quality of mine that you have esteemed for so very long a time," Rebecca said, not quite certain whether she wished to laugh or cry. "So you do not mind that I am an aged spinster of seven and twenty?"

"Actually, I had thought you older than that," Havermill said.

"Nor does it bother you that my face is less than pleasing?"

"What is a face, my dear Miss Creighton, but a pair of eyes, a nose . . ."

"Eyebrows and a mouth, Mr. Havermill, we cannot forget those," Rebecca said, stifling a giggle. Were it not so painful, it would have been wholly ridiculous.

"Indeed, Miss Creighton, indeed," Havermill agreed, "most important features, those."

"You do me great honor, Mr. Havermill," Rebecca said, attempting to keep the sarcasm from seeping into her speech. "But I cannot allow you to make so noble a sacrifice for my sake."

Once again, the sound of brass resounded through the hall.

"Oh, bother," Lydia said. "Sarah and I shall go and greet our guest. Do get up off the floor, Silas, and stop making a biscuit of yourself."

"A cake." Sarah giggled as she followed her stepmother to the door. "He is making a *cake* of himself, Lydia."

Oliver looked up, transfixed by the vision upon the stairs. "You are not . . . Rebecca?" he asked, hoping against hope.

"Of course not," the vision said. "My sister's hair is dark, and her eyes are not blue—you ought to know that."

"You remember Sarah? Do you not, milord?" Lydia asked.

"Fancy that, little Sarah!" Oliver said with a jovial grin.

"Will you tell your sister that the viscount has arrived," Lydia said significantly. She breathed a relieved sigh when Havermill appeared at the top of the stairs. "Ah, Reverend Havermill, so glad you could visit. Do come back again another time. Allow me to present you to the Viscount El-mont."

The clergyman scowled as he came down the stairs.

"As you sow, so shall you reap!" he said, ignoring Oliver's outstretched hand and snatching his hat and gloves from Goode.

"Odd sort of fellow," Oliver commented as Lydia led him up to the library.

"Wrapped up in a sermon," Lydia confided. "My dear late husband was often that way. Rebecca is waiting in the library. She is quite eager to see you again after all these years.

Rebecca stood by the window.

"Hullo, Becky."

Rebecca turned at the sound of the familiar voice. Lydia discreetly drew the door closed as Oliver Rowley, Viscount Elmont, entered the room. Her heart sank at the sight of him. Years of war had honed away the last vestiges of boyish-ness. If the viscount had been sunk in dissipation, as Haver-mill had claimed, then there was no sign of it. Oliver was, if possible, more intimidatingly handsome than he had been a decade before.

Do not let anyone deny your worth . . . Rebecca drew strength from Michael's words. Her value did not rest upon Oliver Rowley or any man. She was no longer a green girl to be stupefied by the man's looks. To her surprise, Oliver seemed as nervous as she was herself, perhaps more so. His hands were shaking, and his gait was stiff as he crossed the room.

"Oliver, thank you for coming," she said softly, gesturing to a chair. "Do sit down."

Instead, Oliver went on to bent knee before her. It was daunting to realize that his head still came nearly to her shoulder.

"Oliver, there is no need to do this, truly," Rebecca said in embarrassment. Twice in one day was twice too much.

" 'Deed there is," Oliver said stubbornly, looking up at

her. "Fairgrove explained that you had the right of it. Got to give you your due as a lady and do it by the book. Said that a bent knee is the only proper way to ask for your hand."

"Who is Fairgrove?"

"Friend of mine," Oliver explained. "Heard you speak. Liked it."

"You do not have to ask me to marry you again, Oliver," Rebecca said. "Not if you do not wish to, truly. I forgave you a long time ago for the other time."

Oliver's expression lightened. "Did you, Becky? Mighty good of you to say so. Wouldn't be the thing to have my wife holding an old grudge against me, would it?" He grinned engagingly, and Rebecca could not help but smile back.

"Fairgrove was right; you do have a pretty smile!" Oliver said. "Didn't see it much the first time round. Always were such a serious little thing. Well, Becky, what do you say? Will you do me the honor?"

Surely you believe that a Higher Power sees to the ordering of all things. . . . What is meant to be, will be. Rebecca looked down at the viscount's earnest countenance and resigned herself to the realization that she and Michael were among those things that were not meant to be.

"Are you certain, Oliver, that you want this?" she asked, allowing him one last chance to ease out of this vise that held them both. "Because if you do not, I shall not hold it against you, and I shall tell your father so."

"Ain't often that a man is offered a second chance," Oliver said. "If you'll give me that chance, Becky, I'll take it."

Seldom is a man offered such riches a second time around.

"Yes, Oliver Rowley," Rebecca said. "I will marry you."

Good-bye, Michael, she added silently. *Wherever you may be I thank you, and I shall pray for you.*

*   *   *

Rebecca sighed as Sarah stood transfixed before the display of hats in the window.

"Oh, Becky, is that not the most cunning bonnet that you have ever seen?" Sarah asked.

"Even more delightful than the one that fascinated you no less than five minutes ago?" Rebecca questioned, but her tones of sarcasm were utterly wasted on her sister and their companion.

Oliver halted at Sarah's side, gazing upon the hat in question with the rapt attention of a millinery aficionado. "Brim's a bit broad," he noted, pointing out the deficiency as if it pained him. "And the ribbon, the color . . ."

"Too blue," Sarah supplied.

"Aye, just so," Oliver agreed with a judicious shake of his head. "Much too blue."

Surreptitiously, Rebecca checked the timepiece that hung at her neck. Sarah and Oliver were in their element, conducting long and detailed discussions regarding the effects of color on complexion, the fashionable shades of green versus their brighter, but less exalted relations.

Rebecca had long ago lost count of the number of millinery windows where they had stopped to gaze at the hatmaker's art with an admiration that bordered upon idolatry. Drapery and napery, ribbons and kerchiefs and furbelows of every imaginable kind, all were examined in tortuous detail.

Four hours, for four excruciating hours they had wandered aimlessly along Bond Street, their purchases piling up in the carriage that traveled discreetly behind them. Yet, even though Rebecca's feet were beginning to ache, she could not very well demand a halt, not when Oliver was playing the attentive swain according to her express command.

In the past few days, Rebecca had felt as if the Scripture had spoken to her direct. By requiring Oliver to act the role of devoted suitor, she had sown the wind, and in return she had reaped a whirlwind of activity. Vouchers to Almack's had arrived with astonishing alacrity just this morning, and the portals to that famed Marriage Mart were now open wide, yet they had hardly noticed the deficiency.

All of their evenings had been filled with balls and routs. Cards and invitations had been flying in the door on Cavendish Square. Between the callers and her new social obligations, Rebecca had barely a moment of peace, much less time to write. And in between she was being dragged on expeditions such as this one, or worse, playing the pincushion for fittings for her trousseau.

The outcome was almost worth the trouble, Rebecca decided, admiring her new sapphire blue walking dress in the window glass. She had taken Eve's advice, choosing jewel tones and clean lines for her new wardrobe. While Lydia had protested, the results were undeniable. Although Rebecca knew that she would never be a diamond of the first water, like her sister, the hues and style gave her a look of simple elegance, making the most of her figure and coloring. If only Michael could see her.

Michael stopped in his tracks and wheeled to face the display in the window of number thirty-three Bond Street. Pulling the brim of his beaver forward, he pretended to study William Yardley's assortment of scented soaps and lavender water. It was risky to remain, he knew, but he stood transfixed, devouring her reflection like a boy staring into the bakery shop. Her new finery suited her almost too well, revealing the well-kept secret of her fine, trim shape and her regal carriage. She turned in his direction, and he saw that her curls had been cropped to frame her elfin face, giving her the look of a mischievous pixie.

Rebecca took a deep breath, attempting to quell the sudden rapid beating of her heart. The dark-haired man across the way at Yardley's shop caught her eye. She could not help but stare, willing him to turn so that she could assure herself that wishful thinking had prevailed once again. It was by no means the first time that she had conjured Michael amid a crowd. There had been all too much of that, these days past.

She would read a phrase in a book and think that Michael would have enjoyed it. A dog's bark would put her in mind of Maximillian. But the dark-haired man disappeared into the door of the shop, and she forced herself to turn away.

By all measures, she should have been deliriously happy. Oliver's face was mirrored in the pane, and she surreptitiously studied her fiancé's profile as she kept the corner of her eye on the reflection of Yardley's door. The years had honed the callow boy that she had remembered, but the golden god was still handsome enough to turn every female eye in envy. Sarah constantly raved over her sister's luck. Was it only Rebecca who noticed the weakness of his chin, the befuddled look that intermittently crossed his eye, or was she just making unreasonable comparisons?

Michael hurried out of Yardley's back door, wondering what he would do with a half dozen bottles of lavender water. No matter that Michael's valet had deemed his master's supply of neck cloths inadequate, it had been foolish beyond permission to risk a trip to Bond Street. Almost everyone, including Oliver, already believed him gone from Town, but his affairs continued to drag on. It gave him surprisingly little satisfaction that DeSilva promised him that he would be a much richer man by the week's end. Oliver's repayment had somehow assumed the weight of thirty pieces of silver.

Rebecca shook her head, determined to change the direction of her thoughts, but it mattered not a whit. Was it not sufficient now that Michael haunted her nights? Must he walk beside her in her daydreams as well? Though she turned to gaze openly at the entrance of number thirty-three, the dark-haired man did not emerge.

"Miss Creighton!"

Rebecca sighed as she saw Silas Havermill dodging carts and carriages to cross the street, his hand raised in greeting.

"You have not been at home," he said, puffing with the effort of his haste. His tone almost accused her of deliberate malfeasance. "I have not yet had a chance to wish you happy."

"I am terribly sorry to have missed your calls, Mr. Havermill," Rebecca said, "but my schedule has become rather hectic of late."

"Your new tract was due at the printer yesterday. Mr. Reed was not pleased," Havermill informed her, his pitch rising. "The cost to us for publication may well be steeper because of it."

"My apologies, Mr. Havermill, but you had not mentioned that Mr. Reed was pressing you. *Cathy of Covent Garden* is completed," Rebecca said. "You may take it to Mr. Reed whenever you choose."

"I had thought that we had discussed this matter thoroughly, Miss Creighton," Havermill snapped, his face flushing. "I had found your preliminary sketch entirely unsuitable and suggested a pamphlet relating to the sin of gossip. We agreed—"

"I agreed to nothing, Mr. Havermill. I will write what I choose," Rebecca said, her voice dropping to a chill whisper. "Moreover, I refuse to discuss this matter on a public thoroughfare."

"Something amiss, Rebecca?" Oliver asked, coming to stand at Rebecca's side.

"Oliver, I believe that you have already made the acquaintance of the Reverend Silas Havermill," Rebecca said.

"Havermill?" Oliver asked, mystified at first, and then his expression lightened. "Ah, 'the sow and reap' fellow. Pleased to see you again, sir."

"I have been fortunate to be able to be of some assistance to the Creightons," Havermill said with a bow of acknowledgment. "It is a pleasure to see you again, milord. Perhaps you, as Miss Creighton's future husband, will be able to make her see the folly of her ways. She has written a tract regarding"—he hesitated delicately—"a woman of er, easy virtue."

"Have you indeed, Rebecca?" Oliver asked, his expression clouding.

"I have." Rebecca nodded, waiting for the inevitable outburst once his look of confusion cleared.

"Look forward to reading it, if I could," Oliver said almost shyly. "Like what I've read so far of yours. Not at all like the prosy tracts that m'father used to make me read. You write ripping fine yarns, Rebecca."

"But . . . but . . ." Havermill sputtered.

"Miss Creighton will write whatever she might wish," Oliver said frostily, folding his arms across his broad chest. "If you are uneasy, Mr. Havermill, it might be that I will find someone to publish 'em myself, fine yarns that they are."

"No, no," Havermill said hastily. "There is no need, I am sure. I simply did not wish for anyone to impugn Miss Creighton's reputation."

"Anyone tries that, and they will have to deal with me!" Oliver said, his chin jutting out pugnaciously. "Pistols for two and breakfast for one and all that."

"I am sure that no one would dare." Mr. Havermill all but twittered, backing away in a sudden anxiety to be gone. "I will come by later for your manuscript, Miss Creighton. A good day to you all." He bowed and proceeded at a near run toward Piccadilly.

"Lord Elmont, you were splendid!" Sarah said, her eyes glowing with admiration. "You certainly told him!"

"I did, didn't I?" Oliver grinned.

"Did you mean what you said, Oliver, about publishing as I choose?" Rebecca asked. "Or was that just to get his goat?"

"Fairgrove said that anyone with your talent should have free rein. 'Twas he that made me read your tracts, Rebecca," Oliver confessed sheepishly. "And they are ripping fine yarns."

"I must confess that I am anxious to meet your friend Fairgrove," Rebecca said. "You speak of him so often."

"Is he truly as wicked as Mr. Havermill claims?" Sarah asked.

"Wicked? Sir Michael Fairgrove?" Oliver asked with a snort of disbelief. "Salt of the earth, the type who would give a friend the shirt off his back. If he is wicked, then I am the devil himself."

Rebecca felt a shiver of reminiscence as she recalled Eve's similar description. But Michael was a common enough name.

"Fairgrove is rusticating in Kent, seeing to his estates," Oliver said. "Didn't say how long he would be there, but from what he said, it may well be months before he gets back to Town."

The prickle of hair at the back of Rebecca's neck began to settle down. Oliver's friend was in Kent.

"Is he well-to-do?" asked Sarah.

"Considerably plumper in his pockets than he was before, now that my debts to him are paid," Oliver said cheerfully.

Rebecca frowned, her suspicions almost confirmed. So that was why Oliver had hounded her for her answer. "As soon as the announcement reached the paper, I take it?" she ventured.

"Exactly!" Oliver nodded, hesitating as he realized his error. "Put my foot in it, didn't I?" he asked sheepishly. "Ain't going to cut up rough about it, are you, Rebecca?"

"No, Oliver, I am not vexed," Rebecca said with a wisp of a smile. "In truth, I much prefer to know where I stand."

"You are the top of the trees, Rebecca, the top of the trees," Oliver declared. "Pity Fairgrove ain't in Town; think you would like him. He's a poet, got a way with words, too. Show you one of his poems if you'd like. Took it from him by mistake last time we met at White's. Meant to get it back to him before he left Town, but I suppose that I ought to just post it to him in Kent."

*　　*　　*

William Reed shuffled into the room behind his printing press, his ink-stained hands balled into a fist as he pounded on the counter.

"Where is it, Silas?" he shouted. "You promised me another Rebecca Creighton tract yesterday! Where in hell is it? Those prosings of hers are solid gold on the streets."

"I have it for you," Havermill said, his teeth clenched as he shoved a page of newsprint into Reed's face. "Have you seen this?"

"I leave the wedding announcements to my wife," Reed said in annoyance. "I want the manuscript, Havermill. If you're holding out for more money again—?"

"You idiot! Read: 'The Viscount Elmont and Miss Creighton of Cavendish Square.' It's Rebecca Creighton who is getting married!"

"Well, wish her happy for me," Reed replied with a sneer.

"You don't understand, do you?" Havermill asked. "A husband will ask questions. He will want to see ledgers, accounts."

Reed paled.

"I take it you grasp my concern now," Havermill said, pursing his lips.

"What will we do?" Reed asked, taking a desperate hold on Havermill's shoulder. "I warned you, didn't I, not to be so damnably greedy. If we have to produce a reckoning, it will be all over for the both of us. Thousands of pounds, Silas, thousands of pounds."

"It would be a shame if something were to happen to the viscount before the wedding," Havermill said, catching Reed's eye significantly.

"Accidents do occur," Reed agreed after a pause, "particularly in London, a dangerous city, is London."

"It is," Havermill concurred. "It most assuredly is."

The two men smiled in mutual understanding.

The rhythm of hoofbeats echoed among the trees. Rebecca had forgotten just how wonderful it could be to take a carriage ride on a spring morning simply for the joy of it. From the rear seat, Sarah kept up a constant stream of inconsequential chatter, so Rebecca was not obliged to speak of the weather or the flowers or the state of the park roads. It was a definite relief not to have to fill the awkward conversational void that seemed to yawn whenever she and Oliver were alone.

"Oh, Becky, thank you so much for allowing Harry and me to come along with you," Sarah said happily. "It is such a beautiful day!"

"It is Oliver that you must thank," Rebecca said. "It was his suggestion that you join us. At this unfashionably early hour, someone was needed to play propriety."

"Thank you, milord," Harry said, surveying the surroundings with delight. "I've never been this way before, and I thought I had been all around this park."

"We ain't too far from Sir Michael Fairgrove's place," Oliver said. "Take this ride often, we do, when he's about Town."

"Do you always take it this slow?" Harry inquired, looking over his glasses.

"Do you want me to spring 'em, Harry lad?" Oliver asked with a laugh.

"Yes, milord, if you please," Harry agreed, leaning forward in his seat.

"Then hang on," Oliver said. "We'll see if Tilbury's nags have any mettle to 'em."

Rebecca swallowed her misgivings as Oliver eased the horses from a slow trot to a run. It was plain to see that her fiancé had an expert hand upon the reins. The carriage picked up speed smoothly, and she held her hand to her bonnet as they bowled down the drive.

"This is famous!" Harry cried. "Absolutely famous."

Oliver touched the whip lightly to the horse's backs when suddenly the animal on the driver's side shied, pulling ahead of the other member of the pair. Oliver fought to rein the recalcitrant horse in, but the beast only seemed to become wilder.

"Hang on!" Oliver yelled. "All of you, hold on until I say 'bail' and then jump!"

With all of his strength, Oliver turned their heads, forcing the team toward the incline. Though the animals plunged onward, the upward motion caused them to lose speed. "Bail!" Oliver cried. "Bail, all of you, now."

Rebecca clung to Harry and jumped, landing on the damp grass. Sarah plunged out the other side of the carriage, rolling down the incline before coming to a halt. Sarah rose swiftly and ran toward the carriage. "Oliver!" she screamed, watching the carriage tilt crazily as it crested the hill. "Oliverrrr!"

Michael stood on the landing and surveyed the trunks lining the entry below, papers, clothes, favorite books. The heaps of luggage represented the sum total of his life, a pitiful statement if ever there was one. His paintings and most of his library had already been crated and shipped to Kent along with the few sticks of furniture he had chosen to keep. The servants had gone on ahead to make ready. He had made his good-byes to the few friends that he had cared to notify more than a week before.

Maximillian scratched at the door of the room that had once been Michael's library. Now that the carters were gone for the day, Michael released the dog from his confinement, letting the animal scamper around freely. The echoes in the empty rooms were oddly discomfiting, rousing once again the hollow ache that had been plaguing him since he had made his good-byes to the Paragon.

He had almost succeeded in convincing himself that he was the victim of his own imagination. Calm, sensible analysis had allowed him to explain away his feelings on that strange and wonderful night. Stress, proximity, tension, and myriad reasonable explanations provided ample rationalizations for the emotions that had beset him. In time, perhaps, he might have managed to persuade himself that everything that had occurred was quite within the realm of the ordinary.

Then he had seen her. Never had he thought of himself as a man subject to jealous starts, but the sight of Rebecca strolling down Bond Street with Oliver had been enough to stir Michael into a green-eyed fit.

For the first time in his life, he had known the true meaning of envy. The biting pangs gnawed at his very soul, and the thought of Oliver holding her, touching her, drove him to despair. Elizabeth had never haunted his dreams and made his nights into a dark hell of empty longing. In the back of his mind, there had even been passing thoughts of mayhem. Heaven help Oliver if he failed to love her, to cherish her.

There was no bamming himself any longer. Perhaps the passage of the years would dull the pain, but Michael knew that the prospect of seeing the Paragon, speaking to her again, would suffice to drive him to insanity. Distance was most definitely a necessity, and he wondered if Kent was actually far enough. Michael vowed that excepting the occasional requirements of business, he would not return.

Only the last few threads of his affairs in the City kept him in London, hiding like a criminal on the run, but it had paid off. Thanks to DeSilva's investment, Michael had more than enough ready capital to implement some of the more expensive estate improvements that he had previously postponed to the distant future. Still, the realization that he was now flush with the ready was less than comforting. Though his pockets were finally full, Michael felt curiously empty.

The clang of brass upon brass suddenly reverberated through the bare town house. Michael hurried down the stairs, realizing that he had forgotten to remove the knocker from the door.

"Yes?" Michael said, looking down at the little boy who was barely tall enough to reach the knocker on the tips of his toes.

"Please, sir, you must help us," the child said, tears streaming down his face. "There's been a terrible accident across the way in the park, and Lord Elmont said to come knock at this door. He did not think that his friend, Sir Michael, would be at home, but if you could please come and bring some other help. The carriage came to rest on his leg, and though we all tried, we cannot lift it. Rebecca said that though the baronet might be gone, there might be some servants left behind."

Rebecca. Amber eyes stared up at him, pleading, and sudden fear knotted the pit of Michael's stomach. *The Paragon's eyes.* Obviously, the boy had mistaken him for a servant; a family trait it would seem. "And your sister, was she hurt?" he asked in a ragged whisper.

"She has a bruise on her forehead." The boy sobbed, too frightened to question how a servant knew that Rebecca was his sister. "We all had to jump, sir. But Lord Elmont stayed on to the last. He said to bring a gun if we could. One of the horses is in a bad way."

Trust Ollie to think of the beasts before himself. Michael kept his voice calm, gently extracting the details from the boy as they hurried to the stables with Maximillian following. Shouting commands and instructions to his groom, Michael led Loki from his stall and hastily put a snaffle on him before hoisting himself onto the skittish bay's back.

"You cannot be thinking to ride that demon without a saddle," his groom said, aghast.

"There is no time for the niceties, Jasper," Michael said, using the reins and the force of his knees to get the fresh horse under control. "Get the carriage harnessed immediately. This young man will show you the way."

Michael rode as though the devil were at his heels, Maximillian following in his wake. Luckily, there was little traffic at this early hour, and the boy's directions were concise. As the boy had described, the wreck was not far from the entry to the park. The carriage lay at the bottom of a small incline. Sarah was sitting by the side of the vehicle, Oliver's head cradled in her lap. One of the horses lay bleeding on the ground, wide-eyed, raw-throated screams pouring from its throat.

"Thought you had . . . left to rusticate," Oliver said as he saw his friend approaching.

"Where's Rebecca?" Michael asked, drawing out his pistol and cocking the hammer.

"Recalled that . . . Bartram, the surgeon, . . . lives nearby. Becky went . . . to get him," Oliver said, lifting his hand and bringing it up to cover Sarah's eyes. "Don't look, Sarah. Michael's . . . going to put the poor fellow . . . out of his misery."

Sarah shuddered as the pistol shot rang out, and the horse gave one horrible final scream.

" 'Tis over, my girl," Oliver said, squeezing Sarah's hand as Michael came to squat beside him. "Devil . . . take me if . . . I know how this happened. Rolling along . . . one minute . . . next thing . . . up in the air playing the bird."

"He is so pale," Sarah said, her face streaked with dust and tears. "I fear that he must have hit his head when he was thrown."

"Lucky thing you . . . were with us, Sarah." Oliver gasped out the words. "Had you not run after me . . . grabbed the horse's head, I'd be . . . making my bows . . . to Beezlebub by now."

"Let us see if we can get this carriage off you, my friend," Michael said, shedding his jacket and folding it into a cushion.

Gently, he raised Oliver's head, allowing Sarah to slip out from beneath. With infinite care, Michael set his makeshift pillow beneath the injured man before surveying the position of the wreck. They could wait for help, but there was no telling what was happening beneath that mud-embedded pile of wood. If Oliver's lifeblood was seeping away, they would have no way of knowing.

"Do you think that you can help me by moving that great ox if I can shift the carriage?" Michael asked Sarah.

"Who do you . . . call an ox?" Oliver made a grimacing effort at a smile. "I . . . can wait," he said. "Sarah . . . too delicate."

"I? Delicate?" Sarah said in astonishment. "I vow, the fall must have affected your eyesight, Oliver. Everyone says that I am a veritable Amazon." She stationed herself by his shoulders, ready to tug.

"Get set," Michael commanded, putting his shoulder experimentally to the box. He dug his heels into the grass and heaved, putting all his weight against the wood. The carriage shuddered and rose, inch by cumbersome inch. "Now!" Michael groaned.

Sarah pulled, straining at Oliver's shoulders. With maddening slowness, his leg emerged from beneath the wreckage.

"Hurry," Michael demanded, feeling the weight slipping.

With a final frantic jerk, Sarah dragged Oliver away, the force sending her tumbling backward. Michael jumped back as the carriage came crashing to the ground once more.

"Sarah . . . you hurt?" Oliver asked, twisting himself to see her.

"Nothing more than a few grass stains on my skirts," Sarah said, brushing herself off. Swiftly, she was at Oliver's side, looking at his leg.

For a moment, Michael thought that she would keel over, but though the girl paled for a moment, she held herself steady.

"Great gun," Oliver murmured, taking hold of her hand. "Delicate thing . . . like you. Who would have . . . thought?" he asked, slipping mercifully into unconsciousness.

"Not much farther, Mr. Bartram," Rebecca said, directing the surgeon toward the rise. "Over there!"

As they topped the hill, Rebecca heard the sound of a dog barking. Apparently, someone else had stopped to help, for there was another wagon on the road. Sarah and a man in livery were spreading blankets on the seat. Rebecca's eyes were drawn to a dark-haired man kneeling by Oliver's side.

Time seemed to slow to a crawl as the surgeon jumped from the wagon and hurried toward the injured man. The dog emerged from behind the wreck and loped swiftly to the sawbones's carriage. Yipping in delight, the cur jumped up, leaning its paws upon the step. It could not possibly be and yet . . .

Rebecca got down from the vehicle as the man beside Oliver rose and turned to face her. She grasped the side of the wagon for support. It was Michael.

"Sir Michael," Sarah called, "I have laid out the blankets. We can put him in your carriage now."

Sir Michael. Shock gave way to pain.

"Your fiancé's leg is broken, Miss Creighton," Michael said, constrained by Sarah's listening ears. The hurt confusion in Rebecca's eyes was like a physical pain. He wanted to touch her, to assure himself that she was all right, but he could not. Discretion dictated that he play the role of stranger. "Since I have not so much as a bed in my apartments and Cavendish Square is close by, your sister has suggested that we move him there."

Rebecca nodded in silent agreement, unable to trust herself to speak.

"We must talk, Miss Creighton. Oliver is a dear friend of mine, and of course I will do anything to increase his comfort," Michael said, certain from the look in her eyes that she was reading his underlying message clearly. "I am, by the way, Sir Michael Fairgrove."

Sir Michael Fairgrove. Pain gave way to rage.

As Rebecca watched Michael and his servant bundle Oliver into the carriage, she knew that her dream had come to an end.

Well before noon, the sun had disappeared and a light drizzle was falling outside the bedroom window. Michael adjusted the pillows behind Oliver's head. "Better, Ollie?"

he asked, gently easing him back. "We were lucky to get you in out of the rain, my friend. Remember all those times on the Peninsula when it rained just before the battle. 'Wellington weather,' we used to call it."

"I cannot like it," Oliver mumbled, his pupils already dilated from the dose of opiate that the surgeon had given him. "Never had anything happened before like that, Michael. I've a dab hand at the ribbons, if I do say so."

Michael bent closer, trying to catch his friend's whisper.

"One horse went wild, all of a sudden . . . took the bit between his teeth and there weren't nothing for the other beast to do but break right along with him," he said, his blue eyes intensely bright. "Tried to keep us upright, but nigh on impossible . . . for a minute there I thought I was back on the field at Waterloo, hearing the horses screaming in fear and pain." A tear glimmered as his eyes drifted closed. "Hated to see him suffer like that . . . poor creature. . . . It should not have happened, I tell you. It should not have happened. . . ." The viscount's voice trailed off, his agitation fading into sleep.

Michael sat, mulling over Oliver's words. When Oliver's breaths came slow and steady, Michael rose, recognizing that the inevitable could no longer be postponed. With a soft sigh he pulled the cover up under his friend's chin and started toward the stairs. His moment of judgment had come, and there was little use in wishing himself to Jericho.

Rebecca stared into the empty hearth, longing for a fire; there was something inherently soothing about staring into the embers. Nonetheless, it was far too warm to justify the extravagance. She reached for the bellpull, reminding herself that she no longer had to count her pennies. Her hand dropped to her side. Old habits were hard to break.

When she heard the hesitant tread of boots upon the stairs, her throat went dry. Half of her had hoped that Michael would prove a coward and flee, avoiding the complications of prevarication and excuses. She prayed that the footsteps would pass, that she would hear the sound of the front door closing.

The sound stopped at the entry to the library, and without looking she knew that he was standing, watching, waiting. Rebecca steeled herself, determined that he would not know that he still had the power to hurt her. All of the scathing phrases and chill remarks that she had rehearsed in the past three hours were ready on her tongue, prepared to hurl at his head.

She stood stiffly, her hand upon the mantel, her head bowed. All the self-serving defenses that Michael had formulated seemed to fade before the knowledge that he had hurt her. He wanted to gather her into his arms, to tell her that he had never meant to cause her grief, but he did not have the right to hold her. He reminded himself that he had never had that right.

As she turned and saw him waiting in the doorway, Rebecca found that she had gone mute. Pain and longing welled up in her throat, strangling her venomous script at its source. One word tried to escape, but she would not utter it. she would not give him the opportunity to deceive her once more by asking him why. Besides, there was little use in asking a question when the answers were already known.

"I have come, Paragon," he said, distressed by the devastation in her eyes. There in those tawny depths, profound anguish transformed itself into fiery rage and then to icy contempt.

Schooling her expression to polite apathy, Rebecca spoke. "An odd appellation, Sir Michael. I find that I do not appreciate it at all."

"My apologies, Miss Creighton," Michael acknowledged with a bow of his head before closing the door behind him.

"Propriety demands a chaperone, sir," Rebecca said, her words stilted.

"We require no one to serve as a gooseberry picker," Michael said softly, "not with my dearest friend lying up in his sickbed."

"A very strange sort of friendship, Sir Michael," Rebecca said, backing away as he advanced.

"You do not need to fear me, Miss Creighton."

"Fear, sir, is not at all what I feel." She spat the words in a bitter staccato.

"I do not blame you if you are angry—" Michael began.

"How very gracious." Rebecca's nails bit into her palms as she tried to keep herself from exploding. How dare he come here and seem so collected and contained when she was ready to fall to pieces?

"You must have questions."

"No," she said, her eyes kindling with fury. "I have answers, Sir Michael Fairgrove, answers that do you no credit at all. First the question: why would a baronet wear the clothing of a servant or a Cit and come to hear a preachy female speak about the evils of strong drink? Answer: Curiosity, to see what manner of titmouse his best friend was being forced to marry."

She clasped her hands before her as if she feared that she would pummel him.

"Hear yet another riddle that I have solved. What could possibly motivate Oliver Rowley, Viscount Elmont, to marry such a pitiful creature with no address, no fortune, and less looks? Answer: Hopelessness. Oliver was in debt up to his ears and the Earl of Elmont finally had the means to impose his wishes. Do I have it right so far?"

"Paragon, listen to me," Michael pleaded, stepping toward her.

Rebecca put up a halting hand. "Do not dare to call me that again, sir. That name is a reminder of a folly that I have come to regret deeply."

"I did not mean to—" Michael began, but once more, she would not allow him to speak.

"Have you ever noticed how the weakest of justifications usually begins with the phrase 'I did not mean to'?" Rebecca asked mockingly, her head cocking to one side as she regarded him with a basilisk stare. "Yet another part of the puzzle falls into place. How is it that a man can pretend to be noble and all that is decency, yet at the same time connive and deceive? This time, you will have the correct reply if you say money. Convince the titmouse to marry your *dearest* friend and receive reimbursement for the vowels that he owes," she said, making each word a synonym for scorn.

"It was not like that—"

"How lucky it was that I fell into your hands!" she said, walking toward the window and staring into the square. "Were you laughing at me all along, I wonder? Chuckling over my gullibility even as you persuaded me to accept that Oliver was my only choice, my only chance for a future." Her voice broke on a sob, and her shoulders began to shake, but she denied herself the refuge of tears. She would not let him see her cry.

"I never deceived you," Michael said, following her across the room. He had convinced himself that he had acted for the good of all concerned, but in the face of her pain, all of his excuses faded into arrogant fabrications.

"I will not deny that I made false assumptions," Rebecca said, drawing herself up proudly. "But you did naught to disabuse me of any of my mistaken notions. Not all iniquity is in the commission of wrong; there are sins of omission, Sir Michael, and it is for those I lay blame. As for the rest"—her face blazed red, but she would not repudiate her share of the fault—"you are not the one who will have to grant me pardon for my sinful and disgraceful behavior."

She lowered her eyes before his steady gaze, unable to face the pity or contempt that the truth would rouse. "There are no excuses, save that for the first time in my life I felt almost beautiful. You are a talented man, an exceptionally skillful liar."

"Rebecca." He reached for her, but she pushed his hand away.

"Leave me be," she whispered. "Just leave me, Michael. We cannot undo what has been done, but pray, do not make it worse. Strange as it might seem, before this morning I believed that the night we spent together was magical, a fairy tale, removed from the reality of time. And though I knew that I was violating everything that I believed in, I was willing to give you . . ."

She shook her head, unable to complete that thought, to let him know how close she had been to yielding herself. "Now all I feel is shame." She mustered a brittle smile, assembling the shards of her dignity into a courteous facade. "I thank you for your help today, sir. But you must excuse me; there is a great deal to be done, and I must see to my fiancé's comfort."

"Oliver was asleep when I left him."

"Is he? I am glad." She prattled, using a barrage of words as her shield as she started for the door. "We plan the wedding soon, as you well know, but you will be gone by the wedding date, I hope. Oliver mentioned that you were bound for Kent. I am certain that you would not wish to alter your plans on our account."

Michael would have barred her way, forced her to listen, but there was a commotion in the hall below.

"Stand aside, Goode!" The Reverend Havermill's voice echoed up the stairs. "She will wish to see me.

"Miss Creighton. Dear Miss Creighton." Havermill shouldered the butler away and hurried up the stairs. "I had just heard the dreadful news. Were you injured?"

"I am quite sound, Mr. Havermill," Rebecca replied.

"And the viscount?" Havermill asked.

"Lord Elmont has a broken leg, nothing more," Rebecca informed him.

"Indeed, we must be grateful for that," Havermill murmured.

"Indeed, we must," Michael agreed, coming to stand beside Rebecca.

Havermill looked searchingly at the man who had emerged from the library. There was something oddly familiar about his demeanor. "Have I made your acquaintance, sir?"

Rebecca had little choice but to perform the introductions. "Sir Michael Fairgrove, may I present the Reverend Havermill?"

"Sir Michael Fairgrove? I have heard of you, sir, though I do not recall where we met before." Havermill said, reluctantly extending his hand.

"Have we met?" Michael asked.

"I rarely forget a face," Havermill said, his eyes narrowing. "I am almost certain that we have met before."

"Anything is possible," Michael said, hoping that the cleric's powers of recognition were none too accurate. "But I fear you must excuse me for the while; I have some urgent business to attend to." There was little chance now of mending matters with Rebecca, not with Havermill dancing attendance. Moreover, Oliver's words had got Michael to thinking. He wanted to look at the carriage before Tilbury sold it for kindling, and he might do well to examine the horse, too. It would be simple enough to determine which knacker's yard had received the animal's corpse.

"A safe journey, Sir Michael, and thank you once again for your assistance today," Rebecca said with the veneer of cool civility.

"Journey, Miss Creighton?" Michael asked.

"Why, Kent, of course," Rebecca said, trying to keep the panic from her voice. He had to leave; she could hardly bear to look at him. "I hope that you enjoy your stay in the country."

"I have had a sudden change of plans, Miss Creighton," Michael said. "It would appear that I will be staying in London for the present."

Chapter 10

" 'Tis just as I thought," Havermill said, standing beside the silent printing press. "When the footman told me that Miss Creighton had sent him off to Marylebone with a note and money for a one-armed man, it confirmed my suspicions. Our informant tells me that there is no Mrs. Eager."

"The question is, where was she?" Reed asked. "Out all night, without so much as a maid. Pity of it is, if you tell the world the truth, you kill your golden goose, Silas."

"I know that something happened. She has changed, dresses like a tart," Havermill said, his voice shaking with anger. "Ever since that night in Covent Garden, she hasn't been the same. Oh, she would balk before, but it was then that she began to defy me outright!"

"Seems to me that we had best put this lay to grass," Reed advised, puffing on his pipe. "Get yourself out before they ken how far it went. The nobs might not bestir themselves if they think it was only a hapenny-farthing cheat, but if they was to find out the full measure of what we done—well I've no great desire to see Van Damien's land, that's all I'll say."

"I have a plan," Havermill said. "I tell you, Reed, those damned tracts will be so much in demand that you will have to buy yourself another press to keep up with the orders."

"Ain't likely," Reed said, knocking the ashes from his pipe. "It's 'farewell and good to know you' for me, Silas. I'm selling out. And if you have any sense at all, you'll put some miles between your back and London before they start asking questions."

"There will be no questions, never fear," Havermill assured him.

"You won't be drawing from that well no more." Reed gave a snort of disdain. "Once she marries, she won't write for you, Silas, and even if she would, her husband or her lover will be looking over your shoulder, minding the pints and quarts."

"No, they won't." Havermill chuckled. "That's the beauty of it. I am in the midst of a few discreet inquiries. As soon as I get the information that I need, Rebecca Creighton will be ready to do anything that I desire."

Oliver frowned as he scrutinized the sharp pointed object in Michael's hand. The viscount's face paled as he leaned forward in bed to touch the wicked point.

"I can hardly believe it," Oliver said, leaning back against the mound of pillows, studying his friend's grave countenance. "So it would appear the accident was no accident at all. And you found wax upon the tack, you say?"

"Luckily, it needed mending, and they had not yet cleaned the leathers. Your assailant's method was rather ingenious actually," Michael said, lowering his voice. "The sharp edges were imbedded in wax, and placed beneath the harness, so that the horse felt no irritation at first, but the hotter he became—"

"Wax melted faster," Oliver said, his mouth thinning in fury. "So as soon I was going at a decent clip, it pierced the poor beast's hide. No wonder the animal went wild."

"Exactly."

"But who would be out to do me harm?" Oliver asked, scratching his head in puzzlement. "All my vowels have been cleared."

"An angry husband?" Michael asked.

"Ain't been plowing in other men's fields," Oliver said indignantly, "not my style at all."

"I cannot bring myself to believe that this was a random bit of malice," Michael said, wrapping the spike carefully in his handkerchief before returning it to his pocket. "Was any-one aware that you planned to go driving with Miss Creighton?"

"Didn't exactly make a secret of it. And I might have even mentioned it at Tilbury's. Wanted a vehicle with room enough to seat us all in comfort," Oliver said slowly.

"Was the carriage unattended at any time?" Michael asked.

Oliver nodded. "Didn't know it needed watching. I say, Michael, you don't think that anyone would be out to do Re-becca harm, do you?"

"It could be," Michael mused. "Cobbett and men of like thinking would not mind it if she never penned another pam-phlet, I will tell you that. But adamant as he is, William would never be involved in a scheme like this. There are, however, those who would not be bound by such scruples."

"What harm can a few stories do?" Oliver asked, bewil-dered. "They are ripping fine yarns, I admit, but trifles just the same."

"Miss Creighton has become very influential," Michael explained. "Because they are such 'ripping fine yarns,' they are read everywhere."

"I vow, it scares me," Oliver said with an uneasy chuckle, "the thought of having a wife who has a brainbox twice the size of mine."

"I will tell you what scares *me*. There has been an attempt made to maim or kill someone in this house. We ought to tell Miss Creighton about this," Michael said.

"And scare the life out of her and her family? Spoil Sarah's Season?" Oliver shook his head adamantly. "Seems to me we might be making molehills to mountains. It was a rented conveyance, after all. One of Tilbury's carriages looks pretty much like another. Just might be that someone else was the target."

"It might," Michael conceded reluctantly. "But then again—"

"It might not," Oliver concluded. " 'Tain't worth the risk

of another try to find out. 'Tis my task to protect her, and here I am, about as useless as teats upon a bull," he said in frustration. "Just have to tell her that she's confined to quarters until I can be out and about."

"Give me at least twenty minutes to be well quit of the vicinity," Michael said acerbically. "I have no desire to be witness to your murder."

"Won't take well to the reins, you think?" Oliver said, grimacing as he shifted his leg.

"She is not the type of female who is easily led, Ollie," Michael said.

"Well, then, there is nothing else for it," Oliver concluded. "I know that you've urgent business in Kent, but I need you here in London till I'm on my feet."

"I mean to keep digging into this business until I get to the bottom of it," Michael promised.

"Ain't the digging that worries me so much as Rebecca," Oliver said. "I want you to keep your eye on her. Squire her about Town. Protect her. For all her brains, she wouldn't see evil unless it knocked her upon the head. Rebecca's very much the innocent."

"I know, Ollie," Michael said, casting about frantically for some way out. "But your fiancée and I seem to constantly be at cats and dogs. Perhaps someone else—"

"There *is* no one else," Oliver said. "Surely, it ain't too much to ask, Michael."

Michael opened his mouth, but any chance at further argument was forestalled by a knock at the door.

Sarah entered, following a footman bearing a tray.

"How are you feeling, Oliver?" she asked.

To Michael's surprise, Oliver moaned.

"Been better," Oliver said. "Feeling a bit weak."

"I must have tired him more than I realized," Michael said apologetically, rising at Sarah's angry glare. "I will do as you ask, Oliver, if she will let me."

* * *

"I will not have it!" Rebecca said as Ellen deftly pinned her curls into a knot. Since they had hired additional help, Ellen had tried her hand at the job of abigail and had proven surprisingly talented. "I had promised to speak well over a month ago. Surely, Mr. Havermill will suffice to squire me."

"After the last incident, I scarcely need to point out his deficiencies as an escort," Lydia said, frowning as she spoke. "Besides, if you are to join us at the Tolliver's afterward, Mr. Havermill cannot bring you. He does not move in those circles, you know."

"You ought not to blame him for what happened," Rebecca persisted. "It is scarcely his fault that a riot broke out."

"To err is human," Lydia quoted, "but to blunder requires a Divine. Besides, I find his present conduct to be disturbing. You are promised to another, yet Mr. Havermill hangs about you these days like a veritable mooncalf. One is forever finding him underfoot, urging you to speak here and there. It is past time to cut line, Rebecca. Those dreadful times are behind us now. You have always hated putting yourself in the public eye. You no longer have to do this."

"I cannot forget what he has done for us, Lydia," Rebecca pointed out, rising from the dressing table. "Thank you, Ellen, that is quite lovely," she said, dismissing the maid.

"And you have repaid him for his kindness many times over, it would seem to me." Lydia said. "Nonetheless, since you insist, I will allow you to honor previously made speaking engagements. But you must take Sir Michael with you as Lord Elmont commands. With all of the unrest in London these days, it is only a reasonable precaution."

"I will take the new footman along if extra protection is required," Rebecca said, picking up her reticule. "He seems a strong enough fellow."

"You know that servants always disappear at the first sign of trouble," Lydia said.

Unwillingly, Rebecca recollected Esther DeSilva and the conduct of their retainers when pressed by the mob. "Very well, then, we shall have to find someone else. I do not want Sir Michael's escort."

"I simply cannot understand why you are kicking up dust!" Lydia fumed. "For all of Mr. Havermill's insinuations, Sir Michael has been all that is proper. No friend could be more devoted, coming to see the viscount every day to keep him amused. I find him charming. In fact," Lydia said, lowering her voice to a confidential whisper, "I think he might be just the man for your sister. 'Tis true he is merely a baronet, but the name is an old and distinguished one. He is not quite as tall as Lord Elmont, but just tall enough."

"If a title and height are your sole requirements for Sarah's husband then he will do just fine," Rebecca said, picking up her fan from the table and unfolding it, pretending to study the delicate design upon the chicken skin. "It matters nothing that Sir Michael might be the most sneaking, conniving, deceitful wretch that ever sold his soul to the devil!"

"Rebecca, really!" Lydia said, coloring with indignation. "If you have proof of his ill-repute, I will bar him from the house, but the inquiries that I have made regarding Sir Michael show Mr. Havermill's innuendoes to be nebulous at best. According to those to whom I have spoken, Sir Michael is a man of absolute integrity and charity. He has an excellent estate to recommend him. As the latest *on dit* has it, Sir Michael has just made a small fortune upon the 'Change."

"Has he?" Rebecca asked, shutting the fan with a snap.

"Oh, yes," Lydia said, warming to her subject. "Someone in the City, an Isaac De . . . De something or other?"

"DeSilva," Rebecca supplied as she added yet another piece to the puzzle of that night with Michael. DeSilva's name had been familiar, but she had not been able to place it until Lydia had made her comment. Though he was not nearly as famous as Rothschild, DeSilva had been instrumental in keeping Wellington financially afloat.

In truth, the comfortable simplicity of the DeSilva home had been deceiving. It was not surprising that she had failed to discern the identity of their host, when he lived with no more display than a moderately well-to-do merchant. No doubt, Sir Michael was chuckling over that as well.

"Yes, that is the name," Lydia said. "Apparently, he had embarked upon some wildly successful venture and only think! Our Sir Michael was one of his foremost investors."

"*Our* Sir Michael," Rebecca repeated, her inflection liberally laced with sarcasm. "Was he, indeed? How wonderful."

"Even Lady Jersey does not have anything unfavorable to say about Sir Michael," Lydia added, oblivious to her stepdaughter's asperity. "And you know how she is—if there is nothing kind to say, Lady Jersey will surely be the one to say it."

"I cannot like him," Rebecca said, wishing that there was some way to explain her feelings without bringing the whole truth to light.

"I know you are forever brangling with him, but he is your future husband's closest friend," Lydia said. "You would be wiser to reconcile yourself, dearest."

"He has assured me that he has no intention of hanging about once Oliver is healed," Rebecca said as she stared at her reflection.

"Oh, dear," Lydia said. "Then we must contrive to fix his attentions upon Sarah immediately."

"It would not suit," Rebecca snapped, rising from the table.

"We shall see," Lydia said. "However, I add my insistence to your fiancé's. Sir Michael ought to accompany you tonight."

"It would appear, then, that I have no choice," Rebecca said coldly.

"Lord Elmont has your best interest at heart, you know," Lydia said, trying to calm the waters. "And so do I, dearest."

"He is not yet my husband," Rebecca said, slipping the

fan upon her wrist. "It would seem that everyone knows what is best for me, but me. Am I a child, that I need to be kept in leading strings?"

"I did not think so," Lydia said as her stepdaughter slammed the door behind her, "until tonight."

". . . and so, I said to Lord Petersham, 'You would do well to read Miss Creighton's pamphlet upon the subject of swearing and blasphemy.' Lord Petersham replied to me, 'Damn me, I will!' " Mr. Havermill said, seating himself upon the petitioner's bench in the entry of the Creightons' home.

Michael gave a polite smile as the man prattled on, sprinkling his conversation liberally with "milord this," and "milady that." He could only pray that the Paragon was not one of those females who kept a man waiting. His efforts to maintain a civil facade were failing, and in a few minutes he would either give the Reverend Mushroom a crushing setdown or, more likely, wring him by his clerical collar.

A door slammed above. Michael leaned against the balustrade as Rebecca descended the stairs, her expression like a thundercloud about to burst. It promised to be an evening in hell. Her dress was the same shade of emerald as the one that Eve had loaned her. Images of the Paragon surged, sweeping him away on a tide of memories. Rebecca laughing, her eyes alight with trust, the feel of her lips, the warmth of her hand. But reality quickly overcame the force of his recollections.

The chill of disdain within those golden eyes froze his very soul; the warm glow of innocent trust had turned to the scorching glare of betrayal. She flinched as he offered his arm, disdaining his gesture of escort. Michael could almost feel the guiding hand of divine retribution—to be near her and refrain from touching her would be the closest semblance of purgatory on earth that he could imagine.

Like Tantalus, he was caught in eternal torment, waist high in the waters of his own passions. Thirst, and the water

would recede. Hunger, and the fruit upon the bank would retreat beyond reach. But his own circumstances were infi-
nitely worse than those of that tortured soul of Greek myth.
There were no all-powerful gods to keep Michael from
drinking, from tasting—only his own sense of honor and the
Paragon's scorn.

"Miss Creighton, you look quite pleasing tonight,"
Havermill said as he took her arm with a superior smile.

"You will doubtless turn her head with such outré flattery,
Mr. Havermill," Michael said, receiving his hat and gloves
from Goode. "You look exceptional, Miss Creighton. That
color has always suited you."

Rebecca blushed, understanding at last why ladies' fans
were fashioned from flimsy materials such as chicken skin
and mother-of-pearl. No doubt men had designed them
thusly so that they were capable of rendering nothing
stronger than a stinging rap upon the knuckles. At the moment she was wishing for something that was capable of
wreaking more substantial damage.

"Maximillian, by the by, sends his best regards. Your
brother was wondering if I might bring him along next time
I come to visit Ollie. Would you have any objections?"
Michael asked.

"Of course not," Rebecca said as Goode drew the door
open for them. "*Maximillian* is always more than welcome."

"I do hope that you are not plagued with mice, Miss
Creighton," Michael said, walking down the marble steps.
"Anything resembling a rodent sends poor Maximillian
shivering into the corners."

"Maximillian's honesty is one of his more endearing
qualities," Rebecca commented. "I prefer a truthful coward
to a lying hero."

"Maximillian Shelby? Lord Lindale's heir?" Havermill
asked, sensing a juicy *on dit* to add to his collection.

"No, not Shelby. Samson is the family name, I am told,"
Michael said in confidential tones, "though between the two
of us, there is some question as to his bloodlines."

"Wrong side of the blanket, eh?" Havermill said disdainfully, filing the information away for future reference. "Of course, I would not speak of it."

Rebecca found it difficult to keep her face straight, but as Michael's eye met hers, inviting her to share the private joke, she knew that she could not afford to yield so much as a smile. He was far too clever at exploiting her weaknesses, and she would never allow herself to be vulnerable to his wiles again.

"There is absolutely no need for you to come with us, Sir Michael," she said in icy tones as the newly hired footman went forward to open the door to the carriage. "You will certainly be bored to tears."

"You are thinking of joining us, Sir Michael?" Havermill asked in a croak of disbelief.

"I would not miss the opportunity of hearing Miss Creighton speak," Michael said. "Who is to know? I might be moved to repent my sins."

"If the heavens opened and the angels began to sing in chorus, I would sincerely doubt their power to sway you, sir," Rebecca said. "I do not fool myself that a short address may change your ways."

"Surely, you believe in miracles?" Michael asked.

"There are a great many things that I believe in, Sir Michael," Rebecca retorted. "However, you are not one of them."

"You wound me," Michael said. While his voice made the words a jest, she could not know how her contempt cut at him. Now that he had been appointed her keeper, he was forced to remain in range of her barbs.

"Miss Creighton," Havermill admonished her, loathe to discourage a wealthy patron, "surely you ought to provide support to a man on the path to penitence." He addressed himself to the baronet. "Dear sir, perhaps you will join Miss Creighton Friday next when she is to give a long overdue talk at Lady Shand's home. The company will be more salubrious, to be sure, people who are more of our own class, you know. Tonight Miss Creighton addresses an audience largely composed of the middling folk, mostly clerks and merchants, not at all the kind of people that you would wish to rub shoulders with."

"You would be surprised who has touched shoulders with me," Michael commented. To his delight, the Paragon's cheeks burst into flame. It was too bad of him, but beyond his power to resist teasing her. "I must insist upon accompanying you, Mr. Havermill."

"Lord Elmont has commanded it," Rebecca said bitterly. "Sir Michael has been appointed to play cart to my pony. I am well and truly harnessed, Mr. Havermill."

"You imply that the reins are in my hands, Miss Creighton," Michael said, "when that is assuredly not the case. Tonight, where you lead, I will follow."

"This is wholly unnecessary!" Mr. Havermill said. "Lord Elmont as much as implies that I cannot be trusted to protect Miss Creighton!"

"You may read Lord Elmont's demand as you like," Michael said mildly. "However, your opinion does not signify. Will you or nil you, I will be the unwanted third if only because it sets Lord Elmont's mind at ease. What with the recent unrest in Town, I cannot blame him if he wishes to assure himself of his fiancée's safety. There is, however, an alternative to my company."

"And pray, what is that, sir?" Rebecca asked.

"So eager to shed me?" Michael chided. "The solution is simple enough. Give up the lecture."

"I gave my word, Sir Michael," Rebecca said. "But perhaps you are unfamiliar with the sacred quality of a given bond."

"Miss Creighton!" Havermill gasped, in shock.

"You do not know me very well, miss," Michael said, catching her hand and ostensibly helping her up the steps to the carriage.

She felt the grip of his fingers. Though his tone was calm and conversational, his touch told her that she had overstepped the bounds. Nonetheless, her reply was defiant. "I know you well enough."

"You know nothing at all," Michael said, wishing that Havermill would disappear. There were so many things that had to be said, but she would never allow herself to be private with him. Michael constructed his phrases with care. "If you knew me, you would never doubt my word. Were I not sensible of what I owe to Ollie—"

"Or what Elmont owes you, or should I say *owed*, sir?" Rebecca said, pulling her hand away and glaring down at him. His dark eyes were molten, flecked with lights of anger. A sense of reckless rage possessed her; if the fuse were to blow, so be it. Perhaps it would be better than this constant dance with fire and gunpowder. "I hear that you are to be congratulated, Sir Michael, upon your recent triumphs upon the 'Change. You have made yourself quite a tidy sum, I am told."

"Have you, indeed," Mr. Havermill said, seizing upon the subject. "I am much interested in the opportunities of the 'Change myself."

"Indeed, the Exchange is a fascinating subject. Perhaps we shall talk about it en route. It is my suggestion that we all make the best of this. As much as possible, I will play least in sight," Michael said, releasing Rebecca's hand, but pinning her with a speaking stare. "But I will be there should I be needed, Miss Creighton. Count upon it."

True to his word, Michael stayed to the rear of the room as Rebecca spoke. It should have been simple to ignore him, but she soon understood that it would be impossible to pretend that he was not present. Those dark, brooding eyes drew her into their murky brown depths.

Time after time, she found herself transfixed, trying to understand what he was silently trying to say. She despised herself for her weakness, for her inability to resist enticement, but although she tried to look away, she could not. His gaze held her in thrall.

Her eyes crucified him; every glance stabbing like a dagger's point. It would have been far easier to endure her contempt if he had been unaware of the suffering behind it. Far better that she believed him an out and outer, that he had abused her trust, he told himself, closing his eyes against the looks that cut up his peace. A mistake. The sound of her voice drew him back to that other night, and he lost himself in a dream of what might have been had she not been bound to Oliver Rowley.

The sound of applause roused Michael from his reverie. This part of the evening's ordeal was done. As the collection plate came round, he slipped a gold piece among the mound of coins. Remaining in his seat, he watched her as she talked to the parishioners and contrasted her to the ill-dressed crow he had first met, little more than two weeks before.

Her emerald dress gave her skin a dusky glow, accenting the gold of her eyes. A cascade of curls tumbled down her back, making his fingers ache to touch the silken memory of her hair. As the vicar went to usher out the last of the visitors and close the doors, Michael rose to join Rebecca and Havermill in the vestry.

"I had warned you, Sir Michael, that you might be bored," Rebecca said. "You slept well, I trust."

"I was not sleeping," Michael said, "but dreaming. You inspire me to dreams of heaven, Miss Creighton."

Emotions vibrated between them, but Havermill remained oblivious.

"I understand that you are off to an engagement," Havermill said briskly. "Perhaps it would be best if I deliver your share of this evening's offerings to your home, Miss Creighton? You would not wish to be carrying any large sums, I am sure."

Rebecca considered. The Creighton family was presently too much in Oliver's pocket as it was. At the very least, she preferred to maintain some semblance of independence. On the morrow, the servants were due their salaries, and the thought of tapping her fiancé's purse to pay her own household expenses rankled. "I would prefer to do it now," Rebecca said. "If Sir Michael does not mind the wait."

Michael shook his head. "Not at all, Miss Creighton. At this hour, the recital will have barely begun. With any luck at all, we may even miss most of the caterwauling. If anyone can make Mozart whirl in his grave, it is Miss Tolliver."

"If you would step outside, then, Sir Michael," Havermill said, putting the collection plate on the table. "This is private business, after all."

Somehow, the coins in the plate seemed to have diminished considerably since his last viewing. Nonetheless, Michael nodded in recognition of the request. "Do you wish me to leave, Miss Creighton?" he asked, taking up his hat and gloves.

Rebecca was about to show him the door, but the cast of his face stopped her. There was nothing flirtatious in that significant rise of his brow. Something was afoot.

"There is no need," she said.

Havermill glared. "Very well, then, if you deem the privacy of your affairs of no consequence." He spilled the coins from the plate onto the table and reached into his pocket and pulled out a leather sack. He poured those coins into another heap. "The sale of the pamphlets this evening," he explained.

As Havermill divided the coins into three heaps, a predetermined sum for the host church, one for himself, and one for Rebecca, Michael did a few calculations of his own. The profits from the tracts had definitely come up short. There had not been a hand in the house that had not been clutching a copy of *Cathy of Covent Garden,* and many had purchased more than one of Rebecca Creighton's other titles. The coins on the table did not nearly reflect those sales. As for the offering, it was entirely devoid of gold, and the gleam of silver was decidedly less bright than it had been when he had seen the plate earlier. Yet, Rebecca seemed delighted by her share.

"This is extraordinary," she said as she viewed her portion. "How kind and generous they were this evening, and even though I know that I was not at my best."

"I had meant to speak to you on that score, Miss Creighton," Havermill said. "You have been rather distracted these days. In the future I expect—"

Rebecca shook her head. "I have promised one more lecture for Lady Shand, Mr. Havermill, and I shall honor that obligation. However, there will be no more after that."

"Miss Creighton, what of the people whose lives you touch?" Havermill said. "There are souls out there, hungering for your words. You must reconsider."

"I will continue to write, Mr. Havermill," Rebecca said. "However, I have never enjoyed being before the public, as you know."

"But I have engaged you to speak before—" Havermill began.

"Oh, dear, you really ought to have consulted with me before you made any promises," Rebecca said, reaching for her portion. "But now is not the time for discussion. We are expected at the Tolliver's."

"Just a moment, Miss Creighton," Michael said, staying her hand. "You will want the rest of your money, of course. Where are the rest of the proceeds, Havermill?"

"S-see here, sir," Havermill sputtered. "What on earth are you speaking of?"

"The gold, Havermill," Michael said. "There was gold in that dish."

Havermill laughed nervously. "Nonsense! We get some silver, occasionally even a sixpence, but gold? In Bloomsbury? We hardly ever see gold when she speaks in Mayfair itself, Sir Michael."

"There was gold in your plate tonight, Mr. Havermill," Michael said, "and I ought to know, because I was the one who put it there. If you would be so kind as to turn out your pockets."

"Are you calling me a thief, sir? Name your seconds!" Havermill demanded.

Michael curled his right hand and delivered a jab to Havermill's gut. "That was my first. If you care now to meet my second"—he folded his left hand meaningfully—"I shall be delighted to oblige you. Your pockets, Mr. Havermill. Empty them, or I swear, I shall empty them for you."

"Miss Creighton," Havermill croaked. "Surely you will not stand by and let him impugn me, that . . . that . . . radical!"

Michael tsked. "Such language, Mr. Havermill, and before a lady, too."

"Is there any reason that you do not wish to empty your pockets, Mr. Havermill?" Rebecca asked softly.

Havermill straightened, his face contorted in rage. "After all that I have done for you. You were nothing! Nobody! It was I who made you all the crack! It was I who transformed you from an anonymous country bumpkin into the famous Rebecca Creighton!"

"I know," Rebecca whispered. "And I am indebted—"

"No, you are not, Miss Creighton," Michael said, grabbing Havermill by the arm and reaching into his pocket. He took a small leather sack and pulled open the drawstring, letting the contents flow onto the table, a shower of silver and a single gold crown. "If anything, I suspect Mr. Havermill is in *your* debt." He held up the crown. "No telling how many of these he has skimmed off the top of the plate for himself."

Havermill stared at the marigold in Sir Michael's hand through a haze of silent hatred. Outside of Mayfair, offerings of gold were rare, so uncommon that Havermill recalled every instance of that breathtaking glitter in the collection plate; twice, in fact, in the past three weeks. His eyes narrowed as he surreptitiously studied Sir Michael Fairgrove and tried to recall the details of that other night. Fairgrove had been dressed differently to be sure. No, Havermill never did forget a face. Slowly, he began to tally the facts in light of this new revelation.

"You will regret this," Havermill threatened.

"I somehow doubt it," Michael commented, scooping up

the pile of coins and placing them in the sack. "I think that you will wish to keep yourself scarce at Miss Creighton's final engagement, Havermill." He placed the bag in Rebecca's palm. "Yours, I believe, Paragon," he said, closing her fingers around the sack. "You will forgive me if we leave you to find your own way home, Havermill."

"But there is not a hackney stand for a mile!" Havermill complained.

"You will get on, I am sure," Rebecca said, regarding him with a mixture of anger and sadness. "If I recall, you have a talent for finding your own way. Farewell, Mr. Havermill."

"I had never expected such gross ingratitude from you, Miss Creighton," Havermill said with a look of pure venom.

"Life does not always go as we expect it, does it?" Rebecca asked, following Michael to the door.

"I made you, Miss Creighton," Havermill vowed as the door closed behind them. "And by the devil, I will break you, you ungrateful bitch."

Chapter 11

Rebecca stared out into the darkness as their carriage clattered up Oxford Street, remembering another ride, another night. However, the coins in her reticule shifted heavily in her lap, deriding her for her ridiculous fancies.

"You must believe me an absolute fool," she said, breaking the silence, turning to regard Michael with a bitter smile. "Havermill had been a friend of my father's, not his closest acquaintance perhaps, but my father held him in some regard."

"People tend to show us what they want us to see," Michael said.

"I have learned that lesson at great cost," Rebecca said. "Havermill, too, told me that I had a gift, something that could be of value."

"He did not lie about that, and neither did I," Michael said, finding it difficult to accept that she now placed him in the same category as Havermill. As always, her eyes were easy to read, and he ached for her, but he dared offer no more than words. "Your tracts do provide something to people, comfort in hard times, hope that tomorrow may be better than today, a faith that can help them endure."

"I had thought you were a Cobbett's man," Rebecca said, her mouth twisting wryly.

"I believe that England will have to change," Michael admitted. "But I am no Jacobin. It would give me no relish to see us go down the path that France trod. But all people need to have something upon which to fix their dreams, particularly when times are precarious. Perhaps that was why you were willing to place your trust in Havermill after your father's death. He offered you hope."

"No," she said, sadly. "I cannot absolve myself so easily."

"Once again, the martyr?" Michael said. "You are above the common cut of mankind, I suppose, beyond the rest of us, who occasionally place our trust in the wrong people."

"It would seem that I begin to make a habit of it," she retorted, eyeing him significantly. "You did sell me in the end, didn't you? Not to a brothel or a white slaver, perhaps, but you sold me, Michael, so that Oliver would be able to pay his debts to you. I understand that. But I cannot for the life of me figure out why it was necessary . . . why you . . ." She felt her throat constricting and shook her head, unable to speak.

" 'Why?' Paragon, 'tis the question that I have been asking myself ever since I met you," Michael told her. "It began as a lark, as you guessed, an opportunity to scout out the territory for Ollie. I never even meant to make your acquaintance that night, much less deceive you. I never thought to see you again, I swear it, but then Ollie was injured—" Michael began.

"And we were brought face-to-face again," she said. "How terribly inconvenient and embarrassing to have your hoax uncovered."

"No," Michael told her, "it was no hum."

"It seemed simple enough from where I stood. A masterstroke, to allow Eager and his make-believe wife to stand propriety for me. There was no risk of you being recognized that way," Rebecca said. "No chance of your tail being caught in the parson's mousetrap."

She looked at him in the dim carriage light, trying to read his expression. While she hoped that he would defend himself against her charges, he damned himself with his silence. The remaining distance to the Tollivers' town house passed without a single word between them.

*   *   *

Unfortunately, when Michael and Rebecca arrived, they found that Lady Tolliver had saved her daughter's performance for the *pièce de résistance*. As Michael hunched uncomfortably in his chair, he considered her caterwauling performance as a trifling form of penance. From time to time, he glanced at Rebecca, but her face was devoid of expression, save a polite pasteboard smile. But the worst torture was yet to come.

"Dancing!" Lydia fairly twittered with delight as Lady Tolliver made the declaration that the Tolliver ballroom had been cleared for those who might wish to take an impromptu whirl across the floor. "What a pity. Poor Lord Elmont does not know what a treat that he is missing."

"Perhaps we ought to go home," Sarah suggested. "I had promised him a game of cards when we returned. I had not expected that we would be out so late."

"Stuff and nonsense!" Lydia said with a frown. "Certainly Lord Elmont would not expect a young lady in her first Season to dance attendance on an invalid. Have you ever seen a young girl with such excellent sensibility, Sir Michael?" Lydia asked coyly, drawing him into the conversation. "I vow, our Sarah has been so kind to your dear friend, though I am sure it has been vexing to a person of her tender years. She is forever reading to him, playing cards or backgammon or some such other game."

"The doctor said that he is not to move," Sarah said, uncomfortable beneath her stepmother's lavish praise. "It is so dreadfully hard for a man like Ollie to stay fixed in one place."

"Patience has never been Ollie's foremost virtue," Michael agreed as the musicians tuned their instruments. "I thank you for helping to keep him in line. Having done that for so many years, I know how very difficult that can be."

"Sarah tells me that you have known Lord Elmont for a long time," Lydia remarked.

"Since Eton," Michael replied. "We have been bosom friends for many years. Ollie is like a brother to me."

Though he ostensibly spoke to them all, Rebecca felt that he was addressing himself to her directly. There was a clear message in those dark brown eyes.

"Ollie is most gratified that you have chosen to stay in Town, despite your pressing affairs," Sarah said shyly. "He would be so happy if you could remain for the wedding."

"I would rather lose my right arm than see Ollie hurt," Michael said, his eyes on Rebecca. "But I think that I shall have to move on as soon as he is up and about."

"That would be a shame," Lydia said, tapping him playfully with her fan. "We must convince you otherwise, is that not right, Rebecca?"

Rebecca refused to take her stepmother's hint. Somehow, the very thought of Michael being witness to her marriage was deeply disturbing. "We cannot in all conscience ask Sir Michael to postpone his departure until June, Lydia," Rebecca said.

"Pooh! Indeed, we can," Lydia said, pouting with disapproval. "And if you do not intend to convince him that nothing would make dear Lord Elmont happier, then perhaps Sarah and I can."

The orchestra began a country air.

Polite conduct demanded that he ask one of the ladies to dance. Michael looked questioningly at Rebecca, but from her expression it was clear that she would refuse any overture. "Would you partner me in this dance, Miss Creighton?" he asked, making his bow to Sarah.

"She would be delighted," Lydia interjected.

Inclining his head in appreciation, Michael took Sarah's arm, and the two of them took their place in the pattern.

"I cannot comprehend why you are being so contrary!" Lydia said, fluttering her fan to cover her annoyance. "I know that you do not like him, but he is a perfectly eligible *parti*. He has looks, a comfortable living, and a title to boot. Look at them! Do they not appear well together?"

Unwillingly, Rebecca watched her sister curtsy as the dancers formed lines, Sarah's blond loveliness the perfect foil to Michael's dark elegance. *If only you knew what he was truly like!* She fairly ached to shout the words, to tell her stepmother that he was a perfidious wretch, how he had used her, deceived them all. Yet, deep within, Rebecca knew that his deceit was not the true reason for her dog-in-the-manger disposition.

Michael and Sarah met in the center of the floor to clasp hands, and Rebecca recognized the sensation that stabbed at her heart. Jealousy. No matter how much she tried to convince herself that he had treated her dishonorably, that she hated him, she could not. If she hated anyone at that moment, it was Sarah. Rebecca raged within, wondering why her sister had been gifted with the loveliness that gained every man's admiration. As Sarah moved through the figures of the dance, her grace and countenance caused her to outshine every other woman upon the floor.

Never in her life had Rebecca disputed divine justice. She had always accepted her sister's comeliness, even taken a quiet vicarious pride in Sarah's looks. *Why?* The anguished question rose in Rebecca's breast. *Why did You give her every womanly charm and give me nothing?* But there was no answer to her appeal, and she could find no comfort within herself, only the knowledge of her own pettiness and envy.

"They do look wonderful, do they not?" Lydia repeated the question.

"Yes, they do," Rebecca conceded, searching the room for some place to run to, to hide herself as she finally acknowledged the truth. If she begrudged Sarah anything, it was her freedom. Sarah could touch Michael, want him, and if he came to desire her, have him. There was little use in denial; her feelings had gone beyond infatuation. Though Rebecca did not know the how or why of it, she had fallen in love with Michael Fairgrove, her fiancé's dearest friend.

As the last strains of the measure faded and the dancers made their parting bows, Michael found himself looking for Rebecca, but she had disappeared from Lydia's side.

"Where has Miss Creighton gone?" he asked, returning Sarah to her stepmother.

Lydia nodded vaguely toward the terrace. "I think that she was seeking some fresh air. You must forgive her, Sir Michael, if she seems a trifle bearish, but it is doubtless trying for her to attend these events without dear Lord Elmont's company. She is so devoted to him, you know. There is nothing to surmount an attachment formed in the first flower of youth. It is most kind of you to act as his surrogate, but it is not the same, I fear."

"To be sure," Michael said, "nonetheless, it might be wise to seek her out. There are more than a few young bucks here who have had more than their fill of Lady Tolliver's fine champagne. It might not be wise to venture out in the garden alone."

Lydia chortled indulgently. "I doubt that you need have any such fears for our Rebecca. You must do as you think best, of course, but I am certain that she is perfectly safe."

Michael kept his annoyance between his teeth. Seething, he gave a short bow and set off for the terrace. How dare they dismiss her so carelessly? Yet, as he left the ballroom, he realized that Rebecca was no less contemptuous of herself.

The moon had waned to a sliver, and Lady Tolliver had set torches here and there for her guests. Their hostess had succeeded in achieving the perfect balance, sufficient light to find the paths, but enough shadow to provide discreet shelter for those who wished it.

"Sir, you will please unhand me immediately."

Michael swore as he followed the direction of Rebecca's voice. He found her near the marble sundial, struggling in the arms of Lord Tolliver's son. Michael crossed the lawn with deadly swiftness, whirling the buck to face him.

"What hey! You have ruined my Mathematical, Fairgrove," Tolliver squeaked as Michael grabbed him by the neck cloth.

"If you were not our hostess's son, you would be using it

to mop up your claret," Michael told him, shaking him like a rag doll.

"Ain't as if she wasn't asking for it," Tolliver said, besotted to the point of recklessness with his father's champagne. "I saw her walk out here alone. A woman don't do that unless she is seeking company, seems to me. Didn't know she was coming out here to meet with you."

"She was not here to meet me or anyone else, you fool!" Michael snapped, letting him loose to fall in a heap. "But she is country bred, unused to wicked city ways, and foolish enough to think herself safe among civilized people."

"It ain't at all the thing, y'know," Tolliver said, stubbornly rising to his feet. "Can't say other than she was asking for trouble."

"Say anything of the kind, and you will regret it," Michael said. "And count yourself damned lucky that Lord Elmont is not present tonight, or I suspect you would be naming your seconds, greenling."

The buck turned white as he rose to his feet. "She is pledged to Elmont?" he asked, looking at Rebecca in confusion. "I thought that he is to be leg-shackled to one of them saints? Hear she is an utter antidote!" He squinted curiously at Rebecca. "She looks well enough to me, but it is dark, after all."

"Look any closer, and you will find your face rearranged, Tolliver," Michael warned, catching hold of Tolliver's neck linen once more and holding him aloft in demonstration. "Now go in where your mama can keep an eye upon you, and keep you out of mischief. And if I hear a single word of this, it will not be Elmont who meets you before breakfast, but me. You may ask at Manton's if you wish to verify that I can shoot the pip from a card at fifteen paces. Do we understand each other?"

Tolliver nodded. "Aye." He gasped out the single word before Michael set him on his feet again. "Your pardon, Miss Creighton," he mumbled. He turned off and ran back to the ballroom without so much as a backward glance.

"Are you unharmed?" Michael asked, addressing himself to Rebecca. She stood with her back toward him, her hand holding the sundial as if for support.

"It seems that you are forever forced to come to my rescue," Rebecca said softly. "Do you ever tire of playing the role of guardian angel, Sir Michael?"

"Standing at the entrance to Paradise with my flaming sword in hand," Michael said, coming to her side. "Though I cannot like Tolliver's methods, his conclusions were not outside the bounds, Paragon. A woman alone in the dark is fair game."

"I cannot understand it," Rebecca said, thankful for the darkness. "Never before have I had any trouble of this kind, and I am no untried girl."

"That was before your disguise was blown," Michael said. "As young Tolliver so gracelessly put it, you look well enough. You are no longer an antidote."

"Tolliver was in his cups. It is not altogether foolish to consider that his vision might be less than reliable," Rebecca said bitterly, trying unsuccessfully to keep the tears of self-pity from falling. "Do you think that if you tell the lie often enough that I will come to believe it? Why can't you leave it alone, Sir Michael, and leave me alone? I am no Sarah— I never will be."

He swept away the tears on her cheeks. "No, you are not Sarah. You are not a charming, sweet little girl who is more concerned with the state of her hair than the state of the nation. You are much more than a face and a smile." Michael pulled a handkerchief from his pocket and dabbed at her face gently.

"But tonight, tonight, I too find myself wishing that you were Sarah," he said in a hoarse whisper, unable to withstand her misery. Most likely his admission would only make things worse, but he could not help but say it. He groaned as he pulled her to him. "Heaven help me, I wish that you were Sarah, because then you would be free."

"You could have had me," she said, looking up into his eyes. "If you had just been honest . . ."

"You do not understand," he said.

"No, I do not," she admitted, her voice low. "For just now let us make-believe that I am my sister and that we have walked out in the garden together because I have wanted you to kiss me. Please, Michael, I know that it is wrong, but I so want you to kiss me."

His lips claimed hers with all the force of suppressed longing. Misery and hopelessness flowed, yet they could not quench the flame that threatened to consume them both. Rebecca held him close, savoring every stolen second.

The lilting strains of a waltz floated out into the garden.

"Dance with me, my counterfeit Sarah," he whispered, his lips nuzzling at her neck. "Let us waltz, my love."

"I do not know how," Rebecca said, flags of color touching her cheeks. "Lydia still considers the waltz forward and risqué. Besides, I never dance."

"All beautiful women dance," Michael said, putting her hand upon his shoulder. "Follow me, just follow me."

" 'Follow me,' cried Captain Barnes. 'Follow me, he cried—' " Rebecca began as they began to whirl.

" 'Though I lead you through hell itself, there's glory in the ride.' " Michael finished the line.

"You know the poem!" Rebecca cried in delight, resting her head in the hollow of his shoulder, responding to the guidance of his hands and the demands of his body until they seemed like one being.

"From *A Soldier's Journey*? Aye, I ought to. I wrote it," Michael said simply. "Do you think, then, that we are treading the road to hell?"

"Oh, yes," Rebecca whispered as they turned to the music, their steps keeping time to the tune, their hearts pounding in tandem. "This waltz is a most wicked kind of capering. Surely, we must be dancing down the path to purgatory."

"No denying it," Michael said, pulling her closer. "But do

you feel the glory?" he asked, coming to a sudden halt and cupping her chin in his hands. "Do you feel the glory?"

"Yes," she said as he kissed her once more, tasting a bit of heaven upon his lips and caring little that the gates of damnation were fast approaching.

"Becky!"

Sarah's shocked tones penetrated the haze of desire. Rebecca broke away to stare at her sister's horrified face. Lydia's look of incredulity changed quickly to disdain.

"I believe, Sir Michael, that it would be best if we go home now," Lydia said caustically.

"Lydia, it was not what you—" Rebecca began, breaking away from Michael's hold.

"Do not attempt to make me doubt the evidence of my own eyes," Lydia said, crossing the grassy swath to take hold of Rebecca's wrist. The older woman placed herself squarely between Michael and her stepdaughter. "Obviously, I was mistaken in your character, sir. We will not breathe a word of this incident to Lord Elmont, of course."

"Of course," Michael agreed, looking at Rebecca's downcast face. "Mrs. Creighton, I . . ."

"I shall brook no excuses," Lydia said, "for there are none."

"I just wish to say that the fault is not Rebecca's, Mrs. Creighton, but my own," Michael said.

"I can well believe that," Lydia said indignantly. "It is not as if her looks are beyond a man's ability to resist, after all! She is not Sarah."

"No," Michael said, his fists knotting as he tried to restrain himself. "You do her a disservice, ma'am, if you say that she has nothing to recommend her. Oliver does not know what he is getting."

"No, he does not know that she is two-faced," Sarah said, her eyes blazing. "Poor dear Ollie. How could you, Becky? how could you?"

Rebecca stood silently, her head bowed.

"Under the circumstances, Sir Michael, I think it best if

you confined your visits to Cavendish Square exclusively to hours when I shall make certain that neither my daughters nor I are at home," Lydia said, shepherding her stepdaughters from the garden. "I do trust you can see yourself home, later."

Oliver leaned back upon his pillows, watching Sarah in puzzlement. For the past few days she had not been herself at all. Her normal ebullience and chattering good humor had all but disappeared. Every conversational sally was met with monosyllabic replies, and his inquiries about the parties and routs that she was attending garnered little enthusiasm. Something was definitely amiss. She drew a card from the deck upon the bedside table and threw her hand down in disgust.

"Busted again?" Oliver asked. "That is five times in a row, my girl, that you have lost to me. Brings my debt down considerably. Only owe you five thousand and four hundred pounds and five pence now."

"Five pence?" Sarah asked, shaking her head.

"Just to see if you are paying me any mind," Oliver declared. "Certainly ain't been paying attention to your hand, Sarah." He cupped her chin in his palm and smiled at her. "Now you might as well tell me about it, my girl, and I won't take no humgudgeon neither. Everyone here but little Harry has been going around with a Friday face for nigh on to a week now. I ain't dying, am I? And nobody wanting to tell me. Been in the army and seen men die of less than a broken leg, y'know."

"No, of course not," Sarah said, startled. "How could you think that I could ever keep anything so terrible to myself! I would be forever in tears."

"Would you, Sarah?" Oliver asked.

"Of course, I would," she replied, her eyes glimmering.

"Well then, if they ain't about to put me to bed with a shovel, then what is it?" Oliver demanded.

"Nothing," Sarah replied.

"Gammon!" Oliver snorted. "There is something afoot, and I know it. Now, I may not have taken firsts at Oxford, as Michael did—"

"Do not think to compare yourself to that wretched—" Sarah stopped her tirade abruptly.

"So it has to do with Michael," Oliver said, nodding sagely. "Suppose that is why he's been walking about as if he's treading on eggshells."

"Lydia and I went to find Becky," she began slowly. "Sir Michael had gone to seek her in the garden. And we came upon him . . . kissing somebody."

"There, there, my girl," Oliver said, patting her hand. "I know that your stepmama had her hopes up, but Michael ain't never been the marrying kind."

"No, no." Sarah shook her head. "It is not on my account that I am upset, but yours. He was kissing . . . he was kissing . . . Ohhh!" She wailed, burying her face in her hands.

Oliver was perplexed. "Well, if you ain't fond of him, then why is everyone in a dither over a kiss? Unless"—revelation struck—"he was kissing your sister, wasn't he?"

Sarah's hands dropped in amazement. "I knew that we could not succeed in keeping it from you," she said. "You are far too smart not to notice."

"Am I?" Oliver asked, gratified by her perception.

"Of course you are!" Sarah said, wringing his hand. "But I am sure that Becky did not mean it, Ollie, truly. She is so inexperienced. After all, she has never had hordes of men all after her to kiss them as I do. And I am sure that Sir Michael meant nothing by it. After all, who would want to kiss Becky?"

"Don't know about that," Oliver said. "Michael ain't the kind to go seeking cupboard love. What is this about hordes?"

Sarah burst into tears. "Lydia told us not to say anything, but I cannot lie to you anymore, Ollie, I just cannot. She says that he did not force her, but Becky is so good, she always takes the blame. Why, when I stole jam from the cupboard, Becky said that she had done it, even though I had jam all over my face. I am sure the kiss meant nothing to her. How could she prefer Sir Michael to you?"

"How, indeed?" Oliver said, his large hands brushing awkwardly at her tears. "No need to turn the watering pot, Sarah. Ain't like Michael at all, though, to do a thing like this. He knows that she's spoken for." Oliver's brows knitted with the effort of thought. "Go to that drawer, Sarah," Oliver directed, pointing to the chest in the corner of the room. "In my waistcoat pocket you will find a piece of paper."

Sarah followed his direction, drew out the sheet of vellum, and handed it to him. Carefully, Oliver smoothed the piece of paper open. "Read it," he told her.

" 'Lady Faith,' " she read the title aloud. " 'Water upon the rock,' " she began. "Why it is a verse! Did you write it, Ollie?"

"Me?" Oliver laughed. "I cannot make moon and June rhyme, m'dear. You look at it and tell me what you think."

Sarah's lips moved as she read silently, her fingers tracing the words until the last line, " '. . . and so I say, in faith, my heart is yours.' " Sarah finished with a sigh. "It is beautiful, Ollie. The poet must love his Lady Faith very much. But I cannot understand what it has to do with that scoundrel Sir Michael."

"Didn't know at all myself until today," Oliver said with a lopsided smile. "I got the poem from him by happenstance, y'see, one morning at White's. Always meant to return his scrawlings to him, but what with the accident and all, I never got the chance. Struck me as odd when I first read it. It ain't in his usual style at all, you know. More in his line to versify about broken heads and battlefields rather than crushed hearts and churches."

Sarah shook her head, still mystified.

"Michael wrote this, puss. Seems to me that your sister is the Lady Faith of whom he speaks. Wasn't sure till now, but if Michael kissed her, that seals it for me. He is in love with your sister, Sarah."

"But she is to marry *you*," Sarah protested, tears spilling again.

"Don't I know it," Oliver said, patting Sarah's shoulder awkwardly. "There, there, love, don't cry, don't cry." He drew her close, brushing her cheek to comfort her. Sarah turned her head, their lips met, and the boundaries of propriety shattered.

Moments later, Oliver held her at arm's length. The two of them stared at each other in shocked dismay.

"Whatever will we do?" Sarah asked miserably, nestling her head upon his shoulder.

"Don't know," Oliver said, his jaw tightening with determination. "Don't know. Michael's always been the one who has got the ideas. Have to think of something myself this time, I suppose."

Chapter 12

Spring had come in earnest. The park had burst into full blossom. Beneath the canopy of the trees, there was more shade than sun as the leaves finally began to unfurl into full growth. The footman spread their blanket upon the grass as Rebecca watched Harry play fetch with Maximillian. Gone was the emaciated cur that Michael had purchased for a sixpence. A glossy coat now covered Maximillian's bony ribs, and the haunted look had all but faded from the animal's eyes. Would that a human heart was so easily mended.

She smiled as her brother got down on all fours, grasping the stick beneath his teeth to demonstrate his expectations. However, when Harry threw the stick, Maximillian would simply stand, wagging his tail. No matter how much Harry shouted and pointed, Maximillian remained steadfast, lolling his tongue, gazing at the boy.

It was often said that dogs adopt the characteristics of their masters. She recalled seeing that self-same look of lofty amusement on Michael's face. If dogs had the capacity for laughter, Rebecca would have sworn that Maximillian was chuckling at her brother's antics. However, Harry soon tired of playing the part of the dog, and the two of them disappeared over the hill, leaving her alone with her thoughts.

Michael . . . impossible not to think of him, even though Lydia had made certain that the two of them had not come face-to-face in the past week. While Rebecca could sometimes manage to banish his image during the daylight hours, he walked through her nights, filling her dreams so that she woke aching, wanting.

Did he feel any measure of guilt? Rebecca wondered. Even now, Michael was at Cavendish Square, sitting at his friend's bedside. How he could bear to face Oliver, she could not fathom, for she knew that she could hardly stand to look her fiancé in the eye these past days. Lydia had been treating her with barely disguised disappointment, and as for Sarah, Rebecca's younger sister's feelings had shifted from undisguised loathing to excessive pity. It was hard for Rebecca to tell which of the two was more difficult to tolerate.

Meanwhile, wedding preparations were proceeding apace, fittings for bride clothes and an elegant trousseau. But though Rebecca hardly recognized herself in Madame Robard's gowns, the fine garments could not disguise the torment in her soul. Indeed, the consciousness that every one of those exquisite dresses was paid for by Oliver's father was a form of torture in and of itself. Though she told herself that it was necessity and honor that drove her decision, her personal sense of integrity had been stripped bare. She was marrying Oliver when her heart and soul belonged to Michael.

Time and again, she reminded herself of how he had duped her, betrayed his best friend. If Michael did have any feelings for her, they were not very strong. He had abjured her hand so that Oliver could pay his debts. Yet, even that did not seem to matter. Rebecca knew that she loved Michael Fairgrove, that she always would.

A shadow loomed before her.

"Mr. Havermill!" Rebecca looked up in surprise and scrambled to her feet. "I am surprised that you have the audacity to show your face."

"You gave me no opportunity to explain the situation," Havermill shined. "After all that I have done for you, Miss Creighton, I am devastated."

"Are you?" Rebecca said coolly. "So was I. You might wish to refresh your memory of the Bible, Mr. Havermill.

Heaven frowns upon those who steal from the widow and the orphan. You and I have nothing more to say to each other."

She was about to turn, but Havermill grabbed her wrist.

"I believe that we do have something to speak about, Miss Creighton. The sin of fornication, perhaps?" Havermill snickered.

She twisted against his grasp. "I warn you, sir, unhand me, or I shall call the footman. He is lurking somewhere about."

"Call whomever you wish," Havermill said, laughing unpleasantly. "Your footman, however, is in my employ. He is waiting for us in the carriage that I have hired. You see, you and I are going to Gretna, Miss Creighton. You are going to marry me."

Rebecca continued to struggle. "When Gunther's sells ices in hell!" She lashed out with her foot, slamming him hard in the knee with her boot, then gathered up her skirts and ran.

"Bitch!" Havermill exploded as he grabbed at his injured leg. "Run if you can, but you will wish you had listened to me when your sister and stepmother are censured in every respectable home in London."

She stopped and turned. "And how do you intend to accomplish that, pray?" she said, trying to conceal a growing dread. There was a troubling look of certainty on the cleric's face.

"Who would wish to wed the sister of a woman who spent the night alone with her fiancé's best friend?" Havermill asked with a sneer. "A woman who has consorted with a known cyprian?" He crowed in triumph as her eyes widened in dismay. "It took me quite some time and more than a little money to trace your tracks from Covent Garden, but follow them I did. Yes, Miss Creighton, you will marry me, or else I will make public the details of your evening as a woman of the Town. I vow, the *ton* will be delighted to hear that you did the research for *Cathy of Covent Garden* personally."

"Do you think that they will believe you, Mr. Havermill?" Rebecca asked. "Especially when it becomes known that you are a thief?"

"There is nothing that will delight the *ton* more than righteousness brought low," Havermill said. "I will be surprised, of course, indignant, sad, but they will want to believe me above you. It is Lucifer who is remembered, not the angels who stayed in heaven. What is more, I have witnesses."

"Do you?" Michael asked as he stepped out from behind the cover of the trees.

"Michael!" Rebecca ran to his side.

"Fairgrove!" Havermill stepped back in alarm, but he quickly regained his control. "Yes, I have witnesses. So do not think that there is a means of wheedling your way out of this."

"Perhaps not," Michael said, taking Rebecca's hand and leaning carelessly against the tree trunk. "But then again, you have done a bit more than dip your hand in the collection plate, Havermill. I have my doubts that you or any of your so-called witnesses will be given credit when it is found that you have stolen upward of ten thousand pounds from Miss Creighton."

Havermill paled. "That is absolutely ridiculous," he sputtered.

"Ten thousand pounds!" Rebecca shook her head in disbelief.

"Your tracts, Miss Creighton. It occurred to me that if Havermill was filching from the petty cash, he would not be able to resist the main chance. I took the liberty of doing some investigation on your behalf. It seems that Havermill and your publisher have been skimming the bulk of the profits and leaving you with a pittance," Michael explained. "Reed has gotten clean away; however, we have gotten hold of the man who was hired to tamper with the horse at Tilbury's."

Havermill began to quake. "I had nothing to do with that."

"A jury might think otherwise," Michael said with a stony glare. "They might very well believe that you tried to have the viscount killed so that your golden goose would have no choice but to continue to produce those valuable pamphlets for you. Attempted murder is a charge far more serious than theft, Mr. Havermill. There has been a warrant issued for your arrest."

"I will take you both down with me!" Havermill promised, shaking his fist.

"You could try," Michael said. "But were I you, Havermill, I would be on my way to the nearest port and jump the next ship leaving England's shores. Even if you do not end up dancing at the end of a hangman's noose, I am told that Australia is a very harsh land."

Havermill uttered a cry of frustration and turned to flee. Maximillian barked as he loped over the hill and followed the dark-clad figure, nipping at the cleric's heels. When Havermill jumped into a waiting closed carriage, Maximillian gave a triumphant howl and raced back in the direction from whence he had come.

"Well, it would seem that Maximillian has finally overcome his fear of rats," Michael observed.

"Ten thousand pounds," Rebecca whispered, looking at Michael in anguish. "We scrimped and saved, froze the winter through because coal was too dear and there was Sarah's Season to be saved for. Ten thousand pounds . . . I would never have agreed, never have accepted . . ."

"Ollie's offer," Michael completed her sentence. He put his arm around her shoulder and eased her down to the blanket.

"Yes," she said scornfully. "I suppose that you could understand my selling myself into marriage. After all, did you not encourage Oliver's suit for similar reasons? He owed you quite a sum, did he not?"

"No, Paragon," he said softly. "Though you may not believe me, I will tell you it was not the money. Let me tell you a story, but unlike your tales, this one has not yet got an ending."

She tilted her head in silent acquiescence.

Michael began. "A young boy arrives at Eton, very small and very frightened. As is the custom in those hallowed halls, he is a legitimate target for every bully and upperclassman. He has an old and respected name, but his family is neither powerful nor wealthy enough to give him the protection afforded by a coterie of toadeaters."

He paused, remembering those horrific first weeks, alone and terrified. "Our lad proves himself to be prime sport, easily cowed, bookish, wanting nothing more than to be left solitary. But they will not leave him to himself. He is everyone's butt, everyone's whipping boy."

He leaned back against the tree, his eyes closed. Rebecca knew at once that Michael had been that sad little boy.

"Then one day, another new student arrives, as big as this young coward is small, and though the big lad does not have the wit of a Socrates, he has the heart of a lion. Even were it not for his family and funds, he would have been a force to be reckoned with. For some reason that only fate knows, our lionheart takes the little craven under his wing and protects him. He also teaches him a thing or two about the nature of bullies and the use of his fives."

Michael smiled as he recollected the first time that he had bloodied a nose. Oliver had been as pleased as if it were his own fist that had drawn that young ruffian's claret.

"The coward and the lionheart grow to be fast friends," he continued. "They go up to Oxford together, buy their commissions in the same regiment, and very nearly die together several times. Then one day in Spain, our coward is captured by the French. He, along with several other of his compatriots are placed in a jail, but as the battle turns, the village empties, the jailers flee, leaving their prisoners to fend for themselves, with no provisions, not even water."

She could hardly bear to look at his face, to see the raw emotion evoked by those memories.

"We tried to chip away at the stone with our bare hands while we had the strength. I watched them die, Paragon, though I prayed that I would be taken first. One by one, day after day, I watched them die, until I alone remained. And then I heard a voice, a voice I never believed that I would hear again this side of hell. It was my lionhearted friend; he had been searching for me, Paragon. When he had not found my body among the dead upon the field, he had come looking for me. He found me there inside that charnel house."

Michael regarded her steadily, with all the weight of his sadness. "Ollie was a soldier's soldier, but peace was his ruination. I saw my best friend running headlong down the path to self-destruction, and I was powerless to stop him. He was near to rock bottom when his father's ultimatum came."

Rebecca looked up at Michael. His voice was shaking with emotion, but he did not look away.

"If you had not consented to marry Ollie, the earl would have consigned him to debtor's prison. If I had been able to stand the shot for Ollie, I would have, gladly, even if it had taken every cent that I could raise. But he had played too deep, and though I am not considered behindhand in my fortunes, I could not bail him out this time. However, for his father to pay, Oliver had to play the game his way. I could see no harm in the match, especially when I found out your nest was not well feathered. But when you spoke of balking at the bit—"

He turned his head and looked toward the hill, unable to face her. "I thought to make you see reason. Many a marriage is made for worse motives. But, prison, Paragon!" Michael turned back to her in anguish. "Can you imagine a man like Oliver Rowley locked away? It would destroy him. People die in Fleet every day, jail fever, poor food, and despair. Can you see why I found that I could not risk turning you from him, no matter what my feelings, no matter how much I—" Michael stopped himself abruptly. He would not speak those fatal words. He had no right, and they would serve no good purpose.

Rebecca sat in silence, trying to maintain control. She wanted to rage, to scream, to tell Michael that he had no right to make her fall in love with him and then disappear. But she understood now, that he was as much the victim of his own hoax as she herself was. No good would be done by pouring out her frustration, her hopelessness. Now that the course was set, there was no honorable way to turn back. And even though Oliver had left her standing at the altar once, she would not repay him in kind.

"I am handing Ollie that which I hold most dear. He has gotten himself a treasure. I suppose that I will be violating the Tenth Commandment for the rest of my days, for I will covet my friend's wife," he said, his voice on the verge of breaking. "That is why I had to go away, why I *have* to go away now. It was not the money, Paragon. If you believe nothing else, believe that."

"I believe you," Rebecca said. "I have pledged myself to your friend, made a promise to meet him at the church. You are trying to do the righteous thing, Michael. I suppose that I can do no less."

They did not touch each other. They did not dare.

"Becky! Becky!" Harry came running over the hill. "I have taught Maximillian to play fetch."

Michael gritted his teeth as Oliver added yet another cravat to the mound on the floor.

"Dash it all, don't know how a man's to keep a steady hand when he's about to get leg-shackled," Oliver grumbled.

"Perhaps if you try something a little simpler than the *Trone d'Amour*," Michael suggested.

"Nope, got to be in grand style, Michael," Oliver said. "Learned that from you, and a good lesson it was. Miss Creighton deserves the best, can't deny that. Know enough French to realize that *amour* means love. Bad enough that I have to hobble down the aisle with only you and a cane for support."

"You seem in excellent spirits for a man who declared that he would sooner go to prison," Michael said, watching another piece of linen drift to the floor. "Unless it is your plan to postpone the nuptials until you finally tie a perfect *Trone d'Amour*. That bird won't fly, my friend; you realize that you will eventually have to marry her when you run out of clean linen."

Oliver beamed at himself in the mirror. "Look at that, will you! Never seen better if I do say so myself."

"Brummel would be envious if he could but see it," Michael said, staring past his friend into the glass. His own reflection was less than happy. Over the past weeks, his face had grown gaunt, haggard.

"Gone to France, y'know, Brummel has," Oliver remarked, his smile fading. "Not a sou to his name. There but for you, Michael, there but for you. It would have been me in France today. Instead, I am to marry the best of all females."

"Do you love her, Ollie?" Michael asked, staring at Oliver's reflection. "Do you really love her?"

Oliver turned and took Michael's hands. "I love Miss Creighton, Michael. Love her more than I've ever loved anyone or anything in my life. And I owe it to you. Just hope that some day I can repay the favor."

"Just be happy," Michael said softly. "And make *her* happy, my friend. Now let us get this over and done."

"Sound as if you are about to get a tooth drawn." Oliver chuckled, clapping Michael on the back. "And you look like it, too. The air in Kent ain't done you a bit of good, from what I see."

"I have barely been there above three weeks, Ollie," Michael said stiffly. "And I would be there still if I had any sense at all. I still cannot fathom how you managed to dragoon me into coming back to London."

"Can't get married without my best friend in the world

standing up with me," Oliver said simply, putting an arm around Michael's shoulder. " 'Tis time now."

"There," Sarah said, pinning the last tendril firmly into place. "I vow, you have never looked more beautiful, Becky. I am so glad that you did not follow our advice. Sapphire becomes you far better than the white that Lydia and I favored."

"Smile, dearest!" Lydia demanded, pinching some color into Rebecca's wan cheeks. "Just think, soon we will all be addressing you as 'milady.' "

Sarah giggled. "Yes, we will, Becky. And mayhap I will be a 'milady' someday, too."

Rebecca managed to produce a smile. Yes, this was what she was sacrificing herself for. With Oliver's exalted connections, Sarah might look as high as she wished. "Yes, indeed, Sarah, I am sure that you will be a 'milady' one day soon."

"Maybe sooner than you think," Sarah said archly, handing her sister a bouquet of flowers. "Just wait until you see Ollie, he looks handsome even with that cane of his. It is too bad that he will have to carry it with him on his wedding journey."

The wedding journey. Rebecca tried to swallow, but her throat was suddenly constricted. She looked to the door in a panic. Soon she would be Oliver's wife in fact. She wanted to run out of the church and keep on running until she came to a place where no one had ever heard of Rebecca Creighton. Now she understood how Oliver had felt on that day ten years ago.

"I cannot," Rebecca whispered. "I cannot!"

"Every bride has her doubts," Lydia said.

"No." Rebecca grabbed her stepmother's hand. "You do not understand. I cannot marry him."

Sarah knelt before her sister and folded Rebecca's cold hands in her warm ones. "Remember what you have always said, Becky. Everything that happens in this world is for a purpose. Everything always comes out well in the divine plan."

For Sarah, Rebecca told herself. *For Sarah and Harry and Lydia.*

"You will be very happy, Becky," Sarah said, her blue eyes shining with faith and hidden secrets. "I promise you that you will be happy."

Rebecca rose, wishing that she shared her sister's unswerving belief.

As Michael took his place at the altar, he realized that he was fortunate that the wedding was entirely *en famille.* Other than Michael himself and the clergyman who was to perform the ceremony, the wedding party consisted of Rebecca's brother, sister, and stepmother and Lord Elmont, Oliver's father. The lack of a large audience was a definite blessing.

Still, as he watched Rebecca coming down the aisle on Lord Elmont's arm, Michael hoped that all eyes were focused upon the bride, for it was easy to see that the smile on his own face was sewn in place. She was as beautiful as all of his dreams, but he knew this moment for harsh reality. He wished that Oliver would cry craven once more.

For a brief second Rebecca's eyes met his, and he thought that he would surely go mad at the unhappiness in those amber depths. He wanted to sweep her up in his arms and carry her away. Instead, he stood rooted in place as Lord Elmont delivered her to Oliver's side to become his wife. Some prayers remained unanswered.

The vicar opened his book to the service, smiling at the assembly. It had been a mistake to come, regardless of Oliver's demands. Michael had been at enough weddings to know the service by heart. He feared that when the time came and the lines were spoken and the vicar exhorted them all to "now speak or else hereafter hold . . . peace," he would not be able to resist.

Rebecca stood besides Oliver, but she was conscious of

the man beside him. Though it was afternoon, Michael was dressed in the dark formal clothes fashionable for evening. His face was drawn, somber, a reflection of her own inner turmoil. She could bear it no more. A cry welled in her throat, and she struggled to get it past her lips. She could not let this farce go on.

"Dearly beloved," the reverend intoned.

"This just won't do!" Oliver said, shaking his head. "Reverend, will you halt for a moment? There are a few matters that need to be put to rights."

"Not again!" Lydia cried, her hand clutching the rail convulsively.

"What are you about, Oliver?" Lord Elmont asked. "You will marry Miss Creighton, by Jove, and right now."

"In good time, Father, I promise I will wed Miss Creighton. Just want to make certain that everything's done right and tight," Oliver said, winking at Sarah. "Read the name on that special license that I gave you, would you, Reverend?"

"Miss Sarah Leah Creighton," the reverend read.

Michael froze.

Rebecca turned to him and saw the reflection of her own shock in the dark confusion of his eyes.

"Now see here, boy," Lord Elmont shouted, snatching the license from the clergyman's hand. "What kind of foolishness are you about? You ungrateful wretch!"

"Sharper than a servant's tooth is an ungrateful child," Lydia said, clasping her hand to her bosom.

Lord Elmont blinked. "That is serpent, Mrs. Creighton, sharper than a serpent's tooth."

Rebecca grasped Sarah's arm. "You minx, you knew all along," she whispered.

"Did you think that we would let you marry the wrong man? You do love Michael, don't you, Becky?" Sarah asked.

"Yes, I love him," Rebecca said.

"I am so glad," Sarah said, falling into a fit of giggles.

"Lord Elmont," Lydia declared. "Your son has humiliated Rebecca yet again!"

Rebecca felt the heady mix of relief, joy, and love bursting within her; tears warred with laughter and laughter won.

"Look at her! Just look at my poor girl. She is so overset that she is having a fit of hysterics!" Lydia said. "I think that I shall swoon."

Lord Elmont ignored Lydia's warning of imminent vapors and took his son by the shoulder. "You made me a promise, m'lad, a sacred oath," he reminded him. "If you do not keep your word, I swear that I shall wash my hands of you."

"I fully intend to keep my word, sir," Oliver said. "Said I'd marry Miss Creighton, and by Heaven I will if you'll let me. Didn't say which Miss Creighton, though!" His face split into a wide grin. "If it's all the same to you, rather have the Miss Creighton who really wants me, and that's Sarah."

"You are a complete hand, Oliver," Michael said, looking at Rebecca and feeling hope well within him. "Damn me if you are not."

"I know that you love her, Michael," Oliver said. "Should have known when I saw the poem you wrote her, but didn't put two and two together until Sarah told me that the two of you were kissing in Tolliver's garden."

"Sarah was kissing Fairgrove?" Lord Elmont asked.

"Fairgrove was kissing Rebecca," Lydia said. "But it was all a mistake, you see."

"Whom am I supposed to be marrying today?" the reverend asked pointedly.

"Damned if I know!" Lord Elmont said, sitting down heavily on the pew. "Do you know, Lydia?"

"Well," Lydia said, "it would seem that Oliver is fixed upon Sarah, and that would fulfill your promise to dear Arthur. After all, your son would be marrying his daughter."

"So he would," Lord Elmont said, rubbing his chin in consideration. "So he would—nonetheless, this all seems deucedly havey-cavey to me, what with Rebecca kissing a man she ain't being spliced to."

"Who says she ain't being spliced to him?" Oliver asked. "Have a special license in my pocket that says otherwise." He pulled the document from his coat pocket and waved it under his father's nose. "Read here—'Rebecca Rachel Creighton'—that's her—to 'Sir Michael Xenophon Fairgrove'—that's him—though I don't know why they hung that Xenophon upon him, for I never seen a man who is less of a Xenophon than our Michael here. Still, wouldn't have been legal if the Xenophon got left behind, much as he might wish it."

"Oh, Oliver, you are so very clever!" Sarah said, clapping her hands in delight. "Who would have thought that he was a Xenophon?"

"Who, indeed, after all the pains I've taken to hide that foul secret?" Michael asked, going to Rebecca's side. "However, you have forgotten one small thing in all your plans, Oliver."

"Have I?" Oliver asked, his gleeful expression changing to one of anxiety. "Got you here. Got the license with the Xenophon on it. Got my license. What did I forget?"

"My lady," Michael said softly, taking Rebecca's hands in his. "You have neglected to ask the Paragon if she will have me, Ollie."

Oliver cleared his throat. "Well then, Becky, will you—"

"Let Michael ask her himself," Sarah said indignantly. "You have done everything else, after all!"

"Quite right, my jewel, quite right," Oliver said, patting her hand. "You really ought to ask her yourself, Michael. Get down on the knee now and do the pretty, just as you said."

"Have I taken a wrong turn and come to Bedlam?" the clergyman asked, but no one heard.

"Rebecca Rachel Creighton," Michael began, sinking down onto one knee and looking up into her eyes, "will you stop laughing long enough to tell me if you would do me the honor of becoming my wife? I do love you, you know that."

"Yes, Michael Xenophon Fairgrove," Rebecca said, wiping tears from her eyes, whether it was from joy or laughter she could not say. "I will marry you if you want me."

"Oh, yes," he said, rising to his feet. "I have wanted you for a very long time, my Paragon." He pulled her into his arms and touched his lips to hers.

Oliver tapped him on the shoulder. "That part don't come yet, Michael. You kiss her after the 'I dos' are done. That is when you get to kiss the bride."

"Quite right, Oliver," Michael said, bringing Rebecca to stand before the altar. "Quite right. Let us get to those 'I dos.'"

"May I begin now?" the vicar asked, his spectacles sliding to the edge of his nose.

Oliver linked his arm with Sarah. "Fire when ready!" he said.

The vicar started with a sigh. "Dearly beloved . . ." he began.

Historical Note

Dear readers,

In *The Poet and the Paragon*, I have taken the liberty of creating my own little riot. Unemployment, rising prices, and rapid economic and social change created the powder-keg situation that I have described. While the disturbance in Covent Garden never really happened, the fear of civil unrest and outright revolution in the years after Waterloo was very real indeed. I enjoy hearing from my readers. If you would like to write me, please address your mail to: Rita Boucher c/o Alice Orr Agency, 305 Madison Avenue Suite 1166, New York, N.Y. 10165.